DON'T

GABRIELLA BATEL

Crown of Thorns and Roses Press

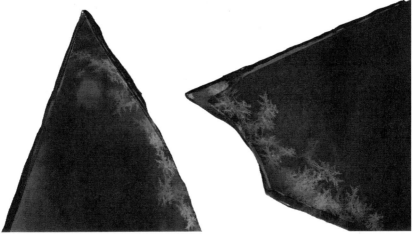

ISBN: 978-1-959831-00-6

Cover Design by Stefanie Saw at Seventhstar Art
Interior Design by Gabriella Batel using Adobe Indesign

Published by Crown of Thorns and Roses Press
https://www.gabriellabatel.com/

Bible quotation taken from USCCB Online Bible.

For Mamma:

You saw and nurtured the writer in me before
even I knew she was there.

DON'T

BY GABRIELLA BATEL

"Abba, Father, all things are possible to you.
Take this cup away from me. . . ."
—Jesus Christ, Mark 14:36

1

FOUR A.M. IT MUST BE if the pain's this intense.

I sit on my mattress, my temple rested against my bedroom window, a fuchsia headscarf protecting my smooth scalp from the frost-edged glass. A small wooden crucifix dangles from my fingers as I wait for my phone to chime. Not that I know how I'm going to tell him.

My eyes slide closed. Where there should be a set of eyelashes scraping against the window, there's a void. At least my heartbeat seems normal today.

If this next treatment doesn't work, then…

My grasp closes around the crucifix until the wood bites into my hand. I shift my gaze to the small statue. A dart of pain splits the backs of my eyes because of it, but I force myself to focus on the iron corpus, on the icy glow that stray light from the porchlights outside gives it.

I brush my thumb over His marked hand.

"Please," I whisper. It's not much more than a breath between my dry lips. I'm never sure what I expect to come of it—nothing came of it last time. So I force out that one word and hope the prayer means more to Him than it does to me.

There's the chime.

I contain a grimace as I twist toward my glass nightstand, where my phone sits screen down. My tactical knife is folded behind it.

I extend my arm. The small expansion of my chest grinds, and my smooth heart rate spasms, but I manage to get ahold of my phone. Its light cuts through the dark, and I blink as my lock screen comes into focus. The three of us at the wedding six months ago: Tristan in a white tuxedo; Mercedes in a long, periwinkle dress; me in a maroon gown to match my headwrap. All of us with our arms around each other. All beaming like the world was perfect. It was.

Where did that go?

I unlock the screen and go to my texts.

From Tristan: Awake?

I swipe a response with my thumb. Always.

I send it, then kill the screen so I'm sewn up in darkness again. The house is so still that the only sound is my wheezy breathing—until a second later, when a door creaks almost imperceptibly down the hall.

Tristan's long strides approach, socks deadening the noise against the laminate floor, and there's a tiny knock, more out of decorum than anything.

I adjust my grasp on the crucifix as my doorknob twists and my stepbrother's tall frame slips in. I could swear the space he needs to get in becomes smaller and smaller each time. He's still strongly built, but he's thinner ever since what happened to his father.

Tristan's head is tipped down, hiding his eyes—in the sun, they're bright green—behind thick, dark blond lashes. He shuts the door, careful to turn the knob so it doesn't click and wake up Mercedes downstairs. And maybe my mom too; she should be on the graveyard shift, but the pregnancy's been harder lately, so I can't assume.

Tristan strides across the room—past my glass desk and dust-filmed laptop, my ebony-stained dresser, and the bathroom—and draws back my thick, dove-gray drapes. The fabric gives a sandy swish as it slides along the curtain rod. The whole time, Tristan clasps a folded pocketknife in his hand.

He sets himself down on the foot of my bed. And never looks at me. His line of sight is fastened outside.

Everything is covered in frost. The young trees, leafless in dormancy. The cookie-cutter houses, encased in pastel vinyl. And the square of cement in front of our house where my mother held his bleeding father.

Tears spring up in my eyes. I blink them back.

My bare feet, on top of my fleece blankets, tingle from the chill. My temple is numb from the cold and the pressure of the glass. I shift in my propped position, and as I do, a jab threads across my sternum down my wrist. This time, I can't contain a wince.

Now Tristan looks at me. In the moonlight, half of his face is deathly pale; the other half is shaded to pitch black. On both sides, his eyes are tight at the tips.

His shoulder shifts. Next thing I know, his hand rests on my foot. His fingers are warm and leave soothing lines on my skin as he gently squeezes, careful of my tender bones.

I wait for the side of his mouth to twitch back the way it used to. It was never to tell me that I would get better, but he was promising that he was there, and that was enough.

It never comes.

Dew has collected on the corner of the window as if the glass is mourning. I flex my jaw. "We set the date."

Tristan's green eyes search me for a few seconds, but nothing else about him moves. Not even his chest as he breathes.

When his lips finally open, it's like watching a fracture in ice. "When?"

"Two months. I fly out March 9th. The procedure's going to be two days later."

For another moment, he doesn't move. When he does, it's only a wordless nod. I see through the calmness, though. A muscle-bulge under his ear. A fidget with that pocketknife his father gave him. The shift of his gaze to and from me like he can't bring himself to meet my eyes but is afraid I'll be gone if he doesn't.

Then he looks down; I drop my eyes to the same place just as he wraps both of his hands around one of mine, the one with the crucifix, and braces it around the wood. I didn't realize I was shaking. His cedar body wash fills my sore lungs.

I sigh quietly. "Tristan—"

My hand slips loose, trembling again once his touch is gone.

Tristan's gaze shoots out the window.

The motion catches my eye too.

2

THE SHADOW OF A TEENAGE BOY paces across my lawn—he must have come down the street from behind our house. He meanders onto the sidewalk and into the gutter next to the sewer drain, wearing nothing but a soot-colored T-shirt and a pair of black cargo pants. A skinny-necked bottle is roosted in his hand. I pinch my eyes shut. Something pangs in a deep, safeguarded room inside me. I thought he was getting away from that. What happened that he's resorting to it again? Something new? Or the same thing that left my family like this?

Luiz takes an almost delicate sip from the bottle while a breeze plays with his onyx hair and his shirt. He stares across the street, but I can't tell what he's looking at—assuming it's anything specific. His narrow chest stretches in an inhale; when it collapses, a thick cloud of white releases from his nose.

He tilts his head up in the direction of my window. I can't tell if he sees me—but I think his eyes clear up.

I glance at Tristan. His hand's a fist around my flannel bedsheets, so tight that teal veins light up on the bulges of his knuckles in the moonlight. It tightens further when, from outside, there's a shout. One I recognize even through the barrier.

My hand clenches around my crucifix. My heart pulses irregularly as heat simmers in my jaw, my stomach, my neck. Luiz looks over his shoulder before the closest thing he ever gets to a smile glides over his face. The ground turns to graphite where his footprints have cleaned away a dusting of frozen mist. Luiz waves his older brother over.

"Close the curtains," I tell Tristan. "Please."

"Just relax, Paityn," he says tersely. His shoulder blades are tense, his breathing stiff, his pulse stark in his neck.

I frown. "What's wrong with you?"

Tristan flashes me a sidelong scowl just as a second shadow appears outside. I can't make out this one's features, only his stiff hair and a thick jacket, its hood glistening with condensation. His hands are in his pockets. The hands that I know pulled that trigger four months ago.

He's speaking to Luiz, and the next thing out of Luiz's mouth must be a joke if his expression's any indication. Tony laughs, his shoulders shaking. Tristan's knuckles are white—I imagine his skin rupturing under the tension and releasing blood.

My heart rate stammers, and my vision crosses; I swallow a wave of dizziness, but it doesn't let me go. My bedsprings fluctuate with my balance. It must be at least seven seconds before a new sound breezes into my ears: Tristan exhaling. A few extra seconds later, my vision straightens, and I search the ground outside. Blown pine needles, ochre with age, crosshatch the gutter. The brothers are gone.

I release my chokehold on the crucifix. Bruising blushes over the craters in my skin.

Tristan never stops scanning out the window. Maybe he's waiting for police lights, like I do. Waiting for them to spark the night with blue and red, and for the shrill notes of sirens to pierce the silence. Praying that my mom and the baby she's carrying aren't in one of those cars.

Minutes pass. Young twigs sway on the hibernating maple out front. After almost an hour, the pain ebbs enough that I think I might be able to sleep. Hazy lilac effuses from the horizon, and a runner jogs up the sidewalk. He seems young, but he's tall with long, confident strides. Like clockwork, every morning.

I ease myself onto my mattress. Forget the blankets—I don't have the energy.

Tristan doesn't glance sideways. He'll stay until he knows I was able to fall asleep. He always does.

3

I WRAP MY FRESH HEADSCARF, this one black and decorated with magenta and lime swirls. My foot's wedged under me as I sit on my bed; my weight packs it into the velvety spare blanket I woke up under. The one that Tristan tucked around my shoulders after I fell asleep.

I inhale deeply—carefully, but deeply. The pain's not as bad as usual. Not bad at all, actually; better than I've had in a while, now that I've slept off the worst of this morning.

With my thumb and middle finger, I tweeze a fuchsia thread from the hem of my curtain, then ease to my feet, slide on a pair of leather boots and a wool swing coat, and cross the room to my door. My hand hesitates on the chrome knob until the metal grows warm.

She'll be here. She will.

I twist the knob and inhale a spicy waft of ginger tea—and I smile. My mom's the only one who drinks that. She and the baby made it back from the graveyard shift.

I follow the scented steam downstairs. The bottom of the stairwell meets the front door and switchbacks me down a short hall to the living room that takes up half of the bottom floor, where a blue paisley rug cloaks the chestnut laminate. The kitchen is adjacent, blocked by the wall from where I am. Two voices murmur from around the corner.

My eyebrows twitch down. Mercedes is usually at school with Tristan by now.

As I turn the corner, I run my fingertips against the drywall, nicking the bottom of a framed sketch hanging there: Mercedes, Tristan, and me penciled in thread-thin lines. In the kitchen, Mercedes is sitting on one of our dining chairs, her turquoise hair hanging loose around her neck. My mom's pecan-toned wrist, several shades darker than mine—I've got lighter, chai skin because of her first husband, who left when she was two months pregnant and promptly died DUI—is settled on Mercedes' forehead.

My mother faces me. Mercedes' gray eyes follow; she's almost able to hide the wince.

Still angled toward me, my mom gives Mercedes' cheek a stroke before she lets her arm hang by her side. The other hand hovers at her midsection—it has been for the past four months.

"You're up." She smiles at me. I return it, albeit tiredly. Yes, I am. Finally. First time in, what, a week? Mercedes smiles too, but her elbow is propped on the table, and her head leans on her alabaster fingertips.

"What's wrong?" I ask.

She shrugs and runs a finger down the inner corner of her eye. "Just a headache."

"*Just* a headache." It's more than that if she skipped school for it.

Mercedes shrugs, and from her stifled grimace, the motion wasn't pleasant. "I've had worse."

Sure she has. When Damien was killed.

She only gets one of these whenever she spends all night grinding her teeth. I'm sure this one's because we decided on my procedure date yesterday.

"Anyway," Mercedes continues. She combs her hair behind her ear. "It's better now, but my head was splitting when I woke up, and it's not like it's hard to get my dad to sign me out of school."

My mom glances at her sidelong, and I catch myself just shy of pursing my lips. It's sheer irony that her father has to give consent when he essentially handed Mercedes off to us eleven years ago. I thank God every day we got her, though.

I work through the ache in my swollen joints to stride across the room and take a seat at a diagonal from Mercedes. The table is bar height, mahogany tinted. My mom lifts a stocky mug of tea off it.

"Why are you dressed up?" she asks. Her curly black hair is pulled into a thick ponytail. There are silver streaks at her temples like frost on a raven's wings.

I moisten my lips. "I was going to the cemetery."

The mug stalls at my mom's mouth, then slowly lowers. Something deeper than tears wells up in her eyes as she swallows and returns the drink to the tabletop. "Again?"

I didn't notice Mercedes close her eyes, but now they flip open as sharply as switching on a light. They're pink at the rims; her irises, though, are steel.

"I wanted to get out while I feel fine," I say. "And I can't pick up anything there." My stomach pinches at the thought of what would happen if I do get sick and can't fight it thanks to the immunosuppressants: they'd cancel my procedure. And that can't happen.

My mom runs her thumb over the lip of the mug and gazes

into the amber liquid, then out of a nearby window. The light filtering through is silver from cloud cover, and a few snowflakes float from the sky. Tristan's father—her husband—used to love days like this.

"Don't push yourself," she finally says. "I want you home in half an hour."

Just about the time I need to walk down and back. Perfect. "Thank you."

Mercedes loosely draws her hair through an overstretched black elastic that encircled her wrist. "I can go with you if you want."

"It's fine. I'll go on my own." I slide off the chair. My bones and muscles ache at the pressure of my body weight, and I press my lips together in discomfort, but it's not enough to keep me in bed. Not this time. "You rest."

She makes a face like she finds that ironic coming from my mouth.

"Paityn," my mom says. Her voice is suddenly grave.

"Yeah?"

"Keep an eye out."

"For what?"

My mom takes a sip of her tea, then plucks a finger off the indigo ceramic to point outside. "We've been tracking down a man named Garrett Martin. He's wanted for breaking and entering, assault"—she takes another swig—"and murder."

"Mm. Lovely." Mercedes deadpans it, but she glances at me anxiously. The last murder took the man who was our father.

I rebound the same glance back to her. To my mom, I say, "How close?"

"Close enough."

"Do you know what he looks like?"

"Black hair, blue eyes, average height, and a scar on the bridge of his nose. Most of the time, he gets people to let him in their own doors, but still—don't let your guard down."

"How does he do that?" Mercedes asks.

"He leaves text messages asking to be let in, pretending that he's a family member using a different number in some emergency."

Mercedes scrunches her face. "People fall for that?"

"You'd be surprised."

Floating particles wink in the bleached sunlight. I rerun the list of features through my mind. "I'll be careful."

My mom places her hand on my shoulder and massages a thumb across my neck. She smells like the perfume she put on last night, notes of bergamot and rose.

"Give him our love," she says.

Mercedes looks away. Memories well up in my throat. "I will."

4

THE CEMETERY IS SURROUNDED by a stone wall short enough to be decorative but high enough to make vandalism too much effort. Not much good, though, with the wrought iron gate swung invitingly open.

Cold leaks through the dense wool of my coat and aches down to my marrow. Mist stings my cheeks. The sun glares silver overhead, burning into the cloud cover without offering any heat against the frigid cold.

When I swallow, my throat twinges—there goes feeling fine. I wish I could've driven, but that's not going to happen with my mess of a pulse. Here's hoping I don't regret the less-than-a-quarter-mile walk. Again.

The expansive parking lot's empty except for one sedan powdered with snow. Drifting flakes land on the asphalt for a few seconds before melting and tingeing it charcoal gray. An unoccupied street unrolls past a sidewalk-and-dead-lawn perimeter. Beyond that is a row of houses, all of which are identical to mine. Convenient to live so close to where my stepfather—my father—is buried.

I run my hand along the bumps of the cemetery wall as I amble toward the entrance. Papery weeds pop out of the seam between the base of the stones and the blacktop. Nice and slow. It took me long enough to get here. I'm not going to rush now.

Suddenly, my heartbeat stammers, and the world blurs and quarter-flips around me as blood drains from my head. I anchor my boot on the ground and support myself against the wall. I think the crunch of shoes on frozen grass approaches from inside the gate, but I'm not sure. My mass against the stone grinds my tender shoulder, and a wince of an exhale stumbles out of me.

Myocarditis. Dr. Tahan's voice rings in my swimming skull. Even now, I hate how the medical term sterilizes the fact that my heart is swollen, being repaired with scar tissue rather than healthy cardiac muscle.

My heartbeat continues to sputter. One pump, a break, and two more rapid pumps before it finally quells into a steady pace. I close my eyes and press all the air out of my lungs, as if that can flush out the disease.

That was pretty bad; maybe I shouldn't have come by myself.

"Is everything okay?" says a soft voice.

I jolt. And for a moment, I'm left speechless.

His eyes are gorgeous. They're narrow with long eyelashes, the irises a rich, sweet brown—but that's not even what's most stunning about them. They're so expressive. Gentle and...grieving.

I know the pity I get when people see my sickly frame, my headwrap, my pallidness. This isn't it.

I stand up off the wall. He must have been the footsteps I heard. He's around my age, tall, with copper skin and thick black hair, gelled and slicked.

I softly clear my throat. "Everything's fine. Thanks."

He nods and smiles slightly. The intensity never leaves his gaze. And his gaze never leaves my face.

At the bottom of my vision, his hand squeezes. A thin silver chain, like a necklace, is wrapped around his knuckles. It's pale like a scar and sparkles in the cloud-filtered light. Wind whistles in my ears. I tug back my lips in a quick smile, then take a step to leave, but my hip and knee pulse at the sudden pressure, and I let my weight off a bit prematurely.

When I do, the boy tenses. He pulls his hand up short from extending it to me—like he's fighting a reflex to support me.

I watch him. And he watches me. His breathing is erratic.

"Sorry," he says. He has a charming accent. He pulls his hand—that's still poised to brace me—farther back.

"It's fine." My eyes fall back to the boy's hand with the necklace. It's clenched tighter. And it's shaking.

Just leave it. Just go.

The boy's the first one to leave. He heads to his car, the only one in the lot. I crush the brittle, flaky remnants of a thistle under my boot and keep my weight on it for the whole stride. Then the next stride, then the next.

I stop when I reach the gate.

The boy's standing next to his driver-side door with one weary hand on the roof, gazing at the chain in the other. He's so still that I hold my breath so I don't disturb his reverie.

He sags against the car as if it's suddenly difficult to stand without it.

I turn away and walk into the cemetery.

I approach the thick-trunked oak tree that shelters Damien's gravestone. At the funeral, it was blooming with emerald leaves. Now its branches stab the sky, as lifeless and gray as old titanium.

There's someone standing underneath it with his head bowed.

I slow. What's Tristan doing here? It's right in the middle of a school day—

Oh. Noon. Lunch break and a ten-minute walking distance.

I grimace. If I go up now, I won't get the Tristan who sits with me in the early morning. It'll be someone else completely.

Headstones puncture the unforgiving ground for acres. An oily black crow caws from its perch on one of them. Beneath each, in columns so uniform it's mesmerizing, is a rectangular bulge in the dehydrated sod. Across the landscape, they form a perpetual pattern twirling around me, ready for me to get lost in. A bouquet of lavender, tied in a satiny ribbon, has shriveled on a nearby tomb.

I exhale through my mouth, and it forms a cloud of steam. I won't leave. I won't avoid him.

Ice crystals and hardened grass crackle under my boots as I make my way to the grave. I only get a few steps closer before Tristan raises his head in my direction. And just like that, his expression goes blank. His spine stiffens, his jaw sets, and he looks straight ahead to avoid my eyes.

I stroll up. Tristan's hands are hidden in the pockets of his army-green jacket, and a light wind teases his hair.

"What are you doing here?" he asks the space in front of him.

His shoulder is inches from mine, the wide trunk of the oak tree to our backs. I flex and release my fingers in my own pockets to get some circulation—not that that's very much thanks to the lupus. Even in the fleece-lined gloves, the tips are almost numb.

"Same as you," I say.

Goosebumps roughen Tristan's neck, but he doesn't shiver. His pale lips are rigid. It's like his whole body is trying to shut me out.

"I thought I told you to stay away from me."

There it is.

The words deserve harshness or anger, but there's none of that. Only a tired steadfastness.

I turn to him, knowing he won't reciprocate. Somehow, my voice comes out the same as his. "I don't care what you told me."

He scoffs. Again, not malicious. Just tired. "You should."

Before I can respond, he pushes past me. He shifts his shoulder so he doesn't brush me—so the impact doesn't hurt me—on his way out.

He doesn't go far: close enough that I can hear the breeze skim over his windbreaker.

Snowflakes cling to the lapels of my coat and melt on my cheekbones. The frost is already cleaned off the flat headstone, the curves of Tristan's fingertips preserved at the edges. Underneath, militant letters are chiseled into the granite.

Damien Robert Carson. Husband. Father. Protector.

And that's what he was. Not stepfather. He was more than a marital status, like Tristan has never been my stepbrother. Damien was my father. Tristan is my brother. That's what they've always been, long before the wedding day.

It hasn't changed for me. So why has it changed for Tristan?

I barely have time to finish the thought before Tristan's head snaps toward the other side of the oak behind me.

I frown, and somewhere between curious and suspicious, I pace around the tree. The thick trunk is armored in rough bark so dark you'd think it was charred.

On the other side, standing over a gravestone, is a young man, maybe in his late twenties, wearing a heavy black jacket with mock fur on the lowered hood. He's tall—if I were to guess, my temple would line up with his collarbone—and his coffee-brown curls, almost the same as mine used to be, are tied back loosely.

I use my teeth to peel flaking skin off my lower lip. Where did he come from? I couldn't have missed him when I walked here. The tree couldn't have hidden him that well. I came in from the side, which would've given me at least a partial view of where he's standing. And I didn't hear him either—his footsteps, his breathing, anything.

A frozen flower, once a weed, I think, is as thin as tissue paper over the first letter carved into the bone-colored gravestone he's visiting. I read the name: Cynthia Magdalena Sanchez del Rio.

From the dates, I run the numbers. I calculate twice to double-check; each time yields the same result. Sixteen years. Same as me.

I swallow through my sore throat. What happened to her? What took her so early?

The man catches me staring, and I look up. And when I see his face, I stop.

I think I recognize him.

He has a balanced nose and a trimmed beard, and his eyes are hazel, green in this light, gold in another, then brown as his head minutely shifts, but it's none of that. I'd remember those features. The height, the eyes, all of it. It's nothing about them. It's just him.

He looks at me and smiles with his lips closed. I'm still staring.

"Sorry," I say. I should leave; I'm pushing the time my mom gave me to be here anyway. Tristan takes a cautious step forward, his weight on his toes.

"It's been a while," the tall man says.

So he knows me. And he thinks I know him.

When I take too long to respond, he smiles again, though this time it's a sad smile. His jacket and flannel shirt are unfastened low enough to expose a purplish spot where his collarbone meets his throat—a bruise. How is he not cold?

The man looks back down at the gravestone and swallows; his bruise stretches. "Cancer. She fought for years."

Something about the way he says it makes me think he was right there when it happened. I can't imagine what that's like. I don't want to ever have to know.

"I'm so sorry." I mean it more deeply than most people possibly could. And as I speak the words, I pray this next procedure will give me a different outcome.

The man's gaze finds me again. It's so gentle my heart aches.

"I know," he says.

Everything slows. The swaying oak branches above me, the quivering blades of withered grass, the shy beat of my heart—it all slows under the gravity of his voice.

He didn't say that like a generic conversational answer. He said it almost like he's seen me live this. Lived it himself.

A puff of air leaves his nose. A laugh. "I'll let you go." And he strides away, farther into the cemetery. I don't think there's an exit that way. I watch the man until he's small and obscured by the mist. My knees are throbbing, and I shiver—I need to get home.

I return to the front side of the oak tree. Yards away, Tristan's attentive gaze watches over me. I crouch and brush a few snowflakes off Damien's name.

"We love you," I whisper. Then I stand and head back in the direction of the entrance.

When I near Tristan, he sets in stride next to me. Without him saying anything, I already know he'll walk me home.

As we near the gate, his brow is furrowed, his green eyes thoughtful. He didn't know the man either; otherwise, he wouldn't have seemed so concerned. So where have I seen that guy before? And where has he seen me?

There's enough brisk humidity that a droplet of condensation slides down my turtleneck. The cemetery gate's wrought iron bars support a layer of snow on their spires. Beyond the gate, someone laughs.

Tristan's posture, which was slightly bent against the cold, stiffens. We get to the gate and take one step past it—one foot from the dead grass onto the frosted asphalt—and I bite down a swear. My heart slams against my sternum, and Tristan falters as if he has ice in his joints.

They're between us and the exit.

5

THERE ARE SIX OF THEM. They're all lounging in a cluster farther down the wall. A blond boy, not tall but not noticeably short, named Eddie Davis. A willowy girl named Venus Driver with umber skin and flat-ironed hair to replace what I guarantee are naturally thick coils. Two other boys whose names I don't know, one with a shaved scalp, the other with black bangs that hang into his eyes.

Luiz Suarez. And, finally, his older brother, Tony.

Tony leans against the stone wall a few yards down; when he spots us, his face cracks into a malicious grin, strong white teeth wrenched straight and tight in his head.

"Carson!" he calls to Tristan. His voice is as slick and cool as a sheet of ice.

An icicle dangles from a ledge on the wall a few feet from us. Tristan gathers his coiled frame to his full height, but at six feet, that puts him four inches below Tony. Tristan swallows. His hands are shaking. He's shaking.

Tony smirks, picks himself up from his prop against the wall, and strides over. The icicle on the wall is gray, as if ash were trapped inside; its tip is sharp.

We can't leave. Tony can easily outrun us, and besides—you don't run in front of a predator. So I harden my jaw, my body, myself, as he approaches us, as they approach us, creeping their way around Tristan and me. Flanking us. Especially Eddie, who slides to a spot closer to me.

Tristan eases forward until his body covers half of mine—is between me and the rest of them.

Only two lag behind, for less than a blink's hesitation. Venus, who rolls her eyes, her lips painted a vicious red. And Luiz. A thick scar, the skin turned to ivory, splits the smooth bronze skin across his forehead, swooping near his eyebrow and disappearing in the hair at his temple. A ghost pain slithers down my back.

That hesitation passes, and the two come over. Venus takes a spot at the far corner of the half circle they make around us, her weight on one hip. Luiz saunters next to his brother. He pops a wad of gum between his pale teeth.

Tony reaches us, and the others stand around Tristan and me. Our backs are to the wall.

My heart hammers in harsh contractions, and a fever burns under my clothes. I swallow hard and force myself to breathe in even strokes, hoping that will help my heart rate stay where it should be. I won't let myself get dizzy, not here, not now.

Tristan wedges farther in front of me. He's transformed into glass: hard, unfeeling, and able to drive itself down to your bone if you mishandle it.

"What do you want?" His voice is like glass too. Shards.

Tony raises an eyebrow; there's a scab at the corner of it, and black studs glint in his earlobes. "You still mad at me, Carson?"

After you killed Tristan's father but slipped away because we couldn't prove it? Yes. We both are.

Tristan's eyes are frostbite, but he doesn't respond. A gust of wind swirls snowflakes over the pavement.

Venus scoffs. "Kill the joke already, Tony."

"Shut it, Driver," Eddie shoots back, his sick grin never leaving. Venus glares at him.

The whole time, Luiz's placid attention alternates between all of us, taking us in, evaluating, preparing; and Tony's smile is like a razor, ready to cut us and let us bleed.

"I thought we'd worked things out." He places a thick hand on Tristan's shoulder. Tristan's muscles bulge until I almost think I can hear them grind.

My voice is as steady and precise as the clean cut of a scalpel. "Don't touch him."

Tony's eyes shift to me. The others exchange murmurs and jeers. Except for Luiz: his gaze latches onto me, and it's not observant anymore—it's warning. I see it. I see it, and I step out and forward so that none of Tristan's body is shielding mine. My inflamed knuckles nearly brush his. The rim of Tony's thumbnail is untrimmed and corpse-white but filed smooth. It looks ready to cleave Tristan's skin as Tony stares at me.

"What did you say to me?" A little of the smugness has fallen from his smirk. The ugliness beneath takes its place.

I level my eyes on his, undaunted, unbending, unyielding. I'm everything that intimidates people who expect others to cower before them. "You heard what I said."

A hush rolls across the parking lot. Venus' eyebrows rise, intrigued or impressed. Luiz's foot eases back, and his weight shifts to his toes like he's preparing for a quick move.

Tristan's breathing, which has been silent the whole time, begins to rattle. He watches me sidelong but keeps his stance solid.

Tony stares at me for a few seconds. Then he jerks his chin at me. "You come to see your daddy?"

The air drops ten degrees. Tristan's hand shrinks into a fist. One tail of my headscarf blows over my shoulder like a braid. I don't react. Tony's waiting for pain or fear, weakness, but I won't give it to him.

Tony shrugs and removes his hand from Tristan's shoulder. "Honestly. You're not dead yet?"

Luiz's eyebrows lower dangerously. My heart's at a sprint.

Tony peels his lips farther back, revealing dull canines. "Hurry up and do it, would you? I need—"

Tristan's fist snaps forward. Before my next heartbeat, Tony's head whips backward.

The parking lot is one collective gasp. My clenched hand flies to my lips and presses against them. Luiz's muscles cinch—something between a jump and a restrained lunge.

Tristan looks back at me as if to make sure I'm okay.

Tony swings his face back toward us. All the cruel humor is gone. Gore oozes down his upper lip, and he touches under his nose to examine the dark fluid.

An iron taste spreads over my tongue. I don't know if I bit my lip or if I'm imagining it. Imagining the smell that covered Tristan's hands as he wept in my arms that night.

Tristan straightens his shoulders.

Tony lets his nostril run free, and maroon splatters the floor. The wall is less than two feet behind Tristan and me. Nobody moves. Except when Venus speaks up. "Tony—"

Tristan hits the wall. The collar of his jacket is snatched in Tony's fists, and Tony's forearms crush down on his clavicles. Their faces are inches from each other—Tristan's is contorted in pain.

I surge for my brother, but a hand, vicious and hungry, clamps around my arm and drags me back faster than I can fight it. My heels skim the ground.

"Get off him!" I wrench against the vise on my bicep, but it doesn't budge. I twist around.

Eddie leers down at me.

He raises his waxy hand and strokes the side of my jaw. "Easy there."

"*Get your hands off her.*" Tristan wrestles against Tony, but Tony slams his fists into Tristan's collarbones. Tristan groans as his head collides with the wall. The icicle, the strong, ashen one, snaps and splinters under the impact, and its glossy pieces clatter to the ground.

"Look at me, Carson," Tony says.

Eddie snickers. His breath stinks of leftover marijuana, so close it warms my ear. I tense my arm, ready to dislocate his jaw.

"Stop."

Brassy fingers bury into Eddie's shoulder until the nails turn white.

"Let her go," Luiz says.

He jolts Eddie back to make his point, but Eddie doesn't let go of me. His grip on my arm is like a noose after the body has fallen.

"Make me." Eddie gives him an arrogant grin, which would be less absurd if he weren't five inches shorter than Luiz, whose eyes are sharp enough to slit Eddie's neck.

Tristan groans again, quietly. Tony has his attention on us. No, on Eddie.

"You wanna talk to my brother like that again, Davis?"

My arm slips free.

I pivot to Tristan. When he blinks, it's sluggish and uneven like he's dizzy, but somehow, his eyes find mine and lock in. His green irises are a bullet of color in all this white, gray, bloodred. I take a step toward him.

"Paityn, don't—" He hasn't finished the last sound when Tony thrusts his weight down and crushes a grimace out of him. I stop.

"Think about it," Tony says to me. He raises his eyebrows. "Your choice."

My fists contract until they shake, until my nails cut into my skin, but I shove an exhale out of my body. My pulse rages in my temples. My mouth tastes like salt and metal.

Venus unfreezes from her rigid posture and slaps on an air of nonchalance. "Seriously, Tony?" By that tone, you'd think she was annoyed someone arrived late. "His mom's a cop."

Tony throws a glance over his shoulder and considers her. She doesn't give any indication that she cares, but a shudder runs down my spine for her. Tristan's eyes jump between the two of us.

Tony glowers at her for another second; then he sinks his face closer to Tristan's until they are eye to eye. In a voice so low I almost miss it, he says, "Don't forget."

I stiffen and pray that the others don't notice.

Don't forget what?

Tony uses Tristan's body as a brace to straighten, and his hands spring away. Tristan takes a fast, overdue breath through his nose and supports himself against the rough stone of the wall until he can stand up off it. When he does, he drives his glare into Tony's. Both look ready for blood and bone, but neither of them moves. Venus relaxes.

Tony backs up a few paces. With the meat of his thumb, he wipes the clotting blood from his upper lip. There's more under his shoes.

"Let's go," he says to the others.

He pivots, and I glimpse the tattoo stenciled on his neck over his spine, a black-inked brand. They all have it: three parallel diagonal lines, two thick, one thin. Their fledgling gang symbol.

The others follow Tony. Luiz, though, hesitates.

It's so brief, so subtle I almost miss it, but he raises his hand and traces the edge of the scar on his temple. I nod so he knows I understood. We'll talk later.

Luiz leaves with the rest of them.

6

TRISTAN AND I STAY SILENT until Tony and the others are long gone. When Tristan finally does make a noise, it's a wince.

A chaos of footprints has dirtied the drape of snow on the blacktop. The light flurry from before has stopped; with a flap of taupe feathers, a stray sparrow chirps and lands on a half-obscured parking line.

Tristan releases his fisted hands. His knuckles are smeared with blood, and he's pale. He reaches behind his neck and touches the base of his skull, and when he pulls his fingers forward, they glisten red. Something hot and painful seethes inside me.

"Let me see." I extend my hand to him.

He pushes it away and looks dead at me. His eyes are hard. They also have a faint sheen.

"I told you to stay away from me," he says. "And I meant it."

The words sting, but not like usual. The sparrow pecks at the ground, then flutters its wings, but I could swear the same wingbeats are in my stomach. Why would he bring that up now? What does staying away from Tristan…have to do with Tony?

"What was Tony talking about?" I ask. The sparrow flies away. "When he told you not to forget."

"What do you think, Paityn?" Tristan says—alluding that Tony was referencing Damien. But that's not what he was referencing. If he had been talking about Damien, he would have said it. And Tristan knows that.

"Come home," I say. "Let Mom look at that." And tell us what's going on.

Tristan stains his jeans when he wipes his hand on his pant leg. He begins to turn away. "No."

"You're *bleeding*, Trist—"

He whips around to face me. Anxiety shimmers in his green eyes. "I'm not dragging Mom into this."

I don't know what I planned on saying next, but whatever it was dies in my mouth. In its place, air promising a storm spills in through my parted lips, tasting like rain. Tristan won't involve my mom the way I involved his father. When I got him killed.

And he's never held that against me. There's no blame in his voice even now, just earnestness, but somehow, I hear it anyway. I seal my mouth and exhale firmly through my nose to stay the grief.

Tristan slumps, as if that concerned outburst—because that's what it was—sapped all his energy. He murmurs to himself and runs a hand through his hair.

Without waiting for me to answer, he starts toward the lot exit. The injury at his hairline is scabbing.

"Tristan," I say. He stops and faces me. In my mind, his head hits the wall again. "Thank you."

For an instant, the hardness softens. "You're welcome."

He turns away.

7

TRISTAN WALKS ME HOME at the lethargic pace I can manage and makes sure I get inside. He's jogging away, stamping slushy shoeprints in the snow, by the time I shut the door behind me. He usually drives that distance to school, but I made him late. I didn't mean to.

Apparently, my mom and Mercedes didn't have any doubt that I would get back in time: Mercedes is dozing on the couch, and there's no stirring upstairs.

Good. I have a minute to think.

After I lock up, I strip off my boots and coat, trudge upstairs, and bundle myself in hefty silken-fleece covers. The heating system purrs through the vents and flutters the pages of a hardback memoir I left open. Sleep drags at me, but I fight it. Tony had Tristan pinned in a split second, and Tristan couldn't defend himself. Now he's alone.

I rerun the scenario, and everything makes enough sense until Tony told Tristan not to forget. And until Tristan didn't answer when I asked what he was talking about.

I drag a hand over my face—an acne rash from my medication roughens my forehead, nose, and cheeks. I'm overthinking this.

Tristan and I both know Tony killed Damien or at least helped, even if there was only enough evidence to charge Tony's father. That may be the only thing I need to explain Tristan's behavior.

It doesn't matter anyway. Tristan isn't safe, not after what happened, so I sit up and wait. Luiz wanted to talk to me, and I need to find out if he knows anything. Besides—it'll be nice to see him.

It's a shame that only happens when someone's been bleeding.

I don't know whether I should expect him to skip school or not. Fat snowflakes stack on the ground like cotton wads. A gray cat trots to the middle of the road, licks its paw, then lopes away. Curtains are stolid in every window along the street.

And then, a little over an hour later, there he is. Tall, thin, and in the daylight for once. Well, here goes.

My entire body throbs—especially my chest—as I tiptoe downstairs to the front door. Actually, it's two doors: a wooden black-plum-painted one on the inside and a glass storm door on the outside. I unlock the bolt on the solid one. Mercedes doesn't stir.

Just as well. She and my mom know about Luiz and me, but they don't know him like I do. And certainly not after what happened to Damien. I don't feel like explaining.

I rotate the additional flip bolt, but when I open the first door, he's not there.

I undo the lock on the storm door. The hydraulic hinge hisses as I make a space for myself to get out, and when I plant the sole of my boot onto the concrete porch, a rush of winter air snatches the breath from my lungs. Mercedes' father's place stands in ugly blue across the street, and our solid vinyl fence guards our perimeter, cutting an abrupt corner to my right. All of it's bleached with snow.

I frown. I'm not confused—that was Luiz I saw, and I have the footprints, like oyster-gray ink on paper, leading down the street to prove it. I trace their path—

A tall mass of black cloth slips around the corner of the fence. My body yanks taut.

"Paityn, easy." Luiz raises his hands reassuringly. "It's me."

I exhale and release my death grip on the doorknob. "What are you doing *there*?"

I don't add *lurking around the corner*, but it comes across: the side of Luiz's mouth quirks back like he finds that funny. The glass door swishes shut. Luiz sticks his hands in his pockets. He's wearing an oversized polyester bomber jacket—although, everything seems oversized on him. I'm surprised breathing doesn't break a rib.

Luiz strolls closer, so light-footed I can barely hear him moving. "I knew you saw me. I didn't want someone else to answer the door. I'm not sure I'm"—he rocks back on his heels—"welcome here."

"You realize I tell my mom every time you're here, right? And she doesn't ever stop me."

"That doesn't mean she wants to see me."

I cross my arms for warmth—he's not wrong—and shoot a gander over his shoulder. "Where's—"

"Nowhere near here." His voice is soft and calm, and his breath forms a cloud in front of his face. The tiniest shy smile plays on his mouth.

That's always made an aching place inside me warm and loosen. I wish it would this time.

"What did you want to tell me?" I ask.

What I thought I saw of a smile slips away. Luiz pops that same wad of gum from before. It's exhausted to a pale green by now. Spearmint. "I'm sorry about Tony."

I moisten my lips. The saliva freezes on them. His brother's choices aren't his fault, but he's expecting that apology to make up for the fact that he just stood there. That he stayed silent when I needed his help.

Snowflakes fall lightly on Luiz's jacket. I ask, "What's Tony going to do?"

Those fragile snowflakes fall to the ground when he runs his hand through his black hair. "He hasn't said anything. Not to me."

"Would he? If he was planning something, would he tell you?"

"Maybe." His voice is so quiet it almost doesn't cross the distance between us.

Luiz has never been evasive with me, and there's no part of me willing to believe he'd start now, which leaves me in the dark.

Summer's hydrangeas are brown, spiny, and crooked in our garden. Twin needles worm from my hip to my ankle and back. It was a mistake to strain my joints earlier, let them get stiff, and then push them again. I transfer my weight from one hip to the other, hoping for some relief, but instead, a shot races up my leg, and I wince. Luiz's eyes shift up and down me, as if he's searching for where I'm hurting.

A wave of exhaustion suddenly hits me, like pain that you don't register until long after you realize you're bleeding. I sigh and lower myself onto the edge of the porch, my feet a step down. With no gloves, my fingertips are burning in the cold. It won't be long until I can't feel them. Compliments of lupus.

In the next second, Luiz has set himself next to me. He blocks the light wind, and for a moment, I want nothing more than to rest on his shoulder. "Did the treatment work?" he asks.

I laugh, but it's so devoid of humor that it sounds hostile. I forgot he only knew about my last treatment. It's been that long.

"No," I say flatly, because if my voice wasn't flat, it would quiver. "It didn't."

Luiz frowns gently. That scar practically glints in the wintry light. "So now what happens?"

I linger on his scar. I can still feel him shaking from when I dabbed up his blood. "I have a different one in New York in a couple of months. They'll put me through so much chemo that it kills my immune system. Then they'll fix my stem cells so they're supposed to grow a new immune system without lupus." Supposed to. Just like the last treatment was supposed to work. A ninety-nine percent success rate, and I fell in the other one percent.

I wait as Luiz watches me. I wait for him to let himself break open, the way he only does with me. His face doesn't move. Then, after a few seconds, his chilled fingers come to rest on my cheek. I inhale, and a sweet wave of spearmint sweeps into my nose. Not just his gum. It's on his clothes, in his skin, light and clean.

Luiz's eyes betray nothing except what I'm able to read.

"Hang in there," he says, his voice as still as night.

I can let him be strong for me. I nestle my head on his shoulder. His opposite hand glides with my cheek, his touch never breaking. A ridge of bone juts against my temple.

His closest hand, the one of the shoulder I'm leaning on, is braced on the ground between us, and I blanket it with my own. They both feel so breakable, like birds' bones.

My fingertips go from stinging to numb. I retract my head and sit upright, but he still tenderly holds my face.

"I should go." When I speak, the corner of my mouth brushes the smooth skin on his hand.

He hesitates, and I savor every single second of it. If his thumb stretched a millimeter more, he could stroke the outer tip of my eye.

His fingers leave a cool gap when they're gone. He stands and begins to walk away.

"Luiz," I say. He turns. There's so much—so many things that he knows, that I know. So many things we've spoken without words. "Make sure nothing happens to Tristan. Please."

If he was expecting something different, he gives no indication. He nods, his expression as placid as it was back at the cemetery.

"He'll be fine," he says. He leaves, gone around that fence corner as light-footed as he came.

I go back in and stand in my front hall, orangish laminate beneath my shoes. On the couch far behind me, Mercedes is softly snoring.

Outside, snow sparkles on the grass like pearls. Across the street and one space down, a house is shelled in dull green vinyl: where Damien and Tristan used to live before the wedding.

Luiz said Tristan would be fine, but his word alone isn't enough: he can't stop his brother any more than he could stop his father, who's finally on trial.

Anger clamps my jaw. They won't convict him. Tristan and I are the only ones who witnessed anything, and we only saw them running, but I know the unique body shapes. I know the distinct haircuts, the son's spiked and the father's slicked. I know their individual gaits.

And I know the motive—I helped make it. I helped make it the last time I spoke up against one of the Suarezes.

Tristan wants to keep quiet. I can't risk losing someone else, especially not with the baby on the way—but I also can't lose my brother because I *didn't* say anything.

A tear mounts itself on my cheekbone. I wipe it away as I make my choice.

I imagine my mom, imagine her dozing upstairs with her hand over her midsection. Protecting her children at any cost. Just like her husband did.

———

Two hours into sitting awake, a flareup has already started, and my muscle aches sink deeper, become more piercing. I won't let myself fall asleep, though. Tristan has to come home; I need to see it. I need to know that he's alive, that Tony didn't take him from me before I had a chance to find his smile again.

Dinner spices, savory and homey, come and go, but I don't eat. I can't stomach anything, not now that I've told my mom what happened. Now that it's too late to turn back.

I don't let myself think about Damien's body lying prone on the sidewalk.

The snow has stopped falling. My brother's nowhere in sight.

I shift my gaze from the window to the shiny glass of my nightstand and the items sitting on it: my phone, which Tristan won't answer; my knife, which does neither of us any good; and my crucifix.

I pick it up. It's not a magic charm—it's a piece of wood. A piece of wood I carry while my family continues to hurt and people continue to die. I'm too tired to cry. That would make the pain worse anyway.

"Please." I hold the crucifix and open my eyes, and Tristan's still not there.

———

After another couple of hours, Mercedes crosses the street to her house. I wait for her to return with a change of clothes, like she does most of the time, but she doesn't come back. I scoff. Her dad's on a business trip and must have gotten the random urge to make her stay there to watch the house. The sky glows purple and orange under a thin layer of clouds.

Finally, a pair of headlights thinly illuminates the corner down the block, and our spare car emerges from around the curve. The tires splash snowmelt that has collected in darkened ruts in the road's cold, skeleton-white covering. The car eases into our driveway, and the door swings open. Tristan slings his backpack over one shoulder. His head is dipped like he's tired.

I exhale. He's here.

The relief is shallow, though: if it wasn't today, Tony will find Tristan later.

I curl up under the covers and breathe tightly so my chest doesn't expand too much. My pillow smells like my soap.

He's home. He's safe for now. I hope.

8

DEAD OF NIGHT, and there's a hydraulic hiss from downstairs. I break the layer of dried sleep that sealed my eyelids, and my heart greets me with a fit of irregular pumping. My body warmth leaks from my blankets.

I roll onto my back. That sounded like the storm door. It's probably my mom leaving for her graveyard shift, but that's not usually enough to wake me up. My chest is already beginning to feel swollen the way it does right before Tristan comes in.

I could fall right back asleep—maybe—but for no good reason, I sit up and check the time on my phone. It's 3:30 a.m.

I frown at the sterile light. My mom's shift starts at midnight. She should have been gone for hours by now.

I edge back my curtain. The sky is a piercing black, and in the distance, lightning rips it in two. That's headed our way, I'll bet. Houses, unlit except for ghostly porchlights, hunch like stalkers, but nothing else. No one.

My curtains brush my face, smelling like faded detergent and dust. I inch them farther back and narrow my eyes as if that's going to help me see through the darkness better. I know I didn't imagine that—I heard that door open.

There. A silhouette—lean but well-built, hooded, about six feet tall—leaves our house. His gait is steady and rocks slightly between steps.

That's Tristan.

My mom's gone. Mercedes is at her house. Which means I'm the only one left to figure out what he thinks he's doing.

"Great," I mutter, and I grab my knife from the nightstand.

———

I bundle my down jacket around my neck. My heels work their way into my tennis shoes as the frigid outside air washes over me. Ozone—the storm is definitely coming toward us—fills my nose.

I scan the night, my neck prickling. The shadows are so thick I almost expect something—someone—to slide out and snatch me, drag me away, never to be seen again. My knife weighs down my pocket.

I click the fob to my mom's spare car, and the locks lift with a uniform thunk. I consider going all the way to the sidewalk and searching up and down the block for Tristan, but I'm already too exposed, too vulnerable, so I shut the car door behind me, start the engine, and blast the heat. I leave the lights off, though.

As I brake and shift into reverse, I scan my memory. Which direction was he headed when I saw him from the window? South, I think. The snow on the sidewalk and street has melted, leaving only dark wet patches like smeared paint, so there are no convenient footprints for me to track.

The sky lights up with a jagged rift of lightning, and thunder follows a few seconds later, buzzing in my jaw, putting me on the edge of dizziness. Or maybe that's my ugly heart rate. I shouldn't be driving, but it's not like Tristan gave me much of a choice. I decelerate to a few miles per hour.

One block passes, masked in black. The only movement is the eerie waving of weak tree branches in a light breeze.

Two. Vinyl fencing slithers parallel to the street. It'll end when the block meets a T-intersection ahead. In the daylight, it's white, but now, it's corpse gray.

Three. There are hundreds, thousands of blurred shadows—bushes, landscaped rocks, recycling bins—but none are human.

I adjust my hands on the steering and completely let up off the gas. How far could Tristan have gotten? Did I miss him on my way up? I can't have.

I coast up to the edge of the fence.

I brake so fast I'm afraid the tires will screech.

Not half a block down, on the opposite side of the intersection, standing next to a pine tree that reminds me of a mountain—there he is.

With someone else.

My blood ices.

Tony.

9

ANOTHER BOLT OF LIGHTNING illuminates Tristan and Tony. They turn a spectral white in the flash.

My heart thuds in the silence. I almost jump when thunder joins it, rumbling across the neighborhood like a tidal wave. When the boom fades, the street is gravestone quiet again. My knuckles are bloodless on the steering wheel; the car engine purrs in my spine.

The engine. Tony will hear it—but it'll be worse if I suddenly shut it off. The muffled whoosh of my blood in my ears is steady and echoes the thunder.

I swallow through a dry mouth. Snap out of it, Paityn.

My palms stick before they peel away from the steering. I replace one hand loosely on the wheel; I slide the other into my jacket pocket with my knife. Exhaling raggedly, I flatten my skull against the headrest and turn enough to get a decent view of them beyond the corner of the fence. Too decent. How did they not see me drive up? How have they not noticed my bumper?

Shriveled blades of grass poke out from the snow beneath their feet. Tony's hands are in his pockets. Even in the gloom, I recognize him without a doubt in my mind. The bulge of his nose, the slope of his shoulders, his stance on his hips. Unmistakable. Just like the night Damien was killed.

The fringe light of a lamp pole near the end of the block helps my eyes adjust, even catch a few colors. The pine needles are dense and spiny like quills. A sun is markered in black on the fence behind the two. Tony's lips move. Tristan's move in response. His weight is casually on one leg, his arms crossed. Tony's jacket lifts in an occasional wind. When he jams a finger in Tristan's face, Tristan doesn't react. As if that happens all the time.

What in the—

That thought dies cold when Tristan's collar disappears into Tony's fist.

The muscles in my forearm clench, my fingers curl around my knife, and my mind spins back to the cemetery, to Tristan bleeding out of the back of his head, and when it snaps back, leaving me dizzy, I imagine Tristan after this, dead, sprawled in the same position as his father was, limbs splayed, head lolled to the side, eyes blank. And it would be the same because Tristan looks so much like Damien, his height, his build, and his blood—his blood will be the same deep, broken shade.

Nothing happens. Tony doesn't pin him against the trunk of the pine. Doesn't pull a weapon. Nothing, until Tristan shoves back. It's a familiar shove, the way someone would do it to a homeboy. And Tony lets him go.

My throat goes slack with disbelief.

Tony hands Tristan a wad of cash. It's a sickly sea green. And out from inside his coat, Tristan draws a small plastic bag.

I sit with the air frozen in my lungs.

Please, dear God, tell me that was not white powder.

Tony's head shifts to me.

Not directly at me, I don't think, but close enough that he'll be able to spot the edge of an idling car that wasn't there before. My leg burns with tension as it holds down the brake. My arm itches to throw the gears in reverse and get out, but I can't—that'll make too much noise, and then Tony will *know* he's been seen.

Lightning screams across the sky, and as the whites of Tony's eyes light up, I could swear he's reading my soul.

The lightning vanishes, and the street is submerged in darkness again. Tony's eyes seem to go from demon white to completely black, but by the time my vision adjusts, his attention is back on Tristan. A breeze lifts a few strands of Tristan's hair, then lets them drop.

I count my heartbeats until the thunder, and when it finally booms, I ease in reverse, willing the engine to be quiet. I roll back until I'm hidden far behind the fence, and shift into park. And I stare at the empty street.

I didn't see what I thought I did. I didn't. I couldn't have. Tristan wouldn't…would never…

I press the back of my hand to my mouth. My stomach convulses. I don't know if it's because I'm about to scream or if it's because I'm about to throw up.

I was afraid Tony would kill Tristan for what he did. But I think I just watched something worse.

10

IT'S FOUR. TRISTAN HASN'T COME HOME. I use the heel of my hand to massage the area above the bridge of my nose. It does nothing for my migraine.

What was I thinking? Tony saw me, and I left Tristan there alone, easy retaliation.

The hand between my eyebrows curls into a fist. I left him. Left him to his transaction: a tiny bag of white powder and too much comfort in his demeanor.

The dread coursing through my veins distorts to anger, a slow, cruel burn. My heart clenches over and over, far too fast instead of its usual sluggish grind. So much circulation rushes in my head and ears that the world tilts. I remove my hand from my forehead and press it against my sternum as if that can contain the spasming, as if that can stop my heart from smashing out.

There's a break, a half a moment where the throbbing in my body vanishes before almost immediately starting up again. I suck in a wheeze as my pulse beats, waits too long, beats. I don't know when it regulates, but it does, and I rest for a while. A muscle cramp pinches my right leg. My blankets and clothes smell like salt, like cold sweat. The wind begins to whistle outside.

The next time I look at my phone, it's twenty minutes after four. Twenty-five. Thirty.

That's it. I'm calling my mom, calling the police. He's missing, somewhere he shouldn't be in the middle of the night.

The wind has gone from a whistle to a moan, and a sharp gust rattles the screen in my window. It sounds cold, and my body aches with a fever at the thought. I grab my phone.

It lights up with a call.

Caller ID: Tristan.

I answer faster than I've done anything in my life. "Tristan, where are you? What—"

"Hey, sweetheart."

My breathing shuts off.

"You snug at home?"

That's not Tristan's voice.

It's Tony's.

"You where you're supposed to be?" His voice croons so softly I want to crawl out of my skin to get away from it. Then it changes. Sickly sweet but venomous underneath. "Or out for a drive. You know, bad things happen at night. You might—"

I cut the line.

11

I DIDN'T NEED TO HEAR the rest. I heard what I needed. I heard the message. Keep my mouth shut about what I saw, or my family is dead. My mom. The baby. Mercedes. Tristan. Me.

My heart rate is mangled. My body goes numb, my fingers weaken, and my phone tumbles somewhere in my sheets.

It was Tristan's number that called. There are a thousand ways Tony could have gotten his cell phone. I settle on two.

Tristan's dead. Or Tristan gave it to him.

My head spins, and I must bite my lip, because it begins to swell, and the iron tang of blood sours my tongue.

I lean on one hand, then lower to my elbow while commanding myself to get up. I have to call someone. I grope around for the phone.

My head tips to the side, and my heartbeat staggers before I'm out cold.

———

A memory works its way into a dream—this was a little less than four months ago, a couple of weeks after Damien died.

I'm curled up against the railing at the top of our stairs, my temple propped against the smooth main pole. A single tear drips into the brown-orange wood. The door to Tristan's room is closed a few feet away, and the washing machine and dryer churn in an alcove in the hall.

The grief's different now, not as biting, not as desperate. Now it's an empty, raw gap somewhere so deep I can't reach it.

Chin up, Paityn. That's what Damien always says—said—to me. When I was little and broke my ankle playing basketball. When I was diagnosed with lupus. When I would lie in bed, burning away with fever.

I sit upright and shift my back so the wooden pole parallels my spine. It's comforting to be in odd places. I don't know why.

Footsteps tap at the base of the stairs, too heavy to be my mom's but not heavy enough to be Mercedes'. A few seconds later, Tristan's head appears from the stairwell.

"Hi," I say.

He faces me.

His eyes are bloodshot and swollen like he just finished a fit of harsh crying. His breathing sounds that way too. And the look he levels on me—there's no light. No kindness or pain or sadness or courage. No crinkle at the corners when he's smiling or trying not to cry. None of the depth and sensitivity that I've known all my life, even after Damien was murdered.

These aren't the eyes that stay up with me every morning when the pain keeps me awake. I've never seen these before.

I stand faster than my swollen joints want me to. "Are you okay?"

"You tell me, Paityn." That tone isn't his either, just as angry, just as hard. He sweeps past me without a break in his stride and wrenches his doorknob so violently I'm surprised the mechanism doesn't jam.

"Hey." My voice comes out calm. I don't know how I managed that—all I can register is shock. "Stop. What's going on?"

He's halfway behind the door when he looks me dead on. I search for something, vulnerability, grief, anything.

"You need to stay away from me," he says.

And he closes the door in my face.

I stand there. I can't do anything else. I can't speak. I can't walk. I barely remember to breathe.

I don't know how much time passes that way. Seconds or minutes or an hour; I can't tell the difference.

I stagger a few steps forward until I'm standing directly in front of his door and lay my hand against the wood. It's whitewashed and thin and hollow, and I'm not sure how it's strong enough to support me as I press my back against it and sink to the floor. I hug my knees to my chest and tuck my face into them, trying to breathe, trying to think.

Can he hear me? Does he know I'm still here?

Some part of me knows this is a dream, but it hurts as badly as the day it happened, somewhere deep inside and spreading through every synapse in my body. I listen for any sound on Tristan's side of the door, but there's nothing. He could lie down and die in there, and I'd never know. I'd never be able to help him.

A soft, tender footfall hits laminate.

I inhale with a shudder and furrow my forehead, still buried in my knees. I was alone when this happened. So whose was that?

I raise my head. And I recoil.

Down the hall, half turned from me, is a man: the tall man from the cemetery, the one I thought I recognized. The back of his neck drips crimson.

I snap awake.

My door opens.

Rain rumbles against my window loudly enough to make my temples pound. How did I pass out? How did it get that bad?

My head drains when I raise it off the pillow. Tristan, sopping wet and standing in my doorway, jumps.

I exhale in a shudder as my head adjusts to the new altitude. He's alive. He's safe.

So how did Tony get his phone?

My heart flicks against my sternum at odd intervals. It's sharper than usual, and it sends that same sharpness through my blood.

"Don't leave," I say.

Tristan makes a sound like it pains him, but closes the door. I grit my teeth and lift myself from my elbows onto my hands. My phone is tangled in my sheets, face up. It automatically has the time on the sleep screen: it reads five a.m. Rainwater beads and streaks down the glass of my window.

"I thought you were asleep," Tristan says. His arms are crossed, and his shoulder is leaned against my door. "I just wanted to make sure you were fine."

"What were you doing with Tony?"

My words are articulated. And they're loud.

Tristan stiffens. "What did you say to me?"

"Don't play. I saw you." Speaking is painful, but I don't care. I'm done. "What were you doing?"

He stands up off the wall. "What are you implying?"

"What was in that bag?"

His eyes harden. "How dare you?"

He hasn't denied it.

"Then what?" My voice is shaking. "Explain what I saw."

"Why would I be selling drugs to Tony Suarez?"

Please, Tristan. Just deny it. "Why did I get a stalker call from him right after it happened? On *your phone*."

One chance. He has one chance to tell me this is all a mistake.

He doesn't have time. Right as he opens his mouth, a high-pitched note, fierce and clipped, cuts through the torrent outside. My back prickles, and I jerk around to face my window.

That sounded like a scream.

Tristan crosses my room in three strides and throws back my curtains. Goosebumps rise on his neck. My heart threatens to punch out of my chest, but both of us search the downpour.

If that sound could make it through the thudding rain and the sealed window, it must have been close.

A second short scream hardens every muscle in my body. Where is it coming from?

Tristan's face is lit pale. A river runs in the gutter. Puddles swell on the sidewalk and in the road. Grayish grass springs up as its jacket of snow melts. Rain shimmers and darkens as it falls, a perfect pattern. We wait for almost a full minute.

The pattern of rain breaks when two silhouettes appear from the house directly across from us. Dressed in black, hooded, and indistinguishable in their baggy, shapeless clothes. Obscured by the sheets of rain.

Running out of Mercedes' door.

12

TRISTAN IS OUT OF MY ROOM by the time I get to my feet. Blood lurches through my arteries.

What did they do to her? What did they do to her because of what I saw?

I throw myself onto my joints and into the hall, to the stairs, my feet heavy and unstable. Tristan's at the door, and then he's out, gone, sprinting into the storm. I'm halfway down the stairwell when my heartbeat falters.

My knees buckle, and I slam onto the railing. Pain splinters from the heels of my hands, where I caught myself, up my elbows, shoulders, spine. I gasp.

No. This is not happening again, not now. They did something to Mercedes, and I have to get out there, *I have to get out there.*

I force my legs to support me, get to the bottom step, hurl myself out the door. My toes curl against the icy cement, and my clothes are drenched within seconds.

Tristan bolts into Mercedes' house. I drag my unprotected feet forward, toward them, blinking away dizziness, commanding my heart to stay in line. Thunder buzzes in my ribs.

Get to them.

I stumble to the sidewalk, the soles of my feet grating against the concrete, and someone approaches through the rain, a person I can't see fully, also hooded but wearing a blue raincoat. Going for a run. Like clockwork.

My heartbeat drops.

Hollowness breaks open in my sternum. My vision weeps away. I hit my knees, and the impact rattles up my neck. I fall onto my hands. My heart must be beating again, but I can't feel it; I can't feel anything except my burning lungs.

No. Mercedes is inside that house. Tristan is inside with her. Stand up. *Stand up.*

My heart slips again. I drop flat against the ground. There's black all around me. Black street, black rain, black tennis shoes racing up next to me, splashing through the layer of black water on the ground. The runner. There's a hand on my shoulder, shaking me, and a voice calling to me, asking if I'm okay, I think, but rain and a ringing in my ears drown out every other sound. My torso is tilted off the ground, my shoulders supported by a strong arm. A hand props my head up.

Rainwater streams down a face I think I recognize. Copper skin, jet hair, but not Luiz—I would know Luiz. The world's wet and blurry and spinning. Then it comes into focus for an instant. The boy I met at the cemetery parking lot—the one with the beautiful eyes.

His face fades. A warm palm cups my face; then it's gone again, leaving me at the mercy of the torrent. An arm slips under my knees, and I'm lifted off the ground—lifted a bit too forcefully, like he was expecting me to weigh more.

A gentle sway, my temple against a chest. Somewhere, in the edges of my mind, I remember being in this same position before.

Raindrops drum against a waterproof jacket   almost like a heartbeat   I can't hear mine   the drumming stops   and it's cold   but the water doesn't batter me anymore   a flicker of a pulse from my heart.

I'm lowered back to the ground. There are shouts, and I think it's Tristan and Mercedes. Under the blur of noises, there's whispering. In Spanish, maybe? A constant beat that I seem to recognize. Like prayer.

Black creeps in at the corners of my vision.

I go out like a candle in water.

13

SOMETHING ICY AND STIFF THUMPS against my chest.
Every single muscle, every fiber in my body is paralyzed—including
my lungs. Panic floods me until, just as quickly, everything relaxes and
air rushes into me. Light floods me at the same speed as the pain that squeezes my
torso like iron fingers. A glass door, vinyl siding, a woven chair—
I'm on my porch. The prickly, wet cement stabs beneath me. The
thick clouds are black. The breeze dances over my bare skin where
a large rectangle of fabric has been removed from my shirt. My
vision comes into focus. Two paramedics, both of them women,
lean over me. One holds defibrillator paddles in her hands. I assume
the other is there for modesty's sake.

My heartbeat still isn't right, not completely. Blood jerks in
and out of my head. The paramedics speak to me, and I manage
to gather that they're taking me to the hospital.

There's a cobweb on the porch's overhang, studded with
autumn's last insects and dewdrops sprayed from the storm. I take
an empty breath and roll my head to the side.

A hot, relieved tear melts down my temple and follows my

scalp. Mercedes sits on the sidewalk; red paints the side of her neck and dyes the collar of her shirt. Fight-or-flight is wild in her eyes, and she's shaking, but she's there, and she's awake, and she's alive.

Several yards away stands the boy from the cemetery, the one who carried me here. His eyes are never in one place, but they stay off of me, probably because of how exposed I am. He has his arms crossed, uncomfortable and tense. The hood to his windbreaker is down, and rain drips off it. I can't tell if the beads of moisture along his hairline are from the storm or because he's sweating, or maybe both.

And there's Tristan, standing next to Mercedes, one hand on her shoulder. His jaw muscle is a knot under his ear. His eyes catch mine for just a moment.

When he shifts them to a different angle, there's anger searing inside.

They load me onto a gurney. My heart rate flickers.

———

The blackness changes into another dream. A different memory, from before Damien died. I lie in bed, shivering and sweating under three layers of wrap. Fever cremates my body, and I can't swallow.

My mom and Damien are on their shifts. Mercedes is at her house, but I need someone here, and I need them now, so I reach a trembling hand out for my phone. A moan squeezes from my throat as I speed dial Tristan. He's only in the other room, but I don't have the strength to call out for him—I don't even have the strength to lift the phone to my ear. I lay it on my pillow, next to my face. My room is so quiet that its digital tones come through without me having to turn on speakerphone. It rings and rings.

"Please pick up." My voice is so weak I practically mouth it.

Even though that's ridiculous—it's four in the morning. His

phone should be muted, if not off, but it's not worth the energy to end the call.

Then there's his voice, a soft hum from the speakers. "Paityn? What's wrong?"

An exhale of gratitude falls out of my cracked lips. "Can you come here?" My voice is so frail and raw I sound like I'm crying. I'm on the verge of it, except that crying would hurt too much.

On the other end of the line, there's no hesitation. "Hang on." His strides have already started down the hall before the line goes dead. I fight to keep my eyelids apart as he eases the door open. He slides my desk chair from its place, positions it next to my bed, and sits. Places his wrist against my forehead. Then his full palm. He's calm and in control.

"I'll be right back." Tristan disappears into my bathroom and flicks on the cozy, campfire-like light. He reappears a few seconds later. My nerves twinge under his cold fingers as he tilts my head back so he can place a thermometer under my tongue. Triangles of shadow are on the ceiling in the corners where the walls block all light. There's a fingerprint on my window. A soft beep, and Tristan reads the thermometer. His eyes pinch.

Mine shut. Tristan begins speaking, but not to me—he's on the phone. He mentions a 105-degree fever.

My door swishes, and his voice fades; he must have stepped out into the hall. The conversation or voicemail he's leaving continues, muffled by the wall between us, but less than a minute later, the door opens again, and a damp cloth drapes over my forehead.

"I'm taking you to the hospital," Tristan says.

My mouth is sand. "I can't get up."

"That's okay."

He lifts the cloth and dabs my neck. I moan.

"Breathe, Paityn. Keep breathing." This time, his voice is strained. It's been a long time since that happened.

The cloth turns hot. He removes it. And then I'm lifted in his strong arms, my temple propped against his collarbone. I sway as he carries me down the stairs.

I don't know how he does it. I don't know how he gets us out of the door with me slack in his arms. I didn't hear him undo a lock, but my ears are thick and painful, so maybe I missed it. Or maybe he prepared when he left my room before he came in with the cool cloth.

I don't know. All I know is the thin outdoor air and the warm stability of his torso beneath me. The sky, the sidewalk, the trees, the houses, the flowers are all pitch black in the night, like they've been painted with ink.

Except for one thing: a man—who wasn't there when this actually happened—stands at the base of the driveway. His gaze is toward the other side of the street like he's lost in thought.

He doesn't seem to notice us. It's the same man as before—the man from the graveyard. His left hand is halfway into his pocket. The other is spread across his sternum.

That hand peels back. It comes away dripping deep red.

Tristan adjusts me in his arms. The blade of his forearm spears into my spine, and I wince and close my eyes.

When I open them again, the bleeding man is gone.

There must be an army of drugs in me; I haven't had this little pain in a long time. I fight to surface from sleep. My blood and my muscles are thick. Everything's thick, except for a stinging slice just to the left of dead center on my chest.

I split my eyes open. Thick veins of darkness obscure my

vision, but I make out an IV package hanging above me, a screen that shows my vitals, and a person sitting next to my bed. Mercedes. When she catches me, she leans forward, and a hysterical laugh bubbles from her throat. "You're awake."

I attempt to twitch my mouth into a smile for her, but my facial muscles catch against what feels like a sort of cord that shifts something fixed at my nose: an oxygen tube. Mercedes exhales as if she'd been holding her breath in for hours.

My vision gradually sharpens. This isn't the emergency room, where my bed would be shielded from the hall by only curtains. This room's solid; I must have been out for a while if they already moved me. Underneath a wide window is a body-length padded bench, large enough to sleep on and upholstered with dull blue pleather. It's light outside, the sky a glaring azure.

"What happened?" Rust would sound nicer than my voice.

Mercedes is in an armchair that has, jutting from its back, a chrome hook meant to hold a saline bag. Her hair is down around her face and her neck. She pushes away a turquoise tress.

"Your heartbeat"—her voice catches, and she clears it—"stopped for a few seconds. Elijah, the boy who found you, he was feeling your pulse, and there was a minute when…we thought we lost you."

A tremor tickles my back at knowing that I came so close to dying, but I can't say I'm surprised: I knew my heart was bad before I went out. It was wrong even after the defibrillator.

"They gave you an emergency pacemaker," Mercedes says.

Ah. That explains the slit over my heart.

"Why did you scream?" I wasn't asking about me in the first place. "Why were you bleeding?"

The relief on Mercedes' face stiffens and slowly dissolves.

Grimacing, she reaches up and gathers her hair to one side.

Phantom pain slashes next to my throat. Twin cuts, careless but clean, are crosshatched by stitches on the side of her neck.

Knife marks.

"They were in my room before I knew what was going on," Mercedes says. "Two of them. One pinned me. The other one did this." She taps a filed nail in the general area of the wounds but doesn't actually get close to them. She shivers. "I'm lucky that's all they wanted."

"Lucky?" Though my throat isn't as sore as usual, it's puffy when I swallow.

Mercedes shrugs, causing the red cuts to flex. "It could have been worse."

"Like what?"

"Like that guy Mom's been tracking. Garrett Martin."

I hadn't thought of that. I hadn't thought of anything besides her screams and the figures racing from her house. "How did they get in?"

"I don't know. There was no broken window or anything, but I know I locked the doors. I double-checked before I went to sleep. They must have jimmied it."

"Did Tristan see anything?"

The moment his name comes out of my mouth, Mercedes goes rigid.

"What?" I say.

Instead of answering, she inhales unsteadily and reaches for her pocket, but before she has a chance to show me whatever it is, the door clicks open behind her, and she swivels to look. The oxygen tube snares the skin inside my nose as I do the same.

Two women walk in. First, my mom in her officer's uniform.

Her thin, precise rim of jet-black eyeliner makes her look like a mother wolf. That, or the look in her eyes.

Second, my specialist, Dr. Tahan, a tall woman with caramel skin and intense narrow eyes. Her black eyebrows are thick but threaded, and every time I see her, she sports a different hijab. Today it's black with large roses.

Dr. Tahan's stoicism lightens when she sees me. "Glad to see you awake, Paityn. How is your pain?"

My dry nose stings with each puff from my oxygen tube. "Better than before."

"Good," she says, even though I meant it halfway as a joke, and from her expression, she's not reassured. She nods to acknowledge Mercedes.

Dr. Tahan scrutinizes my vital signs on the monitor. So does my mother. Both have beautiful dark skin. Both are tall and immovable, like two sequoia trees.

Points on Dr. Tahan's face flex and release, as if she's fighting to remain analytical. "You've heard about the pacemaker?" She glances at Mercedes to supplement the question, and I nod. Dr. Tahan's forehead pinches, not bitterly, but tiredly. "It will only work on cardiac muscle. Not scar tissue."

Scar tissue. The only way my swollen heart can recover from the lupus.

My mom cups her nose between her thumb and bent forefinger as if her nose were broken and she was bracing herself to pop it into place. It only lasts a moment, though, before she raises her head, chin strong. "There's nothing else we can do?"

"We're giving her everything we can."

No kidding. A strong immunosuppressant dripped into my veins for hours, sometimes twice a week. The highest dose of prednisone I can take without hospitalization. Large IV doses of other steroids, for days at a time, whenever I flare up. Drainings when my chest cavity fills with fluid. A low-risk treatment that's often successful, except in my case.

And now, a different treatment involving so much chemo that there's a mortality risk. My last shot. Otherwise, we wait for the scar tissue to build up until it's too much. Until the pacemaker stops working.

My mom subtly twists her head as if stretching a cricked muscle in her neck. "Thank you."

Dr. Tahan nods. She checks the vitals screen one more time and purses her lips. "You know what to do if you need anything."

I nod again. Dr. Tahan glances at my mother, and I briefly close my eyes so that I don't have to see the look that passes between the two of them.

Once Dr. Tahan leaves, my mom's soldierly posture slumps. She posts one hand on her hip, the other over her belly. Protecting, as always—her default.

I roll back to my original position with my face to the ceiling, which loosens the tension of the oxygen tube in my nose. Mercedes' forehead is creased; her fingers are still over her pocket, where she was reaching before Dr. Tahan came in.

"What did you want to show me?" I ask. My mom frowns confusedly. "About Tristan."

At that, my mom's alert. "What about him?"

Mercedes' jaw cranks until I think it pops; she pulls her phone from her pocket and shows my mother the screen. Within one second, my mom's eyebrows lower and her eyes widen.

"What is it?" I ask.

Mercedes tilts the screen for me to see.

Tell Paityn that's just a taste.

The sender: Tristan.

A sick ache flushes my gut. My mom takes the phone and reads as if she's certain she must be missing some detail that would explain everything. "Why would he send that?"

"He didn't."

Mercedes' and my mom's attention whips up. My mother lowers the phone, screen down, clutching it so hard I imagine fractures zigzagging through the circuit board.

"Paityn?" An edge razors her voice. Telling me that I need to answer her so she can do her job. A job that I can't protect her from, one way or the other. "What is going on?"

My mother's knuckles whiten as she grips my bedrail. Mercedes' face is just as pale.

I never said the words "drug deal." I told them exactly what I saw. Exactly what I heard over the phone. Nothing more. Nothing less. That's enough.

My mom drags her hand off my bedrail, tightens it into a fist— her knuckles never change from that circulation-deprived shade— and holds it to her mouth. She's who I learned that habit from, except I do it when I'm uncomfortable; she does it when she's been pushed to her limit. Mercedes' fingers hover over the prickly ends of her stitches. Water creeps up her lower eyelids.

"I'll be right back," my mom says. With a stiff hand, she strokes my scalp once—they must have taken my headscarf—and then she leaves the room. Her muscles are so tight as she walks I almost expect them to snap. Knowing her, she's collecting herself so that she doesn't make a rash decision.

Mercedes watches her leave, then looks at me. For once, the

moisture in her eyes doesn't wane so easily. Her jaw flexes and releases. "I should go. School. Will you be—"

"I'll be fine."

I don't ask if she'll be—she won't. She won't be fine after we've been betrayed by the one person we all would die for.

Morphine numbs me for thirteen hours, drowning me in a thick, drugged, dreamless sleep. Not peaceful, but not awake. Somewhere in between. My mother sits with me. Once in a while, she'll caress me, and that grounds me, reminds me where I am, why I'm here, what happened.

At least she's with me. At some point, she speaks to me; I'm too tired to catch all of the words, but it's something about going home before her shift. She mentions Tristan.

At that, an ache blossoms through the painkillers like a poisonous flower.

Dr. Tahan agrees to take me off morphine. I'd rather deal with the discomfort and be able to think straight.

It's only about thirty minutes later that I realize what my mom was telling me before she left. Mercedes slips through the door, and Tristan comes in behind her, his eyes downcast.

That's what she said. They're both going to sleep here. Mercedes isn't safe alone, and Tristan obviously can't be trusted to be by himself.

They both carry bags. Mercedes takes the cushioned bench under the window. Tristan drops his bag on a cot—it must have been brought in here when I was asleep—on my side of the room.

Neither of them says anything to me or to each other. Mercedes' cuts are flushed red, the stitches thorny. She pulls a blanket from her bag and curls up with her back to Tristan, her scars to the roof. Tristan stands by the room's light switch.

What else is he hiding? What other lies has he told us?

He flips off the light and goes to bed.

———

I don't check the time. My torso doesn't hurt as badly as usual, but it's the same type of pain. My body can't help but wake up.

I'm finally free of the oxygen tube. Mercedes' shoulders rise and sink tranquilly, unlike the frayed, stressed breaths from when she was trying to fall asleep. Since then, I don't think she's moved. In my mind, her wounds glow a hot red.

I unclench my teeth when I realize they're giving me a headache. Tony and his lackey left her bleeding out of her neck. And he didn't say it was a warning. He said it was a taste.

Who could the other one be? When they ran, both had men's gaits, so that eliminates Venus, and she seems different from the others anyway. That leaves three: the two I don't know and Eddie.

If they could get into Mercedes' house without a problem, where does that leave the rest of us? Where does that leave Mom and the baby?

I shift my head to this side of the room, where Tristan sleeps as serenely as Mercedes. This is almost how he looked when I met him, except his nose was bleeding then.

I can almost see it again, the few details that are still there. I remember sitting on my bed, so small that I sank into it like it was a foam pit. Peering out the window at a boy around my age playing in his front yard.

A car speeding around the corner. The little boy bounding into the street to chase a toy.

His body crashing to the ground.

Running down the stairs, calling for my mom. Standing on tiptoe to reach the button to open the garage door. Darting into the street, where the car was already gone. Kneeling next to him. Asking if he was okay.

His eyes opening, the first time I realized they were green. He told me his name. I told him mine. And I promised that I'd make sure he was okay.

It's been twelve years, and this is what's become of it.

Tristan wakes up. Apparently, routine has messed up his sleep cycle too. I shift onto my side to face him better, careful of my IV needle and the incision.

"Tell us the truth," I whisper.

He makes a tired sound and shoves his hair back from his forehead. "I'm not doing this. I already told Mom. I lost my phone, and I didn't want to say anything before I tried to find it. Tony must have picked it up."

"Stop lying."

"You don't understand."

"Then talk to me."

"No."

Twelve years. Twelve years of me nearly seeing him die and of him nearly seeing me die. Severed in one day. He closes his eyes again, but they're not peaceful anymore.

This has to stop. And if Tristan won't help me, I'll do it on my own.

14

THE NEXT MORNING, MERCEDES STEPS OUT of the shower in my hospital room, trailing a whiff of her cinnamon soap with her. She surveys Tristan's empty cot—I was awake when he got ready at dawn, and he's been waiting for her outside since. The mouse-gray cot is folded on the wall. Mercedes' hair is swung over her shoulder, dripping wet and soaking into her fleece jacket, covering her cuts.

My phone is in my lap. My fingers start to clench around it at the thought of what they did to her, but I don't let Mercedes see my anger. She doesn't need that right now. "How is it?"

She shrugs with the shoulder on the side that doesn't have any stitches. "Sore."

"But at school, I mean." I know Tony doesn't attend—he's nineteen—but the rest of them do.

Mercedes' face puckers with annoyance. That's a good sign, I think—it can't be anything serious if that's her only reaction. "Yesterday was fine. Eddie and the others left me alone."

Good. Still, I wish I'd been there. I could have gauged their reactions, and that might have told me who Tony's accomplice was.

A pigeon flaps past the window and scrawls a frantic shadow

over me and the beige wallpaper. I run my tongue over my dry lips. There's one person who might know now that it's over: Luiz.

"Oh," Mercedes says abruptly, like she remembered something. Color rises in her cheeks, not quite a blush, but definitely a healthy pink. "By the way, about Elijah"—warmth spreads through me at the memory of him carrying me out of the rain—"he goes to our school, and he asked if he could visit you."

I run a thumb across the grippy rubber back of my phone. I don't know him, but he's already seen me brush against death. "Sure."

Half of her mouth quirks up like she was hoping for that answer. "I'll have him meet me here after school."

"Did you happen to bring my clothes?"

"I did." She rifles through her bag and conjures a fresh headscarf, a pair of khaki shorts, and a wrap shirt with snap buttons that allow easy access to my organs in case of an emergency: that's all that Dr. Tahan requires for me to get out of this hospital gown.

"Thanks," I say, resisting the temptation to wriggle out of this papery, sweaty thing right now.

"No problem." She grins. Under her hair, her stitches stretch.

———

I wait until Mercedes and Tristan are gone, then scroll through my phone contacts until I find the one I need. When was the last time I used Luiz's number? More than a year, I think. It's been that long since he warned me it wasn't a good idea to use it anymore.

A muted ache swells under my stitches. Sun the color of cornsilk pours through the window and spills across my lap, warming me beneath the thin, starchy sheets.

It's strange how much I can miss someone who lives only a block away. Strange how much it hurts to be close enough to reach for him but unable to extend my hand. I think he'd take it if we had the chance.

I exhale sharply, and the twinge it makes in my chest brings me back to the present. Maybe, if I'm lucky, ending Tony's little regime will solve more than one problem.

I type out the message. Meet me.

I delete the conversation and wait for—hope for—a response.

Hours later, I'm enjoying my clean change of clothes when my phone dings. I tilt the screen to my face, and the time fades onto the black sleep screen. It's far past three p.m. Mercedes should be here any minute with Elijah. Tristan won't, though, not since my mom has left to pick him up from school. She said they were going to talk. Does she really think she can get him to open up?

Who knows. Maybe he'll talk to her. Or maybe she's just offering him the chance because he's her son, and that's what she'll always do for him.

I offered him the same chance. He rejected it.

I check the message, but instead of Luiz's name popping up, there's no ID except an unknown phone number.

My mom's words from a couple days ago replay in my mind.

He leaves them text messages asking to be let in, pretending that he's a family member using a different number in some emergency.

Garrett Martin. And while I have no idea how he would know anything about Luiz and me, Tony knows my number now. Maybe Martin gave him inspiration. My phone is fair game.

There's a knock at my door. I plant the phone on my thigh, face down.

"Paityn? You ready?"

Mercedes plus guest.

I shove away an eerie tremor at the thought of Garrett Martin or Tony Suarez. I can't make a decision now. The message will still be there once I'm done with this.

My surgery sutures extend past the neckline of my shirt. I don't bother covering them. "Yeah."

She opens the door, bookbag slung over her shoulder. Elijah's behind her.

His thumbs are hooked in the pockets of a black leather jacket with a pale zipper. That same silver chain is wrapped around his right hand. There's a small crucifix dangling from it that I didn't see before. It bounces in his grasp—his hand's shaking.

My eyes hold his. They're the same as last time, that mixture of gentleness and pain so acute I can feel it in my incision.

He smiles at me. It's strained. "Hi."

I smile back, mine natural. "Hi."

"It was—" His eyes shift up and down me, but not in a demeaning or arrogant way. More like he's recalling something. He clears his throat. "It's Paityn, right?"

"That's me." I manage to work some pep into my voice.

In my peripheral vision, the corner of Mercedes' lip sneaks up until she forces it to be neutral again. She's leaning against the wall with her arms crossed, her hair pulled up, exposing the stitches on her neck. Apparently, she doesn't mind showing him. Then again, he saw her bleeding in the first place.

"I never got the chance to thank you," I say.

"Of course." No, it isn't like he's recalling—it's like he's recognizing something. "I thought we lost you there for a minute."

"Not that easily." I smirk.

He chuckles—somewhat uncomfortably—and sidles closer to my bed, but his attention isn't on me anymore: it's on the vitals monitor, the tubes, the wires, the bland wallpaper. He seems nervous, but not like he's unused to hospitals. It's the opposite. It's like he knows them all too well.

"Are you okay?" I ask.

"Yes, sorry." He clears his throat again. Mercedes frowns curiously at him.

His hand tightens around the chain as he pushes it into his pocket. I can't take my eyes off his, off that look like he knows me from somewhere and never wanted to be there again.

I watch him come back to the present with a blink.

"I should go," he says. His pulse hammers against his neck so hard I can see it from here. He peers behind him at the door as if making sure that it's still there, that he's not trapped. "But I'll come again. Tomorrow, if that's fine with you."

"I'll be home by tomorrow." Thank goodness. Mercedes raises her eyebrows as if wondering why she wasn't let in on that information, and I shrug at her apologetically—Dr. Tahan only told me a few hours ago. "But Mercedes can bring you anytime."

Elijah smiles. The tiniest bit of relief crosses his face. "I'll take you up on that." He turns to Mercedes and raises a hand in a still wave. "See you at school tomorrow."

She extends two fingers in a pretend salute. "See you."

He leaves. Mercedes' gaze follows him, intent like she's trying to see into him and understand. Like she's willing him to know that he can come back. I want him to know too.

After a few seconds, she lets out an airy breath. It's not a wistful sigh, but it's dangerously close. Dry humor hovers on my mouth. Mercedes smiles, pulls a laptop out of her bookbag, and perches on the bench under the window, where she sleeps. Blue skies smeared with sugar-white clouds clash with her turquoise ponytail.

Out of habit, I grope for my phone on my lap. That reminds me of the message.

Mercedes is intent on whatever work she has on the computer. Her backpack is orchid purple and worn at the straps, and a cyan hardcover peeps out: pre-calc.

Seeing the message won't put us in any more danger than we're already in. It might even be helpful if there's anything incriminating written. There's nothing to lose. Still, my stomach pinches as I open the text.

Fine. Wait for another message.

I reread it four times.

My mom said that Garrett Martin makes it sound like the sender's in an emergency. This is telling me to wait. And there's nothing particularly menacing that would implicate Tony. Besides, I don't think Tony knows about Luiz and me.

Am I willing to take that chance?

On the bench, Mercedes grabs a few strands of hair that have strayed from her ponytail and shoves them behind her shoulder. Her stitches flex like fish gills.

I have to take that chance.

Ok.

If it's Luiz, it won't be soon. It'll be tomorrow, Saturday, at about five p.m.

15

IT'S STRANGE TO WAKE UP with a normal heartbeat thudding steadily against my flannel sheets. My room is tranquil and warm around me.

Unfortunately, the pain remains unchanged. Piercing throbs filter from my skin to my bones and back again. Weight pins my ribs against my mattress until the pressure makes it difficult to breathe.

I struggle into a sitting position. The blankets fall from my shoulders and leave me reeling at the change in temperature, but the new position opens my airway until I have enough oxygen. The skin around my stitches pulses with my heartbeat. I'll be back in that hospital for a draining soon. I'll keep going back until it's healed—or until it's futile.

I swallow through a constricting throat, unwilling to give fear a way in. If I let it in, it will corrode me alive.

My mom has always told me to remember this: I need to do whatever it takes to come home safe, but if I can't, there's no shame so long as it was on my terms.

I don't plan on needing the second option. I plan on coming home. I will.

I drowse against the window for a long time, letting my mind wander; my thoughts only break when my phone beeps. I groan, and my hot breath stains the glass with fog. That's one of two people, neither of whom I want texting me at this time.

There's a name with the number. Tristan's. He must have mysteriously gotten his phone back.

My, my. I wonder how that happened.

Awake?

Yes, I am, but I don't want to see him. I don't want to look at him and know that everything he's been telling me is a lie. He won't help us, and because of that, Mercedes is in stitches. Our houses are no longer safe. And I'm waiting on a text message from a strange number as my only way to protect us. I lower myself back onto the mattress, my spine facing my door. I'll deal with the difficult breathing.

In less than a minute, a familiar stride approaches my room. I don't answer the hushed knock. I lie with my back to him, asleep to anyone who doesn't need to know that I'm awake.

My door swings open. Footsteps pad on the hard floor. The air in front of my face warms with a whiff of cedar.

His hand's in front of my nose and mouth. Checking my breathing. The humidity from my lungs bounces back against my face. His woody scent coats my airway.

The warmth lifts away, and then the back of his wrist presses against my forehead. His wrist becomes his whole hand, and his thumb brushes over my cold sweat. Is he remembering the last time we were in this position? Is he remembering when he carried me downstairs and took me to the hospital? Is it playing in his mind the way it's playing in mine, vivid as the dream I had two days ago?

Vivid as what I saw him do. Vivid as the two figures running from Mercedes' house, running from her screams.

I have to get Tony. Him and the entire little gang he's initiated. I couldn't do it for Damien, but this time, there's no other option.

Tristan walks away, taking the smell of cedar with him. He shuts the door.

I have until five this evening before I rule out Luiz. My phone is somewhere in the folds of the fleece blankets that cocoon me as I lie in the quarry-blue cushions of our couch. Mercedes sits at the kitchen table somewhere behind me, doing…well, I have no idea what she's doing. For that matter, she may have left without me noticing. It's an accomplishment for me to keep one thought in front of another, thanks to the morphine pills Dr. Tahan sent me home with.

Light pours in around the neatly tied curtains and bounces around me, silver from the snowy clouds, reflecting off the laminate floor. A quiver runs through me. It all feels exposed, especially since locked doors are moot now.

The comforting rumble of the washing machine and dryer tumbles down the stairs. Tristan's in his room—not allowed to leave, last I heard. I should feel bad for him. Maybe I do. Maybe it's somewhere within me.

I stumble into a half doze, but within less than an hour (unless the medication altered time for me), the doorbell rings. A pair of bare feet tap past me toward the door. I pull myself up off the cushion, my pacemaker flushing blood through my body. There's a window on the inner door, and Mercedes peeks through the slats of the blinds. A ring of keys dangles from her finger. She takes what sounds suspiciously like an excited preparatory inhale.

Ah. I have a guess who's out there. Though, honestly, I didn't really expect to see him again, not after how panicked he was in my hospital room yesterday. Mercedes tries to twist her neck, then apparently remembers the cuts and decides to swivel her whole body instead.

"It's Elijah," she says. "You good?"

I clumsily drag myself into a sitting position and toss away the blanket, plus my phone somewhere inside it. I adjust my shirt, cardigan, and headscarf. No worse than yesterday. Aside from an extra pill. Mercedes answers the door.

"Elijah." It must be brisk out, because her voice is a twinge high-pitched. It's either that or the handsome eyes in front of her. I grin to myself sleepily. And a bit too obviously. Worthless painkillers. Pull yourself together, Paityn.

"Hi, Mercedes." Her name sounds exotic when he says it.

"Paityn's in here." Mercedes lets him through. She's tamping a smile.

So is Elijah. He wears a black and white scarf under the same leather jacket as before. There are snowflakes caught in his black hair and his long, thick eyelashes. He blinks them off, and they melt on his cheekbones.

Mercedes slides her hands in her pockets and opens her mouth to say something, but she's interrupted by a voice from upstairs. It's my mom calling, but I couldn't make out what she said.

"I'll be right back," Mercedes says before dashing up the steps.

When she's gone, Elijah's gaze finds me. His posture is slightly tense, but it's nothing like when we were at the hospital. I do my best to stay awake as he strides into the living room.

"How are you feeling?" he says.

"Better."

"You look tired."

"I think 'sedated' is the word you're looking for."

He chuckles, a low, pretty sound that matches his voice. It's a bit surprised too, like he wasn't expecting me to crack a joke. His eyes don't quite make it into the smile, though—again, it's like he's seen me before, like I'm part of a painful memory.

His arm shifts with a scrape of leather against leather, drawing my attention. He's taken his left hand out of his pocket. The necklace spirals around it.

"That's pretty," I say, gesturing to it. A pathetic lead-in for a question that's none of my business.

A wave of pain crosses his face. "It was my sister's."

"You have a sister?"

"I did."

Did. "Oh. She—"

"She died."

He says it almost tersely, like he can't bring himself to get the words out otherwise.

"I'm so sorry," I say. He's looking at me sidelong, but the intensity's the same. The same as when he found me at the graveyard wall. "Is that why you were at the cemetery?"

I regret it the minute it comes out of my mouth. His face changes and tells me I caught him off guard, opened a wound that shouldn't have been opened.

"Sorry," I say again, silently chiding myself. I hate these painkillers. I hate when I don't think clearly. "I didn't mean to—"

"No, it's fine." He takes a deeper-than-normal breath, but his voice is steady. "And yes. That's why I was at the cemetery."

He smiles as if to put me at ease. I wish I could let him know that I'm grateful he's being so patient, that I really am sorry. Thankfully, before I can come up with another way to embarrass myself, Mercedes comes back downstairs, retying her ponytail.

"Her mom's going to come down before you leave," she tells Elijah.

"Great," he says with an enchanting grin, and the two of them slip into an effortless conversation. Both have tempered smiles and a flush in their cheeks. I tuck my legs into a crisscross and listen.

Until, muffled in the folds of the blanket I threw aside, there's a digital ding.

I come out of the morphine daze in an instant: there's only one reason it would give me an alert.

My mom comes down the stairs dressed in a jacket of broken-in black leather, similar to Elijah's, her gait agile and lithe. Elijah turns to her, and my mom smiles graciously. She also gives him an analytical once-over that probably only I would catch. Elijah meets her halfway. Mercedes idly taps her fingers around her scars. The stitches are vivid black on her light skin.

I mouse my hand around in the thick blanket and pretend to pay close attention.

My mom shakes Elijah's hand. "I'm Faith Carson."

"Elijah. Sanchez."

Where is that phone?

The pads of my fingers brush a bumpy rubber casing. Got it.

Just then, my mom says, "Thank you for helping my daughter."

My hands pause. The ghost pressure of his collarbone presses against my temple, and grateful warmth spreads through me.

Elijah turns around and looks at me. His hand is cinched around that necklace. His knuckles aren't quite white, but they're on their way. "Of course."

Something inside me thinks I'll never know how deeply he means that.

I leave my phone in my lap. My mom goes back upstairs, and Elijah and Mercedes talk for a while. I listen as he promises he'll come back tomorrow. Mercedes is smiling to herself when she closes and locks the door.

Once she's gone too, I pick up my phone.

The same number. So far, I'm still right.

I' ll come at 5.

16

I HAVE TO BE RIGHT. Luiz is the only one who would know that my family is at Saturday Mass at this time. That I'm alone since lupus won't let me go. And the only reason he knows is because he lucked out last time—when he came to me bleeding, when that scar across his forehead was a fresh wound.

I sit at the base of my stairs, the last of my morphine finally worn off. Sweat mists my headwrap, and nerves pop like sparks in my stomach. Evening has already begun to creep across the sky, clouds eclipsing any early stars.

What if I am wrong? What if Martin or Tony somehow figured out more than I think? Martin would be happy for another hapless victim. Tony would be more than happy to get rid of the only witness to any crime he's ever committed.

I exhale slowly, methodically. This is my chance to end it. Luiz might be able to give me enough information to uncover real proof, enough to keep his brother away from my family for good.

I jump when, at five o'clock sharp, knuckles rap on the door.

I stand, careful with my aching joints, pain heating a line down my chest. My pacemaker is stable, but it's solid, as if it can sense my unease.

Calm down. If it's not Luiz, I don't have to open the door. I can call the police and end it that way.

I peer through the slats of the blinds and strain to put a face on the figure in the porchlight. I mentally run the list of features for Martin: black hair, blue eyes, average height, and a scar on the bridge of his nose.

He slowly comes into focus. Black hair. Brown eyes. A scar, but not on his nose—across his brow, pale like starlight.

I exhale. Let's do this quickly.

I open the solid door. Luiz stands with his side to me, the hand facing me tucked in his pants' pocket. He's not wearing his aviator jacket, or any kind of jacket for that matter; a thin shirt is the only thing covering his long arms. Hot clouds billow from his nose like swells of smoke.

Luiz shifts his eyes to me the way he would to a leaf blown across the sidewalk. I scan past him. As always, there's no one.

I flip the lock and lever the handle, and when the door opens, I imagine the hiss of heat and cold touching. "Get in."

He's quick. The moment his second foot is through the door, I yank it shut again and throw the lock home.

"Why did you text me from some weird number?" I shut and deadbolt the inner door. My incision traces out from my shirt, and I do my best not to visibly favor it.

"I told you not to use my number." Behind me, his voice is low, but it seems almost brittle or like it's ready to light on fire at any second. "You can't show up on my phone."

I turn around. "What choice did I—"

I stop. He's not the only one favoring something: on the side that had been facing away from me, his arm hangs limp. The ball of the bone sags and bulges below the joint, dislocated.

Bloodstains are damp on his shirt. A protective heat rises in my voice. "Who did that to you?"

Luiz pops his perpetual gum. "Tony's not like my father if that's what you're implying."

That's exactly what I was implying. And I'd beg to differ, but I humor him. "Then who?"

Before he answers, there's a sharp vibration, like a trapped insect batting its wings. Luiz swipes his phone out of his pocket and mumbles something unpleasant. His thumb hits the screen for the passcode: dead center and near the bottom, then to the left, stretches straight up, and finishes on the opposite diagonal.

He touches the screen a few more times. Just when I think he's not going to answer my question, he slots his phone back in his pocket and says, "Some drunk."

"What did he look like?"

He scoffs. "Drunk."

I frown at him. He's never been sarcastic or curt with me. It's like he's annoyed that I even asked.

He stifles a wince. His shirt is soaked through and is leaking small scarlet droplets on the floor. Some of the drops reflect the sleepy yellow hall light. The ones in his shadow are almost black.

"I'm not going to fix this if that's what you want," I say. "Call the police."

"I told you I was coming before this happened." Luiz glowers at me sidelong. Again, a look he's never given me.

"Why are you acting this way?"

He rotates to face me. Queasiness tweaks my stomach at the sight of his shoulder swaying out of its socket.

"I don't know if you've noticed," he says, "but things have gotten more complicated between our families."

If I've noticed. *If* I noticed Tristan making a deal with Tony. *If* I noticed Mercedes bleeding out of her neck.

If I noticed that his father and brother killed Damien.

"Why did you come here?" I ask. Something in me begins hardening, closing off.

"Whatever you're thinking about doing, stop."

I stare at him, speechless. It's a few seconds before I wrangle my voice. "Are you kidding me? Your brother attacked her."

"You want to protect them?" His dislocated shoulder swings. "Leave it alone for once."

For once.

The words hit me in the diaphragm. Darkness seeps into my voice. "Do not go there." I jab a finger toward him. "I was helping *you*. Damien was helping *you*. And Tony and your psychopathic father killed him."

Luiz's posture hardens, his muscles turning to stone. I search for any sign of the boy I've known—or thought I've known. There's nothing.

"Then pay attention," he says, "and stay quiet this time."

"Get out of my house." It's a cool command, almost tranquil, as if I weren't raging inside.

Luiz tosses back a strip of hair from his forehead. "Fine."

He turns away from me. His tattoo of three slanted lines, the ink so dark it's almost black, is bold, as if it were a layer of polished stone embedded in his skin. He doesn't leave, though. Instead, he pinches the side of his shirt and reveals a few inches of his back. I almost turn away my eyes for modesty's sake, but then I realize what he wants me to see. My breath catches.

Scraping the entire length of his back are raised scars, bright as lightning against a night sky.

Luiz lets his shirt drop. "That's the man who trained Tony."

I try to blink away the burning picture of the scars. "If you want to help me, tell me what Tony's been doing. Help me get him away from my family."

His last chance. His last chance to take everything back.

He rests his fingers on the lock. There's dried blood in his cuticles and under his fingernails. "I just did."

He flips the deadbolt. When he opens the storm door behind it, a rush of frostbitten air envelops me. I hardly feel it.

He looks back at me. Looks into me as I look into him. And he lets the storm door swing shut behind him.

I stand in the hall, my back stiff. Luiz's blood leaves a trail on the sidewalk and follows him into the twilight.

My friend. More than my friend, I thought. And now, by his own choice, my enemy.

I lock the doors and sit on the ground, curled with my knees to my chest.

I swallow, tears burning in my throat. I won't cry over him. He's not worth it. I wasn't worth it to him.

17

RIGHT ON TIME, A KEY grinds into the lock.

I raise my head from where it was propped on the couch. My knees are sore from sitting on them, and bleach fumes from my hands burn in my nose.

Mercedes must be at her house for the moment, because she doesn't come in with them. Tristan, his jeans dressed up with a blazer, opens the door for my mom. My eyes and his meet until I break mine away. He walks upstairs.

My mom, in her pantsuit, watches. Her heels click against the hard flooring when she crosses the room to me. "You ready?"

It takes me a second to remember what she's talking about. I nod, and out of her pocket, she withdraws a round gold-plated container. A pyx. She pops it open, and inside is a thin, circular wafer.

I open my mouth for Communion. My mom places it on my tongue, and it begins to melt away.

It looks like rice paper. It feels like rice paper. It tastes like rice paper. I believe it's more, though. He's present in it. His real Body. I should pray, thank Him like I've been taught, but the words don't come. Only Luiz's cold voice echoes in my memory.

I swallow. "Thanks, Mom."

She closes the pyx with a snap. "What's wrong?"

I hate that cutting tears rise up. I swipe my hand across them, then tell her everything.

She shows no surprise as she listens. When I'm done, she considers for a moment before responding, and I brace myself for her to say something about how I should have told her.

Instead, she says, "We're going to stop this. I promise." My mom. Always brave. Always strong when I can't be. "Paityn." She places her hand on my knee and gestures upstairs. "Don't let them split you up."

I shoot a look in the same direction. "He split off."

He swapped drugs with the person who helped kill our father. He won't tell us anything. He won't let us help him.

Solemness crosses my mother's face as if her wisdom and strength from all her years comes over her at once.

"That's why he needs you," she says. "And you need him."

I wince. I owe it to my mother: she's suffering from this as much as I am. So I'll give him the chance. Besides—I want my brother back.

Things can't ever be the same, though. Not after what I've seen. Not after what he's done.

"All right."

My mom smiles. I wish I could smile back.

I stare at my ceiling, the white paint almost black in the early morning. Rain patters against my window. My chest throbs in sync with the pacemaker, and I imagine pressure cracking it from the inside out. It's not that bad yet, but it won't be long.

Neither will Tony's next move.

Tell Paityn that's just a taste, texted from Tristan's phone. Tristan knows what's going on. He knows the danger we're in, and yet he stays silent.

I can't just wait around for the police to catch Tony at some random crime. It'll be too late by then. I need to find some evidence myself.

Noises sneak through the house. Tapping raindrops, wind creaking through the neighborhood trees, clicks that I could swear are the locks.

I grit my teeth and sit up faster than I should. My stitches are hot, but I haul myself out of bed and grab shoes and a jacket. Even in the pitch black, I get around effortlessly. Same four walls, same desk, same dresser, same everything. The same room where I have an excruciating fever or see my stepbrother leave in the middle of the night or hear my best friend scream.

I need out, out of this house.

I tiptoe downstairs, past Tristan's room, past Mercedes drowsing on the couch. In my pocket are the spare car keys my mom lets me use.

———

I don't remember when Tristan, Mercedes, and I started calling this place "the underpass"—a culvert, a large open drain, running through a small hill a few miles from our houses. When we were six, maybe?

As I gear the car into park, a wry smile fades onto my face. We used to imagine what kind of monsters were inside the cement pipe or where the tunnel would lead if we followed it. Daring each other to see how far in we could go. I can't remember if it was Damien or my mom that caught us and told us that raccoons might be in there. Probably Damien—he'd say something like that.

I shut off the headlights but leave the heater running. Here, the road runs through a lone strip of underdeveloped land. There's housing within less than a mile in any direction, but right around me, it's a perfect area of dirt and wild grass. A large thicket of trees is to the north, where there were even more dares, more adventures. Back when everything was innocent. Back before any of us knew anything about fledgling gangs and murder and lost fathers, before drug deals and lies.

A migraine drums behind my eyes, so I rub my hands over them. It soothes nothing. None of this makes sense. Why would Tristan deal drugs? Why would he deal drugs for *them?*

I keep my face hidden in my hands for a few minutes. When I finally drop them, the rain has almost stopped, just a few crystal droplets drizzling from the charcoal sky.

Strolling through them is a person.

My mouth goes dry. Heat rises in my stomach.

Tony?

My hand freezes on the gearshift. I can't draw attention. If he sees me driving away, thinks that I was spying, assumes that I know more than I should—

Wait. No, that's not him. I know his body shape, and that's not it. I frown.

Whoever it is wanders closer, not coming right at me but meandering toward the underpass. Closer. Closer. The figure reaches into his pocket, then raises his hand, and a spark jumps away from his thumb. A lighter.

Another spark, and this time, there's more of a flare before it dies, but not enough for me to make out his face or anything else about him.

He hides the top of the lighter behind his cupped palm to

protect the flame from any wind and tries one more time. The fire glows over his face and stays there.

Black hair, greasy and cut at his neck. A trimmed beard. Jeans, and a blazer under a gray windbreaker. About five foot ten, if I were to guess.

He raises a roll—too loose to be a cigarette—to the flame, only about twenty feet from me. And unless I'm imagining it, the thick, bulging line of a scar lights up his nose.

The flame disappears, and the man continues his stroll. He never gets any closer than when he lit his joint. The tip of it glows orange and hot. Embers fall to the wet brush below.

I only exhale when he melds with the gloom. And when he's gone, I charge the engine and pray that it's not as conspicuous as it sounds to me.

I get on the phone with the police and report a sighting of Garrett Martin.

———

I pull into my driveway. Unease churns in my stomach.

Breaking and entering. Assault. Murder. And he was standing within feet of me.

I shake my head and exhale forcefully. Stop. Panicking over something that didn't happen does me no good. I've got bigger things to worry about.

I stop the engine, but before I get out, somewhere nearby, a car door thuds shut.

Across from me, parked on the street, is an old SUV. And from it, a young woman walks.

18

VENUS DRIVER.

My nails dig into the nylon armrest. Instincts clash in my mind. She's not like the other ones. She never enjoys Tony's cruelty. She even has the nerve to speak up against it; she did with Tristan.

That doesn't erase the tattoo on the back of her neck.

In the night, her skin is a striking shade of onyx. She crosses the sidewalk and the lawn, and saunters up to my car. She's in sweats—that's a first—and a denim jacket, and her lips are ruby red.

She and I stare at each other. No hiding. And no trust.

She stands with her hands in her pockets for a second. When I don't make a move to exit the car, her face pinches with annoyance, and she swings a finger around in a loop to get me to hurry up. I scowl at her—does she think I'm dense?—and she must take a hint because she rolls her eyes and slides her jacket off her shoulders. In the light from my porch, her smooth arms are riddled with goosebumps, and now she only wears a tank top, snug enough for me to tell she's not hiding a weapon underneath. She turns out her pockets. I can't see behind her, but if she had a gun, she'd have shot me by now. If she has a knife...

I search around her. No one. I pop the door.

Venus shrugs her jacket back on and scans me up and down. I can't tell if she's evaluating me as a minimal threat or if she's judging my clothes that hang so loosely on my frame.

"Didn't think I'd see you," she says.

She doesn't say it sarcastically, but I have a hard time believing pure coincidence brought us here. Then again, how would she know I'd be here now?

I'm not sure it matters.

The cold cuts right through my jacket. The ground smells like leftover rain. "Talk."

She sticks her hands in her pockets. "Not all he's cracked up to be, is he?"

"Who?"

"Luiz."

I stiffen. "How did you—"

"Don't trip. No one else knows."

How did *she* know I had met with him? And how did she know how I felt about him? "Why are you here?"

When I ask, something glints in her eyes, something dangerous—but something I like. She leans in. "Keep your eyes open. You're not the only one who wants out."

"What are you talking about?"

Venus touches her thumb and index finger together and uses the tips to punctuate each word. "Keep. Your. Eyes. Open."

She says it like I'm a child, but her eyes tell me otherwise. I nod. Once I do, Venus checks behind me as if to make sure we're still alone. I do the same. The worst thing back there is an empty purple recycling bin with its black lid flung back.

"Get going," she says, and I turn back to her. "Tony wanders."

"I know he does."

I lock my car, and the headlights flash, highlighting jewels of water dripping one by one from the roof gutters.

Venus pivots, but when she's halfway across my lawn and I'm halfway to my door, she stops and faces me. "Hey."

I listen. The red canvas of her shoes is wet from trekking through the grass. A single raindrop soaks into the shoulder of my shirt, and my skin warms it.

For once, she's displaying no bravado, no attitude. Her mouth is relaxed, her stance evenly distributed on her feet. "Tristan's not trying to hurt you."

My dry lips part, stretching the thin skin on them until it feels ready to split.

Why would she bring that up to me? And why would she say it like that? Like she speaks to him. Like he's told her things he hasn't told me.

"That hasn't stopped anything," I say.

Venus hesitates, like she wants to argue it but realizes she can't.

Voices start up inside the house, first hushed, then louder, and a light flips on. Venus tenses but doesn't leave; she shoves her hands farther into her pockets and waits as the front door unlocks.

Tristan's the first one out. His eyes narrow when they find me, not angry so much as surprised and confused. "Paityn, what in the—"

Then he notices Venus.

Mercedes comes up behind him, and Tristan steps out to give her some space. She props the door open with her hip. Her eyes flit to me, Venus, Tristan, and me again.

"Venus," Tristan says. There's nothing defensive or wary in his tone. In fact, it's vulnerable. "What are you doing here?"

"I was driving by. Saw your sister." Not stepsister. Sister, like she knows us well enough to know how close we are. Were. Are. "Thought I'd stop."

She smiles. Not the fake one she puts on around Tony that looks like it's glued onto her face. It's a hesitant smile, identical to the one Tristan gives her back.

They look at each other for a moment before Venus shrugs. "I'm getting out of here," she says.

She strides back to her SUV. Tristan waits until she's securely in before his attention comes back to me. He gestures for me to come inside. My hackles don't lower until I'm deadbolted in.

Tristan scans me over as if searching for injuries. "What were you doing out there?"

"Thinking."

I prepare for a scowl at the spiteful response, but I never get it. Instead, he sighs and climbs the stairs, leaving me with Mercedes.

"What was all that about?" she asks. Her irises are tinged with gold in the yellow hall light.

My gaze follows Tristan. I don't speak until his door shuts and locks. "I have no idea."

I don't get back to sleep.

I see no reason why Venus would trick me. I see far less reason why she would help me, but for now, she's all I have. Venus, a total stranger, may be the one to help me. Not my own brother.

With nothing better to do, I start playing a mindless game on my phone. The snowboarder avatar lands a flip when a notification appears at the top of the screen. Four a.m. already, and I stare at the same message as always.

I sigh and press my head against the glass of my window, which does nothing but hurt me. I don't want him in here. Every time I look at him, I think of the lies and the blood running down Mercedes' neck.

My mom's words from last night hum to me.

Don't let them split you up. And, *That's why he needs you. And you need him.*

I do need him. I've always needed him, and I won't let Tony take him from me, not without a fight.

I text Tristan back. Come on.

I put down my phone as I hear his strides. The rhythmic sound somehow comforts me, even now. That sound has always meant that everything was all right. Everything was safe.

When he pushes my door open, a wave is etched in his forehead, and I get the distinct impression he's surprised that I asked him in. Surprised that I don't pull my eyes away. I don't say anything; I just wait as he takes his usual spot across the bed, and then both of us watch out the window.

After a few minutes, Tristan looks at me again with that same mild astonishment, as if he's trying to fathom why I would bring him back.

We share gazes, and I don't look away, and neither does he. How long have I been wanting this to happen again? For us to see each other without turning away.

I'm not sure which one of our gazes drifts out the window first, but at some point, it happens.

Tristan sets his hand on my foot.

An hour later, there's the scrape and swing of the front door opening downstairs.

My eyes whip open. The sound creeps across my muscles, sets them buzzing and ready to contract at a moment's notice. Tristan's hand becomes a cage around my foot, and he leans forward to search out the window. The moonlight bleaches him like a corpse.

Then he relaxes and chuckles.

I haven't heard him laugh in such a long time. Months. I had almost forgotten what a sweet, mellow sound it is. I certainly didn't think I'd hear it when our door just opened at five in the morning. I push back the curtain and search for what I'm missing.

Our daily runner—Elijah—stands in front of our driveway with his hands in his pockets. A turquoise ponytail bounces down to meet him. She's dressed in running clothes.

They both grin, then take off down the street.

I let out a hushed laugh, just a gust of air through my nose. Tristan looks at me like it's been a while since he's heard that from me too. And I think he smiles.

19

AFTER EIGHT DAYS, MY FLAREUP finally burns out; I should've known I'd regret my little joyride—unless Venus somehow comes through.

I gag down a cup of green tea. The sky is a tart blue outside the kitchen window. My ears are cool even in the house, but at least my body's in less pain. It ought to be by now. I haven't gotten out of bed aside from showering or sitting up when Elijah visits. Daily, like he said he would. A soft warmth covers my face, a smile.

The garage door opens a few minutes later. When my mom walks in, her face doesn't have enough color, as if all her arteries have faded to a grayish white. One hand supports her back.

"Rough morning?" I ask.

She nods but smiles through her bated grimace. "Worth it. I have a doctor's appointment on Monday."

"Check-up?"

"Yeah."

I glance at my mother's midsection, the tiny life hidden inside. A girl, if my guess is right.

"Listen to her heartbeat a couple extra seconds for me," I say.

My mom's smile broadens. "I will."

Two days later, I'm tapping the toes of my tennis shoes against each other while I sit on the couch. I'm surprised how well my joints can handle the impacts; the pain hasn't been this low in a while. Can't say the same of my chest. It's like a pocket of water is expanding inside me, pressing against my pacemaker and my scarred heart.

I rub my eyes, which feel thick. How long did it take me to get to sleep this morning? Usually, I'm out right after Elijah and Mercedes go running, but no such luck the past few days. Today it was an extra hour at least.

I could ask Tristan, but I won't.

There's the knock at the front door I've been waiting for. I stand, stiff and unstable on my knees at first, but after a few steps, I get going. When I answer the door, Elijah brightens.

"Look at you up and about," he says.

We both laugh. I'm about to invite him in, but the sun glows on my face. It's warm for the middle of winter.

"Want to go for a walk?" I ask him. "It'll be short."

He smiles. "Let's go."

Before I can step out, though, a voice comes from the top of the stairs. "Paityn?"

Tristan's standing there questioningly—I'm not sure how I missed his door opening—but when his line of sight skims over my shoulder to Elijah, he relaxes. Elijah acknowledges him with a nod. Tristan opens his mouth like he wants to speak, then closes it and disappears.

I walk away—he never gives me any other choice.

On my porch, the winter air flushes out my lungs with a rush, a buzz. In the far distance, the mountains grasp at the sky from the west horizon. They're like smoky, dusky paint over a fresh blue backdrop. As I let the door swing shut behind me, Elijah gives me a concerned once-over—I have the sense he thinks I don't notice—before he glances behind me, through the storm door, then at Mercedes' house across the street.

"Oh," I say as we set into stride down my driveway, "she's got a head cold."

All that running in the morning. I tamp a grin.

Elijah cringes. "Really?"

"She says she's fine. She's just at her house for the day. She didn't want to give it to me."

I don't tell him that if I catch an illness, I can't fight it.

He nods. Why do I have the feeling he remembers being that careful for someone else?

"You all right?" I ask him.

It takes him a moment to answer; somewhere, wooden windchimes knock together. "I just came from the cemetery."

I internally wince at the thought of the last time I brought that up; at least this time, I'm sober enough to keep my mouth shut. For a few strides, neither of us speaks. Elijah's left hand bulges in his pocket—squeezing that necklace, the one that was his sister's.

"She died from cancer four months ago," he says.

I slow and look up at him. I didn't expect that. Not only because his sister died so recently. Not only because it was about the same time as Damien. And not only because I was never expecting to hear that it was cancer, a long fight like mine. I was never expecting to hear it at all. He barely knows me, and he opened this up to me.

Telling him that I'm sorry doesn't seem right, doesn't seem enough. He's offering me something. The same thing he offered when he looked back at me after my mom thanked him. When he helped me. When my head was rested against his heart.

"What was her name?" I ask.

"Cynthia."

I almost stall.

Cynthia. And Elijah told my mom that his last name was Sanchez. Cynthia Sanchez del Rio. The name on the gravestone that the strange man was visiting, the man who keeps showing up in my dreams, who was the first one to say she had cancer.

I shake my head subtly so I can bring myself back to the present without drawing Elijah's attention. It's not that important.

"You can tell me to mind my own business." He sounds like he's debating whether he should continue or not. "But…what do you have?"

He was vulnerable with me. Now it's my turn.

My next inhale is crackly. When I let it out, the words come naturally, as if I were talking to someone who's known me his whole life. "I have lupus. It's been damaging my heart. Badly."

Elijah's eyes take on the same light they did when he first visited me in the hospital. Almost afraid.

Now it all makes sense. He *has* seen this before. And he knows how it ended for the last person.

My legs begin to gently throb, and from the way he's looking at me, I could swear he can sense exactly where I'm aching.

"Let's go back," I say. I'm not ready to think about any of that.

We've made it to the end of the bent street. I could go farther—could probably run if I needed to—but I don't want another flareup right after I got past the last one. Voices float from around the bend, so someone must be on the other side, but they're so low that they're unrecognizable. I guess I'll find out when we have to cross each other on the sidewalk, though it's probably a couple of strangers on a stroll.

Elijah and I trace the blind curve that hides my house from this end of the block. Then he asks, "Who were you visiting?"

"What do you mean?"

"At the cemetery."

Oh.

My first reaction is to shut down, close off, tell myself that I don't want to talk about it, but that's not true. I do. Being near him—it makes me want to let it all out. He was holding me when my heart almost stopped. There's nothing I have to hide from him.

"My father. He was killed."

Elijah's pace slackens. "Killed?"

"Yes. He was trying to help a friend of mine, but—"

I cut that thought short when a voice from around the sharp bend, much closer now, raises. My stomach clenches.

Here comes that dear friend now.

The brothers come around the corner. Elijah and I have no place to go.

Someone fixed Luiz's arm, though it's still stiff by his side. He's gesturing angrily with the other one. Tony's mouth is, surprisingly, shut. Elijah takes a step in front of me and says something in Spanish that I don't understand. I have the distinct impression it wasn't something he intended for me to hear.

I don't pick up all of what Luiz is saying, just that at the end of the sentence, he says the name Martin.

There are plenty of people named Martin in the world, but I have a hunch that Luiz—for reasons I don't pretend to know—is talking about Garrett Martin.

I can't place Tony's expression. Not quite bored, but not his eager ruthlessness either. Almost...concerned.

I must have a fever if I'm seeing that.

"Are you sure about this?" he asks.

"Yes," Luiz snaps back.

Just as he finishes the last sound, his eyes shoot to me, bringing Tony's with them. Tony smiles.

"Hey, girl," he calls to me. Shudders slither down my spine at that voice. No longer digital over the phone, but just as smooth, just as disgusting. "How's your friend?"

A deadly combination of fear and anger heats my skin. Luiz's expression doesn't change. Distant, lifeless, heartless. There's nothing left of who I fell in love with.

Elijah's hand clenches into a fist. Not the one with the necklace—the free hand. He jerks his head to move the two along. "We're leaving."

Tony smirks. But to my surprise, he steps off to the side.

Luiz doesn't. Anger radiates from his jaw, his shoulders, every one of his features. He scans Elijah and me—no, *Elijah*—and stays where he is. He's far enough to the side for us to pass, but only if we're the ones who avoid him.

I level him with a glare like his own as his last words to me echo in my memory. *Stay quiet this time.*

That just gives me one more person to get arrested.

Elijah continues forward, and I keep near him. My neck tingles as we approach. Tony towers over me; he's even taller than Elijah, thick, strong, and hardened. Able to snatch me and split me on a whim. Sweat soaks into the back of my shirt.

Make sure the last thing they see is that you have no fear in your eyes. Damien's words from so many years ago whisper in my mind, gentle yet firm as the day he first said it. And then told me over and over until it was a constant chant inside me.

That didn't die with him. So I match Tony's eyes as I pass.

My challenge leaves no surprise on his face, no intrigue, nothing but that smirk. Luiz's brown irises are on me, gliding with me as I pass, so intense that I almost jump when they shift from me to Elijah.

Hatred slips into that glare. I don't let myself shiver.

Elijah and I make it past them. I could swear Luiz's stare spreads ice across me. And then, Tony says something in Spanish and chuckles.

Elijah stops. Turns around, unnervingly placid, as though a hunter's instinct has awakened inside him. Luiz shoots his brother a worthless scowl.

Elijah starts speaking in Spanish, his voice low. Tony stops smirking. Luiz's face changes—becomes dark, dangerous.

Tony speaks again, and Elijah replies coolly, all in Spanish. And Tony stares for a few seconds, his jaw suspended half open, the exposed corners of his mouth a fleshy pink. The silence feels ready to electrocute us. Leave us all dead.

Elijah places his hand on my shoulder to guide me away. Before we leave, Luiz pops a knuckle. His interest isn't on me. It bores into Elijah.

I've never seen that look before. And I hope I never have to again.

I let Elijah lead me away, but my back doesn't stop tingling. Even though I shouldn't, I twist my neck and strain to peer behind me. Tony and Luiz are both watching us, every so often exchanging glances. A dozen or so paces later, they haven't moved.

A new dread sinks inside me.

Another couple dozen, and though the brothers are still there, I know for a fact we're out of earshot. Without making eye contact with Elijah, I ask, "What did he say?"

Elijah's hand is still protectively on my shoulder. I don't think he realizes he's squeezing hard enough to hurt. "You don't know?"

"No."

He relaxes, but it's forced. "Good."

I bite my lip before I ask him to translate. He's right. I don't want to know. "Thanks."

He nods, releases my shoulder, and stretches his fingers. He doesn't know what he's just gotten into. He challenged Tony for me. He's involved now.

We get back to my house and hike onto the driveway, which puts Tony and Luiz in my peripheral vision. They're still on this side of the blind curve, but they've lost interest in us, thank goodness. They're back to their conversation.

Elijah opens my front door—I must have left it unlocked, genius—and waits for me to walk through. I stop when the brothers finally move.

I've already indulged my curiosity too much. It isn't worth it.

I shift my head to the side just enough to figure out what they're doing.

They must think we're long gone, because Tony has placed his hand on Luiz's shoulder as if reassuring him. Luiz's chin is set. He's almost as tall as his older brother.

My foot steps forward without the rest of my body following. My neck cranks as the strange sight gets stranger.

That can't be an embrace. It looks like it, stiff and brief as it may be with the two breaking as awkwardly as humanly possible, but that can't be right because Tony is cruel, and Luiz would never let anyone get that close.

The brothers move on and disappear around the bend.

Elijah's voice breaks me from my stare. "What are they doing?"

"I don't know." I rub my arm, as if that will soothe the tension coiling inside my stomach.

I don't know anything. I don't know what's going on with my family. I don't know what to make of what I just saw. I don't know what I've done to Elijah now that he's in the crossfire, because I know he is; I know it.

And I'm not sure what will put him in more danger. If I tell him. Or if I don't.

20

AS I LIE FLAT on my back in my room, I imagine a clock ticking through the night. Through my open curtains, the sky has faded from heather to a sweet, syrupy black. If it's the time I think it is, it's been at least six hours since I talked to my mom about what happened on the walk today. And six hours later, I have yet to shake the sinking feeling in my gut.

The worst part isn't going to be telling Elijah what's going on. If I'm lucky and his mom told him once my mother called her, he'll already know. No, the worst part is going to be telling him that I'm trouble. That he might be safer keeping his distance. Or that it might not make a difference.

Stars twinkle next to a waning moon. I stare at them until they become blurry, until everything's blurry, and all that's left is the strange hollowness in me. I've only known Elijah for two weeks, but the thought of losing him hurts. Somehow, I already miss him.

I thumb the incision line on my chest, a crevice in otherwise smooth, soft, warm flesh, despite the fact that I know I shouldn't be touching it. The last thing I need is for a germ to weasel directly into an open wound.

Elijah said his sister died after years of fighting. I've never let myself think about that possibility. Not really. It's always been in the back of my mind, a scenario to be aware of so it couldn't crush me if it ever became a reality, but at the same time, I was never willing to believe that it *would* become a reality.

My throat constricts with tears, and my ribs feel as though someone has cinched a rope around them, but the moment that happens, I force the fear out of my mind. I force myself to swallow. I force myself to inhale. I don't have time to waste my energy on a situation that doesn't exist yet.

The doorbell rings; digital notes buzz through the house.

I sit up.

Who in the world?

I search outside the window. The street is empty. Absolutely no signs of who could be wanting to get into this house.

I grab my phone in case I need it. Mercedes is already at the front door by the time I get there, peering between the slats of the blinds. Her stitches are gone, but the wounds are ready to split.

"Who is it?" I almost flip on the light but stop myself in time.

"I don't know." Her sinuses sound clearer than they did on the phone this morning, but she keeps a cautious distance when I come near.

Someone's standing out there, and after a few seconds, the silhouette takes shape.

It's not Martin or Tony. Too short, not to mention shaped like a woman.

"Venus?" I say to myself.

The figure outside places both of her hands in front of her, and a soft glow emanates from them. A phone.

Mine buzzes.

"What is it?" Mercedes asks as I check my messages.

An unknown number, but I immediately recognize one thing: the last four numbers are the same as the one that Luiz texted me from earlier. There's no signature.

Now' s your chance. Open the door.

She's got a hood up, and its shadow completely obscures her features, even with the light from her phone and the porchlight.

I text back. Tell me what' s happening.

I send it when Mercedes suddenly stiffens. Without warning, she shoots up the stairs two at a time.

"What's the matter?" I call after her, but Mercedes doesn't answer; by that time, she's at the top of the stairs. And Venus—if I'm right and that's her—tips her phone up, reading my message, I'm guessing. Then she spins and walks away.

From upstairs, Mercedes' voice shakes. "Tristan's gone."

21

"*WHAT?*" A SICK THRILL runs through my pacemaker.

Mercedes starts back down the stairs, her steps thundering. "His room's empty, and the window screen's popped out."

I press the heel of my hand to my forehead as I fight down panic. Not again. Do not do this to me again, Tristan. Do not—

My phone vibrates.

There's a package on your porch. Hurry.

"What are you looking at?" Mercedes asks, her voice taut.

I show her the message and explain as best I can. She frowns and searches through the glass on the door again. Frustration and anxiety saturate every one of her movements. "I don't see it."

"It's there." One of them picks locks. There would be no reason to lure me out for some kind of package. Tony may not know me well, but he knows I'm smarter than that. Venus must be making good on her promise.

Mercedes adjusts the blinds so that the slats parallel each other and there's more space to see between them. She must spot that package, because she tips her head back and groans as if doing this opposes every instinct inside her. She digs a ring of keys from her pocket—she must have grabbed them when the doorbell rang—

and opens the door. Her hand darts out, snatches an envelope on the floor, snaps back in, and she bolts the door again faster than I've ever seen her move.

She hands me the envelope. I tear it open. It's a typed note:

B/E, menacing, possible assault.
Group effort.
4463 Holland St.
11 p.m.
Information about Garrett Martin.

That location's five minutes from here. I read the top-right corner of my phone: 10:53 p.m.

A thrill runs through me. It'll be enough proof if we catch them in the act. We can get there before the police.

Mercedes' eyes are wide. She jams the keys back into the deadbolt. I call my mom.

We step out barefoot. Mercedes clicks the fob to our second car, and its taillights glow a dangerous red. She tosses me the keys, then dashes over to her house to take her dad's spare car since neither of us has had a license long enough to carry passengers.

I'm not supposed to call my mom when she's on shift except for emergencies, so she answers sternly. "Baby, what's wrong?"

"Tristan's gone," I say. Across the street, an engine—Mercedes'—starts. "But we've got them."

***

If my memory isn't completely shot, my mom says the average police response time is about twelve minutes. That means they should finally get here in five.

The headlights are off as Mercedes and I sit in my car, parked a little way outside the address that was on the note, the car Mercedes left behind parked farther back. There's enough distance between us and the house that Tony and whoever else shouldn't notice us, but we're close enough that we'll be able to see any movement. Hopefully. Police dispatch crackles with static as they wait for the moment either of us sees anything.

Cracks stretch across the asphalt, painted with icy moonlight. The house we're scoping out is the same cookie-cutter as ours, but the yard is thistles and crabgrass. Scrap is on the porch and tucked off to the side. There's no fencing, and the porchlight is off, same as every other house on this block. How can there be such a difference within a mile of the same neighborhood?

If I'm right, the police won't start their sirens, not yet; they won't alert Tony and the others, but that leaves me with no idea how close they are.

Suddenly, Mercedes stiffens and points.

A figure emerges from behind the corner of the house. The clothes are so baggy that they cover any hint of a body shape, but the head, the hands, the height…

That's Luiz.

I tell dispatch. I say his name and tell them how I know, but since I can't see anything well, I know my word alone isn't convicting.

Luiz crouches and puts his hands to the knob. About three minutes pass before he stands and opens the door like the locks never existed. Mercedes' cuts burn in my own neck. That's how they got into her house. It was him all along.

My jaw coils until my teeth slide against each other. Luiz waves someone over. And from around the corner come six of them.

Mercedes covers her mouth. Stifling the dread contorting inside me, I count again. The tallest, Tony. The only feminine shape, Venus. Three others with just about the same build, Eddie and the other two.

And one more. He's crowded around the others, and he has a large hoodie, all obscuring him enough that I can't be sure. But there's no one else it could be.

"Oh, Tristan." Mercedes' whisper is in tremors.

Luiz, Tony, Venus, Eddie, and the one I think is Tristan slink inside with a motion like shadows melding. The other two, I'm guessing, are scouts.

There's a shout from the house.

A light flips on, then off. A scream cuts short.

My heart rises in my throat. I don't know what kind of person is in there, but I know I don't want them dead, no matter who it is. And I don't want Tristan to have been a part of it.

Down the street, a mass passes as smoothly as liquid. A police car. Two. Mercedes' head whips around. Two more, and a fifth drives in from a side street. Enough to deal with seven armed teenagers.

Please, God, don't let Tristan be armed.

From their nonchalant stances, the two boys on the porch are gabbing, but then one pricks up and smacks the other on the arm to get his attention. They spot one police car. They swivel as they catch the others.

As they bolt into the house, the police park, their car doors open, and ten officers have their firearms at the ready. I don't see my mom, but I can't be sure she's not there.

My throat closes. Come quietly, Tristan. Don't make the police…don't make Mom—

Windows shatter like a thousand angry bells. One must be on the far side, opposite Mercedes and me, because two shapes leap from it, shards stuck to their clothes and glittering in the moonlight. At the back, where I can see it from our angle, more glass explodes outward, and four figures run. One of them is Venus, one Luiz, and I can't make out the two others, but none of them are Tony—which means he's the only one left in there.

A window facing us blows open, but no one exits.

Police officers yell, firearms poised. Three of them take off after the two who ran from the far side of the house. Four others pursue the ones escaping from the back. The remaining three approach the house. One shouts their presence.

Where's Tony?

The three officers brace themselves at the front door. Enter, disappear inside.

Motion in the window nearest us.

A gunshot, a flash. A cry of pain.

Mercedes crushes a hand over her mouth. I gag down a yell. A large frame climbs out of the window, tall and unmistakable.

Running down the street we're on.

I crush my skull against the headrest as a swear word tries to wedge out of my teeth. Mercedes says it for me.

He'll see us. He'll see us and know that we brought the police.

A spark and a bang burst from the window. Tony stumbles enough to make me think they got him, a skim shot maybe, but he picks up stride with hardly a break. Closer to us. Mercedes grips the armrest until her fingers are as silver-white as the diluted moonlight falling in here.

Twenty feet from our car.

Ten. I don't breathe.

Five. Close enough that I can make out the sweat beading above his lip.

Don't look over here.

Another shot from the house, but this one must miss. Tony twists around, fires a return, runs.

And as he passes our car, those dark eyes—

Land right on mine.

22

TONY DOESN'T SHOOT. He doesn't get the chance: another bang forces him to sprint past us with a limp in his strides. Two officers pursue.

I'm not sure how much longer it is until I breathe, but when I do, Mercedes' neck is an iron bar. The half-healed cuts ripple as her tendons tighten, release, and tighten again. I wonder if my incision is doing the same thing.

The two of Tony's gang who ran out the far window have stopped, and their hands are raised away from any weapons. The officers who were chasing them have their firearms presented, and now I have a better view. It's the boys that I don't know. Not Tristan. And not the ones I needed.

The police chasing the four from the back have gone far enough that I can't hear their shouts anymore. One of the officers handcuffs the two boys with a nickel glint in the moonlight.

Mercedes exhales in tremors. "He saw us."

I don't let myself look at her scars. "I know."

———

I park in my driveway. Mercedes pulls into her place behind me. My hand shakes when I place it on the car handle.

I pop the door, slam it shut behind me, and rush to the porch. Mercedes sprints across the street and reaches me just as I open the lock. The warm air swoops over us when we get in, and Mercedes slams the door shut so hard the blinds on its window slap against the glass. I sit on the floor with my knees bent as I catch my breath; it gets short too easily. And it wheezes, and it hurts. Breathing hurts. Mercedes barricades the door with her body.

Neither of us talks for a moment. Then Mercedes says, "We're not safe."

I prop my elbows on my knees and hide my face in my hands. We should never have gone. I wanted so badly to catch them, to ensure that they wouldn't get away without leaving proof, to end this. This is my fault. My choice. My family is at gunpoint because of it. Again.

"I'm sorry," I say.

A warm, skinny hand perches on my shoulder. Mercedes tries for a smile; she doesn't do very well. She opens her mouth like she's about to say something. Instead comes a hushed, muffled voice: someone either talking to themselves or having a conversation on the phone.

Tristan's voice.

A fierce, disbelieving heat sparks in Mercedes' eyes, and she thrusts herself upstairs. I follow her. Tristan's one-sided conversation stops. Mercedes has reached the top floor when his door opens.

He's in the clothes he normally wears to bed. His face is clean. His hair is combed. No signs of a struggle or a run.

Except he's pale going on anemic. His hand quivers.

"Where have you two been?" he says. "You scared me."

"Oh, you suddenly care?" Mercedes shifts her neck so the cuts on it stretch, widening the thin red ribbons, and points downstairs. Points outside, to the place where this happened to her, to the danger we've been in. To my mother and the baby, somewhere on shift with Tony on the loose. "You did this."

Tristan doesn't harden, doesn't shut off like he's been doing to me every day for months. Instead, hurt pinches every part of his body. He doesn't respond.

Mercedes' arms are so rigid they're shaking. She tucks back a strand of hair that came loose from her bun, then exhales, pivots, and hurries past me, back down the stairs. The steel of her eyes is surrounded by pink.

Tristan looks at me, waiting for something I don't give.

I go to my room.

As I lie in the dark, I try to block out the memory of the pained cries of the officer that Tony shot. It wasn't fatal, they said. At least that's one thing I haven't done. That doesn't ease the fact that they haven't caught Tony. I wish I knew how he's able to hide so well. Where does he go?

I itch to fiddle with something. Venus' note, maybe, if I hadn't been told to hand it over when the police were questioning us.

Information about Garrett Martin.

Why would they need that?

My body crashes and burns, so lost that the lupus doesn't wake me. And by the time I wake up, the black sky is light purple, and I've missed the four a.m. text message.

For once, I fall back asleep.

The pain wakes me up early the following morning, but at least I'm awake. I missed all of yesterday in a half delirium.

I don't remember the last time it was this bad. Every time I open my lungs, a pang claws through me.

The clock turns to four. No message.

A groan gurgles out of me, half pain, half dread. I give him three minutes, and when the message still doesn't come, I slide out from under the covers and pad through the hall until I stand in front of his room. I raise my arm and knock on his door. The impact sends shots through me.

There's no answer for a few seconds—but there is a sound coming from inside. It's so muffled I'm not sure, but I think he's crying.

I rest my forehead against his door and listen. It's a sound that makes my heart ache worse than the illness, worse than the betrayal. A sound I never wanted to hear again.

I stand upright and raise my knuckles to knock again, but just before bone claps against wood, he opens the door.

He's wearing a mock neck shirt. He's not as pale as yesterday, but his eyes—they're bloodshot, and tear stains rim them. His breathing is in tatters.

"Tristan, what's happening?" I ask.

He swallows hard. Behind him, on his nightstand, moonlight reflects off a small photo. I don't think I've ever seen it before, at least not in his room. It's difficult to see the picture because of the glare, but it's definitely the three of us—Tristan, Mercedes, and me—with trees in the background. I think there's also a strip of gray on the side, but I can't make it out well.

"I'm fine," Tristan says. His voice cracks.

"No, you're not."

He looks at me for a second, and it's there: a flicker of vulnerability, of openness. Hope sparks inside me, hope that all of this will stop, that he'll open up and be my brother again. It burns inside me, almost tangible.

He drops his gaze and eases back into his room. He begins to close the door.

I stop it. I plant my hand against it and grimace as a blade of pain drags through my torso. It doesn't matter. I'll take it. That's nothing compared to the first time this happened. Nothing compared to if he does it again.

"Please." Desperation creeps into my voice. "Don't shut that door again."

His swollen eyes well up, and for a moment, I see him again. See the boy I knew, the boy who trusted me.

He bows his head. And closes the door in my face.

I stand there for a moment. The pain is the same as the first time. Worse, I think, because now I can hardly register it. I stare blankly at the thin white wood in front of me. Then I press my back to the door and slide down. Same as before. Except this time, he's crying on the other side.

And something else. Something else is different.

A smell. One I recognize, but not his cedar. It's pungent and tangy. Familiar. Powerful. Dangerous.

I think I smell...

Gunpowder.

I'm piled on the couch in a fortress of blankets when my mom gets home from her shift, rubbing her eyes. Her hand is over her stomach more firmly than usual, pinning her shirt against her body. The fabric is contorted into waves around her fingers.

"Is everything okay?" My throat is so tender that I almost can't talk. I sit up, and aches spread across my skin. My sternum squeezes when I inhale and throbs with pressure when I exhale.

My mother removes her hand. She's smeared her eyeliner. "I'm all right."

"The baby?"

She shrugs. "Just a little tough this morning. And last night was eventful."

I hate it when she says that. "What does that mean?"

"Garrett Martin."

I tense at the name, at the memory of the drawn face in the lighter fire. "What about him?"

"We found him. Dead. Shot."

Any blood in my head drains into my stomach and leaves me sick. "Oh."

I force my face to be neutral. I can't let my mom see the fear raging inside me. She must be too uncomfortable to notice anything, because she keeps her hand against her stomach and goes into the kitchen. I lie back down.

Information on Garrett Martin.

And Tristan smelled like gun smoke.

———————

I count the next twenty hours. I don't sleep for a single one of them. Not with Tristan hiding in his room, not when I'm praying to God with every heartbeat that I'm wrong.

My chest is ready to burst. I imagine blood and fluid leaking out of my ruptured bones and skin, staining my clothes, my blankets. Even sitting up, my breathing isn't enough.

Tristan texts. I answer.

When he slips through my door, he's calmer than yesterday, and he doesn't put quite the usual distance between us. He's wearing a gray hoodie and rolling his pocketknife over and over in one hand.

My throat is thick. I'm shivering, shuddering. And Tristan recognizes it. When he sits at the other end of the bed, he frowns.

My voice is so quiet I'm not sure he'll be able to hear me. "Please tell me I'm wrong."

The small knife freezes in his grasp. He slides on that practiced hardness. Only now, there are cracks in it. I see them.

"I don't know what you're talking about," he says.

"Did you kill Garrett Martin?"

He goes completely still. He says nothing.

A tiny corner of white fabric peeks at me from the neck of his hoodie: a bandage. "What is that?"

"It's nothing." His muscles constrict on themselves.

I brace myself for the pain. Reach out and pinch the edge of the bandage. He flinches away and stands so abruptly that my bedsprings bounce. The bandage yanks out of my grasp with an adhesive peel.

Tristan backs away and fumbles behind him for my doorknob. I watch him. I watch him as he turns to the side. As the back of his neck is angled toward me. As the stripped bandage exposes the square of skin underneath.

Stained with a forest-green tattoo. Three slanted parallel lines. Two thick. One thin.

An initiation.

Tristan looks at me with pure dread.

And runs.

23

I THROW MYSELF OUT OF BED, and a harsh groan rips out of me—I almost think my sternum is going to break—but I don't let it slow me. I stagger to my door and into the hall, and as I round the corner, he bursts out of his room and takes the stairs. He's down by the time I reach the top.

Downstairs, Mercedes gasps awake and shouts, but I can't make out what she says because ringing and the thunder of my blood have flooded my ears. I pitch down the stairs and reach the corner just as the back door opens. Mercedes calls Tristan's name, and her footsteps slam after his.

I'm near strangled. No keys, so I bypass the front door and take the garage, jam my fist into the button on the wall, and duck under the door as it rumbles open. My vision swims. I try to inhale, but it's choked off as if a knife were stuck in my ribs.

At the corner of the house, Tristan lands on his feet from jumping the fence. The small blade from his father is clutched in his hand. His eyes lock with mine.

He sprints. Trying to outrun what he's done. Trying to outrun my gaze.

He never sees me hit my knees.

I wish I could cry out as my bones spear into the concrete, but the pain cuts it off. Behind me, the door to the garage creaks open. Mercedes.

I can't lower myself to the ground this time. No air. No air. My shoulder collides with the porch.

Pain. And darkness.

Another dream. Another memory.

I exit through the back door to our church and find myself in a small prayer garden. The midday sun blazes, and everything is in full bloom—a willow tree, hydrangeas, rosebushes—but I stand all in black, my cheeks sticky with salt stains. Somewhere inside, my mother and Mercedes are dealing with mourners who have no idea what it is to mourn. And, visible through the slender leaves of the willow, my brother stands in a black suit.

I stroll across the grass, the heels of my pumps sinking into the soft earth, and push aside the willow's green curtain. Tristan leans against the trunk. He's twirling a leaf by the stem when he sees me, and stands up off the tree. A clear liquid bead sparkles on his cheekbone.

And then I'm in his arms, and he's in mine, and I hold him like he's going to break apart if I let him go. He holds me like he'll never let anything take me away. Like he's promising that he'll never let anything hurt me.

His shoulders shake, and his chest shrinks beneath me in hollow sobs. Mine do the same. He holds me against him until his shirt is soaked with my tears.

For a moment, I open my eyes. And through the branches of the willow, I see someone who wasn't there. That same man from the cemetery. He wears a suit with a white shirt, minus a blazer. Off to the side of his tie, over his heart, the starched fabric is soaked and stained with light red streaks.

Tristan's hand tucks my head against him. I inhale his body wash, cedar and frankincense.

This was the last time I saw him cry. I think it was the last time I saw my brother.

My eyes open, and I'm surrounded by three women in sterile, nauseatingly blue surgical wear. A sickening waft of disinfectant and latex washes into my airway, and the all-too-familiar stiffness of an IV is slid into the back of my bony hand.

My upper body is unclothed and cold as if wet, and I smell medical alcohol. Electrical cords are stuck to my torso. My limbs are heavy, drugged. I'm on a sedative; I know it.

The tallest doctor, a woman with round eyes and a narrow face, notices me first. Without making me ask, she says, "It's okay. We're going to drain your chest."

I figured—I was awake the last time they did this. The one who spoke to me, the surgeon, gestures to one of the assistants, who hands her a syringe. She unguards the needle, which glints in the blinding fluorescent light, and tips it to my skin. A shudder threatens. Stay still.

A prick and a sting flares through every nerve it can reach. A few seconds later, it becomes a lighter sting, a coolness. And finally, nothing. An entire section of my body is left numb. It's not enough, though. It never is.

The syringe comes out, and one of the assistants hands the surgeon a small pestle-like sensor, which she runs across my sternum. On a screen in my peripheral vision, my chest cavity is spread in different shades of white, black, and gray.

Then comes a different needle, one attached to a thin tube. The surgeon's concentration alternates between my chest and the echocardiogram as she plunges the needle into my body. A dull, heavy ache grows through the anesthesia. Even sedated, I want to gasp or fidget, but I can't, not with that needle near my heart. One wrong move and I'm done.

One of the nurses speaks to me. I think she's telling me that I'll be fine, that it's almost over, walking me through each moment, but it's difficult to register while I envision the needle grinding and popping through bone and sinew and cartilage as it injects deeper and deeper. Then the doctor withdraws her hands. All three of them watch my vitals for a couple of seconds, and the surgeon tells me that someone will be back to check on me soon. They leave as translucent liquid pumps into the catheter. And I'm alone.

I'm alone, and my brother's gone, and I don't know where he is, and I don't know if he's safe, and I don't know what he's going to do now. He killed someone.

Where's Mercedes? And our mother—does our mother know? Have they found him?

Will they find him?

I can't cry. I can't shake the catheter. So I let the tears noiselessly spill, streaming down my temples until the sides of my pillow are soaked.

God, don't let him be hurt. Killed.

God, bring him home.

God, what has he done?

━━━━━━━

The sedative keeps me in a half sleep where I can almost see Tristan's face and can partially hear Dr. Tahan and my mother discussing my procedure.

"Her heart is taking more and more damage." Dr. Tahan's voice. "The flareups, the stress. The scar tissue is growing. And"— Dr. Tahan releases a terse breath through her nose—"her body's weak. I don't know what the procedure will do to her."

She doesn't know what it will do to me. She leaves out what she *thinks* it will do to me.

My vision is fuzzy. I'm too tired to find the origin of their voices, but I picture my mom pressing a fist to her mouth, her lips going pale. Her voice, albeit sturdy, is hoarse. "How much scar tissue?"

It's not the question either of us expected, by the way Dr. Tahan takes a moment to respond. When she does, she says, "Enough that she will likely have persisting issues."

So. Even if I make it through the treatment, it may not be enough.

Tristan held my shaking hand when I told him about it. I wonder if that was a lie too.

———

The EKG wires are gone. My drain puncture burns like fire every time my ribs expand, but my wrap shirt is satiny against my skin. Sun streams in the window.

Tristan's out there somewhere. It's about the time he'd usually come from school. He'd only sit wordlessly across the room, but at least he was here. At least he was safe.

Mercedes brings Elijah.

Her eyes are bloodshot, like she didn't sleep all night long, but since she slept at our house in case Tristan would come home, I wouldn't know. Elijah's posture sags, but it's nothing like the first time he came to see me. There's no panic. Did he have to prepare himself beforehand? Or did he resign to it? Again.

Mercedes' pale scars flex. "I'll let you guys talk."

Elijah doesn't stop her as she slips out of the room. She probably doesn't want to hear this again. I don't blame her.

Elijah drags a chair next to my bed and sits on it backward. It's too short for his long legs. "I heard about your brother."

I knead the center of my forehead with my knuckle. It tickles. When we were young and immature—and sometimes when we were older and immature—Tristan would brush his finger there just to get me to jump back.

"He left his phone," I say. "There's no way for us to find him." The only things he took were his keys and his father's pocketknife. I brush my knuckles across my lips. "How much did your mom tell you?"

He shakes his head. "You don't have to—"

"Yes, I do." I've put it off long enough.

The ache in my body grounds me—that's a sterile pain—and I tell him everything. From the beginning. Starting with the night I helped Luiz, and everything since.

Elijah listens. After I'm done, he doesn't say anything for a few seconds.

Then he extends his hand as if asking for mine. I slide it in, and it almost disappears inside. His fingers are warm and long. "That's what you've been going through?"

I nod. And as I do, I notice the silver necklace hanging from his neck. "You're wearing it."

He takes his hand from mine and clasps the crucifix. "Yes." His eyes get lost in memory again. I feel like if I could dive into them, I could live the whole life they've seen. "She always said it was God's promise that He wouldn't leave her. Then—" His voice breaks. My heart breaks with it. "Then she gave it to me."

"Elijah." My courage falters when a small tear falls from the corner of his eye.

He sweeps it away. "She's with Him now."

I'm silent. His sister's with God now. So is Damien.

Being with God doesn't bring either of them back to love and laugh and share life with. Elijah and I both asked for miracles. Neither of us received them. They're gone. Nothing changes that.

"Paityn," he says, but he stops as if he's not sure he should say or ask what he's thinking.

"Go ahead."

He exhales tightly. "Mercedes mentioned that you have some kind of operation in a month."

Ah.

I drape a hand across my drain point. The warmth and light pressure are soothing. Elijah's eyes flicker to the movement, then back to my face, and for a moment, I imagine his own hand covering the wound. I imagine him taking it onto himself, protecting it. Protecting me. "I don't know."

"What don't you know?"

"If it'll work." I swallow the knot forming in my throat. "This one could…" I don't want to say this. Not to him. I don't want to cause him more of the pain I've seen him in—but it might hurt him worse if I hide it. "It could kill me."

Something hidden comes over that placid face. Dread, I think.

"And if you make it through but it doesn't work?" Elijah says.

I had never admitted that as a possibility. I never wanted to admit the truth. I never have. "Then we wait."

Elijah starts shaking the way he did when I first met him—or maybe I'm shaking. Or both of us.

He touches my jaw to adjust my face to him. "You'll make it."

I match his pained smile, but I know we're both thinking the same thing. He can't promise that. No one can.

I imagine him telling his sister that. Even right before she died.

24

I STARE AT THE HOSPITAL CEILING. Panels the color of eggshells spread blankly over me as the same question runs over and over in my mind: where is Tristan?

We're almost the same age, but he's always been my older brother, my protector, the one strong enough to defend me when I needed it. He did that by taking the blows for me. With me. And now he's alone. What happens when he takes a blow he can't recover from? What happens if the police find him but it's already too late?

I try to cut off an image of his body sprawled on the ground. The way it was when I found him, but with no chance of him coming back. I fail. The picture prints over my closed eyes as clearly as if it were real, as if I were seeing it right now.

That won't happen. It can't.

My ears ring in the stillness, a quiet yet shrill tone. I wish Mercedes were here and not staying at our house in case Tristan comes back. I don't let myself think about the fact that Tony might discover that.

Rain runs down the window. Specks of city lights smear against a black backdrop. Sleep drags at me, and I'm almost ready to give in—and pray for no more nightmares—when my door opens. A nurse, I'm guessing, since there's no reason why it would be anyone else. I give the backlit silhouette a moment to unblur.

It's him.

I try to get onto my elbows, but my drain site isn't healed, so I fall back onto the pillow. Tears spring into my eyes.

"Tristan," I breathe.

He tries to pull on the smile that I've loved for so many years, but it's dragged away. He looks bled out, like he's been given an impossible weight and is being whipped and beaten to carry it. Rainwater peppers his clothes with smoky dots. He's wearing a mock neck shirt again. To hide the tattoo from everyone else.

Relief swells in me until it hurts. He's safe.

He approaches my bed and rests his hand on the rail. The skin on one of his knuckles is split. "I was hoping you'd be awake."

His broken smile cuts me open deep inside. Tired lines are sketched under his eyes.

He hasn't spoken to me like this in months, and now he does after he runs away?

"Where did you go?" I say.

He swallows hard. "I can't tell you."

"Tristan, stop it." Hot tears rush down my temples. "You can tell me anything."

Anything. That you killed someone. That you've been dealing drugs. That you're in pain.

And he wants to. I know he does. I can see it in the way his hand curls around my bedrail, the way he stretches his jaw as if he's clenched it until it's injured, the way his chest and ribs tighten around his breathing. Each one is so subtle, but they're enough for me to see. Enough for a sister to recognize.

"No. Listen to me. I'm leaving." His eyes change. They become desperate. "And don't come looking for me."

No, they aren't desperate. They're pleading. Pleading like he's begging for his life. Begging for my life.

I untangle my hand from my sheets and ignore the stabs in my side as I drape my hand over his. His is so strong, mine so thin. The rough line of a scab on his knuckle scratches my palm.

"Please." Let him see me cry. He has so many times before, just like I've seen him. "We'll figure it out, just—" My fingers put soft pressure on his rigid tendons. "Just come home."

He holds me with a gaze that makes my heart ache. Then he lowers his head like it hurts to keep it up anymore. My hand tightens around his as if that can keep him from slipping away.

"Please," I whisper.

He raises his head. His eyes have taken on a painful, crushed shade of red.

"I made my choice," he says. "I'm not changing it."

No. Tristan, don't do this, please. "Why did you come here?"

He doesn't say anything. Instead, he leans down and softly presses his lips against my forehead, light as being nicked by a butterfly's wing.

It's like being kissed by a spirit. By someone you've lost forever.

"Goodbye, Paityn," he says.

"Tristan, please—"

His hand pulls out from under mine. He pivots on his heel and strides out of the room. A nurse greets him on the way out.

Tears close up my throat. I want to call his name, to stop him, but that would only make him run faster.

I call the nurse. I call my mother. I call Mercedes.

None of them catch him. He doesn't want to be found. He made that clear.

I'll never stop searching.

————

I sit on Tristan's bed. Night colors filter through the windows, blue and purple giving way to black. I recline against his wall and inhale; his blankets still smell like cedar. Across from me hangs a metal crucifix, pale silver like the pendant on Elijah's necklace.

God's promise He'd never leave her.

What does that mean? What does that even mean?

"Don't leave him," I say. "Bring him back this time."

I don't want some reassurance that everything will be all right or that there's a plan or whatever it is that makes Elijah so peaceful. I don't want any of that. I want my brother.

When my head starts throbbing, I realize I'm crushing it against the wall behind me; the throbbing continues even after I ease up on the pressure. After a few moments, I lay my hand on Tristan's nightstand, the wood cool and smooth beneath my clammy palm.

I sit until a series of soft rushing sounds—weeping—edge through the door. That must be Mercedes finally letting it all out.

I unfurl my legs. Should I let her alone? Nothing I can say is going to fix what she's going through. Then again, maybe fixing it isn't what I need to do.

I stand and open the door, but when I find the source of the sound, my mouth slackens. It's not Mercedes.

"Mom?" I ease down the stairs, where she's sitting.

She turns around quickly enough to make me think I surprised her and inhales shakily. Her eyes are swollen.

"Baby." She wipes wet streaks off her face. "I didn't hear you."

"What happened?" I sit a few stairs above her.

It's a moment before she responds, almost as if she doesn't believe she can get the full sentence out unless she gathers herself. "That sample of Tristan's hair we gave the police."

My stomach pinches. She sighs—it's hollow, like there's a gap where her son tore out her heart and ran away with it.

I bow my head, knowing before she speaks.

"It matched," she says.

25

MY BREATHING'S CLEAR NOW. There's no reason why I should be at my bedroom window at four in the morning. Except for one.

I watch across the street, where Mercedes is staying tonight, and cradle my arms around my drain point. It's better than lying awake, staring at my own walls and driving myself out of my mind.

Tristan's out there. And he's alive, and he can be found. I have to believe that.

"Don't leave him. Keep him safe," I whisper. Fog from my breath frosts the glass.

I repeat it over and over in my mind for a long time. It forms a rhythm with the throbbing in my side. A golden light glows in a window on Mercedes' top floor, then fades off. The far mountains rise in black masses, almost curling like smoke from the ground; they're even darker than the sky behind them.

Something moves. My heart thrills for a split instant, thinking—hoping—it's Tristan.

It's not. That person's too thin. And he brandishes a bottle in his hand.

He strolls across the street and wanders up to the porchlight of what used to be Tristan's house before our parents got married. Luiz looks up at my window, but my curtain's too far closed for him to see in. Apparently disappointed, he downs a gulp. What I feel now isn't compassion like it used to be. He could have helped me stop this a long time ago. He had—has—the information I've needed. Instead, scars harden on Mercedes' skin, and we have no proof of who did it. Tristan has killed a person— for what? a handy initiation thanks to some petty feud between Luiz and Martin?—and ran. And Tony roams unchecked, ready to harm any one of us at his whim. If Tristan isn't already dead.

Luiz finishes his bottle, produces another from his jacket pocket, drains that one, and stares up at my window.

Disgust scrapes over my vocal cords. I lie down. The darkness is better than seeing him.

Sleep comes quickly.

———

The memory's from over four months ago. I'm sprawled on my bed, gazing out the open window. The September sky is a watercolor of blue, yellow, and orange. The first stars pinprick duskier areas. I wonder if any of my family at Mass are seeing the same sky I am.

My body aches, but I'm beaming. Already a month since they got married. Since I became a sister and a father's daughter. Of course, it was always that way; it's just legal now.

A soft breeze flutters my curtains and rustles the lime-green leaves of an ash tree.

Then there's a different sound.

I frown and listen. There it is again: a harsh breath, like a wince, close by. It sharpens, becomes a groan. I sit up, blink against a headrush, and peer through the window. I find a tall, thin young man with bronze skin and obsidian hair.

Luiz is doubled over as if it's too painful to stand up all the way. His hand is clamped against his head, and his pale teeth are exposed in a grimace. When he takes a step, his leg goes out from under him. Red dots the ground in a trail behind him.

I'm downstairs and out the door within seconds. Luiz has dragged himself to my lawn. In his wake, the grass is scarlet.

I drop to one knee next to him. Blood pours from under the palm on his forehead; a bruise takes up the side of his face.

"Luiz." I place my hand on his shoulder. "What happened?"

He lets his hand fall. My heart catches in my throat. A slash runs from the center of his forehead to his temple.

"My father." He coughs at the last sound, then groans and curls in on himself.

"You need a doctor." My hand on his shoulder quakes. No, that's not my hand shaking. He's shaking.

"I can't," he says.

"You don't have a choice."

"Please." His eyes land on mine. "Help me."

I want to help him. I want to keep him safe. I want it more than anything. None of that means hiding this.

He winces, and that brings me back. He's bleeding. I can fix that first.

I stand and extend my hand to him. "Come on."

He exhales, and the tension in his eyes lessens.

Together, we get him to his feet and sling his arm over my shoulders, though I'm not sure how much help I am. His bones are hard across my neck. His body's hot, almost feverish, and he smells of spearmint and blood.

When we get into my house, I flip on the light and release myself from his arm. "Sit down. I'll be right back."

He nods, though he sways when he does it, and supports himself against the wall as he lowers to the floor, exhaling in relief once he's seated. A burgundy handprint smears the white drywall. I go upstairs and gather hydrogen peroxide, rubbing alcohol, cotton balls, an old rag, and my mom's first aid kit; then I head back down. When I get there, Luiz raises his head from where he had it between his knees. I kneel next to him and unload gauze, scissors, and medical tape from the first aid kit.

"I've never done this before," I say as I pour hydrogen peroxide onto a cotton ball.

"I know."

When the cotton's soaked, I raise it to the wound. It's a clean slit—like a sharpened knife made it.

Anger threatens to blur my vision, but I force it down. He doesn't need me to be angry for him right now; he needs me to help him heal. I take a cleansing inhale and center myself with the spearmint that lines my nose.

I apply the cotton ball. Bright red dulls to brown, then white with fizzy bubbles as the hydrogen peroxide hits it. He scarcely reacts as I dab all the way across the wound.

When the hydrogen peroxide is exhausted, I toss the used cotton ball and fill up another one. Clean the wound, the side of his face, his neck, his hand. I clean it all. His rigid body loosens until he's slack against the wall.

I toss the last cotton ball to the side, and it rolls until it runs into the rest of the pile. I've used seven of them, each now dyed maroon. Then I take the old rag and the rubbing alcohol, and saturate the cloth until the alcohol's acrid tang buzzes in my nose.

"This is going to sting."

His eyes are closed. He nods.

"Ready?"

He swallows dryly. Sweat and leftover hydrogen peroxide glisten on his hairline. He's pallid. "Yes."

"Here it comes." I plant the cloth over his wound.

His fingertips grind against the ground until they go ashen under his nails. His face doesn't move, though; he doesn't make a sound except for a ragged exhale.

"All right." I pull the cloth off. It's stained livid pink. "The worst part's over."

His eyes open sluggishly, like he's barely able to stay awake. I trim off a square of gauze, delicately pinch together the edges of the gash, and tape on the gauze to hold the skin together.

"Okay," I say. "Done."

I place my hand on his cheek. He looks up at me with the eyes of a child.

It takes a minute, but eventually, the expansions of his chest steady, and he tilts his head into my hand.

He has no idea. No idea how much I want him to know that this—that I—could be his if he'd just let me.

"Where else are you hurt?" I ask.

"Nowhere you can fix. Just bruises."

"What about your leg? Why were you limping?"

He draws himself into a better sitting position, and I withdraw my hand. My fingers reel from the absence of body warmth.

"I rolled my foot when I ran," he says.

I sit back on my heels and curve my sterilized hands over my knees. "Tell me what happened."

I know the answer, but I want him to say it.

He runs the tip of his tongue over his lower lip and shifts his gaze to a distant spot on the floor. "It was a knife."

My fingernails bite into my knees. "Luiz, don't keep this quiet."

He gives a bitter laugh without his face moving. "And then what, Paityn?"

His blood is drying on my hands. "We'd figure it out."

We would. Together.

His eyes hold mine with the force of gravity. They're a deep brown, surrounded by long lashes, and so steady that I can see my reflection in his irises. I wonder if he can see his reflection in mine.

I take his hand, and our fingers interlock in a swirl of bronze and cream. I cup my other hand around the back of his head. "I got you."

A wet sparkle slides down his face, and he lets me hold him. He doesn't weep out loud—he's not even shaking anymore—but tears transfer from his cheek to mine for a long time.

He still pulls away too soon. "I should go."

I can't stop him from going back. If I could, I would. "Be safe. Please."

He cringes but doesn't say anything. I help him stand and let him out. He limps away.

I could wait until my parents get home from Mass. I could.

I hike upstairs to where my phone is and dial Damien, who, as far as I understand, has dealt with domestic abuse more than my mother has. As it rings, I look out the window for no reason in particular.

There's a figure below. The same one as in all of the dreams, with his dark, curly hair ponytailed. He's standing at the base of the driveway, gazing down the street where Luiz went.

His blood joins Luiz's on the cement. This time, the stain is on his sleeve, starting below his elbow and extending down the front of his arm.

I blink, and he's gone.

The phone stops ringing. Damien's voice comes through.

"Paityn? Is everything all right?"

I push the man from my mind. "I have to tell you something."

———

My cheeks are wet. My body aches, and I'm cold.

There's shuffling in the hall.

I peel my head off my pillow just as my doorknob turns and a hooded silhouette stalks through my door.

26

MY KNIFE IS IN MY HAND before he can close the door.
The blade whirls open, and I plant myself into a ready stance. My
drain point seeps fluid, but fight-or-flight has numbed that area; it's
numbed my whole body. I scan the figure and hope I'm not using
this knife to face down a gun.

He raises his gloved hands as if to calm me.

This isn't Tony. He's way too short. In fact, even in the baggy
clothes, the body shape is off: it's not square enough, not like the
he I've been thinking of. A woman's body.

Sweat absorbs into my cotton headscarf. I fight to make a shape
of the face hidden beneath the hood.

"Venus?" I whisper.

She nods. Places one gloved finger to her lips and lowers the
hood. Her straightened hair is tied in a low ponytail. Every part of
her body is coiled: her jaw, her shoulders, her hands.

"I'm not here to hurt you," she says so softly that she's just
shy of mouthing it.

"How did—"

Venus' body tension triples. Mine follows suit.

She gestures downstairs. "We're not alone."

My voice was quiet before, but I lower it even more until it matches hers. "What's going on?"

She slides two fingers in the front pocket of her jeans. They emerge with a ring of keys. Keys to my house.

"How did you get that?" Without needing her answer, though, I know. Tristan. Those are his; that's the only way she could have gotten them.

She extends the ring for me to take, which I do. I grip it in my spare hand, a piece of him returned home.

"Tristan's fine," she says. "He knows I'm here."

"Why?"

This time she reaches into her back pocket.

"I'm not going to hurt you," she repeats. And she offers me a folded knife. "I just need some blood. And a piece of your shirt."

Proof that she killed me. A bloody knife and cloth from the wound site. Tony's revenge for getting his two homeboys arrested, now that Tristan's not here to get in his way.

I nod but don't take her knife. I have no idea where it's been, what's on it. Instead, I touch the tip of my own knife against the front of my forearm. It tickles.

Just another needle.

I submerge the blade tip. Pain, white-hot and ice-cold at the same time, writhes down my nerves. Keep going, deeper, and drag it. They need deep blood, and we need it now. In the darkness, the liquid bubbling out may as well be black oil spreading across my arm and falling to the floor.

The slit sears as I use that same hand to bundle the collar of my shirt. Blade into cloth, I cut around the V-neck so they can see the shape, so they're sure it came from a fatal spot. The cloth tears with a shredding sound so loud I'm scared her partner—whoever it is—will hear it downstairs. I plant the fabric over the gash and let it absorb all it can handle before I toss it to Venus. It's so wet it sprays droplets on her clothes when she catches it.

I gesture for her knife. She passes it to me handle first, and I flip my arm over the blade.

"Who's downstairs?" I turn the knife over and let my blood stain the second side.

"Not the one you want. " When I purse my lips, she raises her finger so I'll pay attention. "If they find out I lied, I'm dead. So—"

"It won't get out." She saved my life. My family's lives. Tony thinks I'm dead. His grudge against me is placated for now, which takes the others out of the line of fire. I return the dripping knife to her. "Thank you."

"Don't thank me yet." She flicks the knife, and beads of blood splash on my shins. It seems unnatural how warm they are.

Venus disappears out my door.

My heart pounds in my neck, my wound, my drain site as her light tread rolls down the stairs. I wait to hear the door. Instead, I get voices.

There's a vent in my floor across the room. I kneel next to it and lower my ear to the decorative holes. Heated air blows onto my face. A translucent filament or strand of spider silk is stuck to the deep-brown metal and waves like a flag.

"Huh." The voice is muffled, but it's not Venus. I think it's Eddie. "I wasn't sure you had it in you."

"Shows what you know."

A grunt. "You jumped at the chance pretty quick."

"And you didn't. Get over it. You're a better lookout anyway."

Thick silence follows. She must have hit a sensitive spot. Slippery liquid collects under my hand.

"Let's go," Venus says.

The door shuts behind them. Only then do I sit back on my heels. Blood soaks the shins of my pants, and I'm quivering. I need to bolt the door. I have the key, so they can't get back in.

Right. Just like they couldn't get into Mercedes' locked house.

I leave sticky footprints as I stride to my door, checking every corner along the way. The logical part of my mind chides me. They're not here. They left, and if there were some kind of ambush, Venus wouldn't have gone through the trouble of that charade.

When the deadbolt on the front door stops, I push harder, practically grinding it into the wooden frame. I could switch on the light, but I don't know how close they are; Eddie might notice a window brightening.

I climb upstairs, backtracking the drip trail I left, and collect hydrogen peroxide, alcohol, and some bandages. I drench a rag in the hydrogen peroxide and let it fizz on the blood. Thankfully, this stuff doesn't sting, just tickles. Then the alcohol goes on the next rag.

Don't think. Just do it.

I clamp it on. A gasp rushes into me as the pungent liquid burns away any infection and frays my nerve endings. I hold the rag until the sting becomes a throb, then let go and wrap myself in a bandage as well as I can manage with one hand. I might need stitches, but that'll have to wait until my mom gets back. At least tonight, there's no one seeking her life.

I clean the blood I spilled over the floor before I go to the mirror and check my drain site. It doesn't seem torn—it's no longer seeping, and whatever fluid did come out was transparent. I take a hot shower, careful to keep my bandage out of the water, then slip into some new clothes and throw the ripped, bloody ones away. Bleach and alcohol fumes are still burning in each inhale by the time I return to my bed, where Tristan's keys are splayed on my nightstand.

He ran. He's alive. He found out they wanted to kill me. And he saved me, but he won't come home.

I made my choice.

What was that choice?

I slide the keys off and cradle them in my palm. My body throbs from exertion.

I lie down and hold the keys to my heart.

27

THE HUM OF THE GARAGE SNATCHES me from a restless half sleep, part of my mind always awake, always waiting for Tony to break in and realize I'm alive.

A second hum as the garage closes. Mom's home.

I spring up, which is a mistake: I inadvertently put weight on my cut arm and stretch my drainage points. There's moisture on both spots. I hope I haven't bled onto my sheets.

I stumble out my door, down the stairs. My mom stands in the kitchen.

"Baby, are you okay? You're—"

I bunch up my sleeve to reveal a crimson-stained bandage.

My mom's eyes narrow. "What happened?"

She examines my cut. It seals and gapes open at different pressures of her careful fingers. It seemed shallower last night.

"You need stitches," she says. Her tone is diagnostic, but her face is somewhere between anger and sadness.

"Can you do it?" I ask.

She frowns. "Why?"

"So nobody sees me." After all, he wanders.

My stomach squeezes as if a hair-thin needle were sinking into my diaphragm. Venus' life is depending on Tony thinking I'm dead. I can't let him find out I'm not.

That needle-pierced feeling sharpens. What happens when he recognizes that my murder isn't on the news or anything? Will he suspect what Venus did? What then?

I close my eyes. Calm down. Venus knows how to survive Tony. She wouldn't have tried something like that if she didn't have everything covered. I have to trust that.

I bring myself back to the present. My mom's solemn face takes a definitive tilt toward anger. Not at me—I know that. She flattens her lips into a line, and I can almost hear the debate in her mind: risk my life or let me hide?

It's not just my life. It's everyone's.

Judging by her expression, she doesn't like her decision. "I'll see if I can find what I need. If I can't, I'm taking you in."

I nod. My cut is beginning to ooze.

My mother checks her watch. "I need to get going."

"How come?"

"Ob-gyn later today." Her hand floats toward her midsection.

I almost forgot. After Tristan ran, I haven't thought about much else. "How are you feeling?"

She hesitates. Then says, "I'm not feeling much."

She's at twenty weeks. They told her that she should expect to feel the baby long before now.

I tamp the panic before it can come; it doesn't help anyone. Not the baby and certainly not my mom.

She brushes her thumb alongside my cut one last time. "Lock the doors and get some sleep. I'll be back with sutures."

Elijah and Mercedes study the four stitches in my arm as the three of us sit at the dinner table.

Mercedes cringes. "Does it hurt?"

I shrug. "Not really. The lidocaine helped."

Helped. Didn't eliminate the pain completely. I run my tongue over a raw patch on the inside of my lip where I bit it for stitch number three.

Elijah regards my cut with a furrowed brow. His crucifix hangs toward the ugly red line, and I briefly imagine its pure silver dipped in thick redness. He opens his mouth to speak when the garage opens. All three of us jump at the sudden noise.

We can't keep doing this. Walking on knives, unsafe in our own houses. Nothing has happened to Elijah, despite whatever he said to Tony, but how long will that last? Venus bought me time, but this can't last forever. We still have to get Tony.

My mom's thick hair is loose, playing around her shoulders instead of being in its usual tight ponytail. There are heavy circles under her eyes.

"Excuse us, Elijah." She adds a smile for gentleness's sake, but there's no room for discussion.

Elijah's eyebrows twitch up as if he didn't expect that, but he stands and nods politely.

"I'll come tomorrow," he says to Mercedes and me.

"Be careful," Mercedes says with more gravity than she should ever have to.

He smiles and tucks a strand of turquoise hair behind her ear before he leaves.

When he's gone, my mom takes a seat and folds her hands on the table. She's not wearing any eyeliner, but she's just as beautiful without it. Maybe even more.

"What's wrong?" Mercedes asks.

My mother pinches her lips together. She takes a full breath, as if she has been so concerned with other things that she forgot she needed oxygen.

"The baby's not growing as much as we'd like," she says.

It shouldn't be possible for my heart to skip a beat, not with the pacemaker, but I could swear it does. Mercedes has her lower lip between her teeth. When she lets it go, the usual pale pink leaks dark red.

This is because of everything that's happened. The attacks, Tristan running. And now the baby's suffering for it. Maybe even—

No. I won't think about that. I can't.

"But," my mom says, "I did find out something good. We're having a girl."

It's strange—I laugh, despite what my mom just said, despite everything. "We were right."

Mercedes smiles too; we all do for a moment.

Mine begins to harden.

I have a baby sister. And I won't lose her.

———

I could curl up and let sleep take me back for once. My body begs me to do it: it only hurts when I'm awake.

I sit up, draw my blankets around myself, and watch through the window behind the edge of the curtain. I have no reason to think Tristan will come past here, but he would stay up for me, so I can stay up for him. Even if there's just a chance.

I wait.

There's no motion on the street until, as always, a tall, skinny young man strolls into view with a bottle in his hand. He throws his head back over and over, downing the liquor, and from what

I can tell, he's no less stable for it either. And between each drink, he looks up at my window.

What is that about? He must know I'm dead, or so Tony and the rest think. Is this his version of grieving?

Whole lot of good it'd do me if Venus had done what they told her to.

Luiz leaves, and if I see correctly, he's unsteady. I don't even want to imagine how much alcohol that must have taken. I ache to curl up under my covers and sleep while I can.

Stay up. One hour. Tristan did the same for me. Despite how it's ended up.

I clamp my eyes closed. He's killed someone. His chance at a future is over, but if he'd just come home, we'd be here. I'd be here.

I exhale against the glass. It rebounds onto my face colder than it left me. We have to find him first. We'll bring him home.

I lose track of how long it is before I open my eyes again. They hover unfocused over the night below.

And he's there.

28

MY SENSES LIGHT UP LIKE FIRE.

I'm not tired, and I'm not seeing things. That's Tristan in a patch of Mercedes' porchlight across the street. He's wearing an oversized jacket, brown, I think. He must have gotten it since he left. Someone must have given it to him.

His face is angled toward my window. Toward me. And as I stare out, he presses one hand over his heart.

He's here. He's back.

I forget the lupus. I forget pain, I forget everything else, and I pitch off the covers. In my peripheral vision, I think Tristan tenses, even recoils, but I don't stop. I snag my keys as I run. No shoes. No time.

I skip two stairs at a time on the way down and tear around the corner. My view skims the vacant couch before I jam the keys into the front door, release each latch with a dull clack, lever the handle open, get out there, I have to get out there before he's gone.

The night unfolds before me through the storm door. Frost runs around the perimeter of the glass. I don't see him.

I flip the second lock. Cold crawls up my shins when my toes touch the cement.

"Tristan?" I call as loudly as I dare.

The door swings shut behind me. It clicks closed.

And from the edge of the fence to my right, a dark form pounces.

The front of my jacket is in his hands before I can leap back, and he hurls me down. My back flattens against the floor. The air is slammed out of me and refuses to come back.

He presses his foot on my chest.

Eddie.

"Well, well." He grins. "Look who it is. Alive."

He was waiting for me. As if he knew I'd come.

Sickness twines in my stomach.

Did Tristan draw me out?

I try to scream, moan, make some sound, but my ribs are paralyzed. Eddie crouches to one knee, never taking his foot off. Pain explodes up my neck.

Eddie tuts at me. "I have to say, Venus had me convinced, but"—he shrugs—"for some reason, Tristan didn't seem too upset. Then he wandered over here." He leans in closer to my face. Faint marijuana fumes fill my nose. Not as if he'd been smoking it, but as if it's perpetually stuck to his clothes. "Like there was someone he wanted to see."

So Tristan didn't know. Eddie followed him.

I grab his ankle and thrash, but he's too heavy, too centered. My drain scar burns like acid. He adds more weight, forcing a groan out of me.

The dull, low click of a knife's metal joint locking into place. The razored glint of steel in the moonlight.

Eddie's grin spreads. "How about I finish this?"

No. Don't let him. I writhe.

His foot becomes his knee. His full body weight. My vision leaks black except for the white blade that glides past until it's poised over my throat. My skin hums where it will land.

If I move, he'll sink the knife. If I don't move, he'll sink the knife.

I swallow a girlish whimper. I don't want to die, not like this, but he feeds off fear, and I'll give him none.

Make sure the last thing they see is that you have no fear in your eyes.

Eddie's are a wicked blue, gleaming like the knife. I imagine mine, brown like my mother's, lit with fire, the ones Damien always said flaunted strength.

My hand snatches his finger. I have no advantage over him, but I have speed, and I have leverage. Twist, and there's a sinewy, fluid-bogged crack.

Eddie groans, almost screams, and both of his hands jump back from me in shock, slipping out of my sweat-slicked grasp. The hovering knife yanks back. He stares dumbfounded at the swollen appendage that used to be his index finger—bent sideways at the second knuckle.

Something to remember me by.

The sneer is wiped from his face, and the viciousness underneath surfaces. Somewhere, a car engine hums, approaching. A witness.

Threatening tears burn hot, but I won't let him see. Eddie flips the knife in his hand, changing his grip from slit to stab, and swings his arm back. I grab his broken finger.

Eddie yells, higher pitched this time, and I wrench sideways. It's enough to throw his aim. The blade clangs against the concrete next to my face.

Eddie snarls over me. His knee drills into my sternum, into my drainage wound, crushing my bones, crushing my organs, crushing my pacemaker. Cartilage pops.

Tires scream to a halt. Eddie stops cold as a car door opens, and there's the snap of a handgun's slide racking.

"Drop your weapon."

Graveyard shift. Mom.

Eddie blanches. He's staring down the barrel of her pistol. He has no response for her. And no way out.

He glares down at me with pure hatred. My fingers stay clenched around his maimed one.

Danger rings in my mother's voice. "Drop your weapon, or I'll shoot."

Eddie lowers the knife until his arm is slack by his side, but he doesn't release it. It's near my open hand. His knuckles are waxy. His eyes flash left and right. As if he's wondering whether he can run.

I clap my grip across his knife hand and pin it to the ground next to my side. Metal pings against cement, and Eddie flinches, but he's smart enough not to wrestle for it. If I have his knife trapped against the ground, it isn't a threat—so long as he doesn't fight. If that knife moves again, my mom won't hesitate.

"She doesn't miss," I say.

The tendons in his wrist tighten to cords. He wants to drive the knife into my side, stick it between my ribs, watch the life trickle out of me. He wants it. And I can't stop him. The point is less than an inch away from my lungs.

A clink. The knife falls against the porch.

I release his wrist. Eddie places his hands on top of his head.

29

I PUT MY HANDS ON MY HEAD as well. I know protocol. She's more an officer now than my mom. When she says to raise your hands, you pay attention. I'm no exception. I pull away from Eddie, get into a sitting position, and place my freezing palms against the top of my scarf. Invulnerable thing—I was almost stabbed, and it hasn't moved.

My mom advances, pistol extended, smooth, elegant, deadly, like an anaconda. Frightening to be on the other end of. Sweat gleams on Eddie's lip. He swallows as though his mouth is dry. The tip of my mother's gun sparkles in the dim light.

I'm not afraid. That's not a deadly weapon, not to me. Not in her hands.

My mother reaches us. She holsters her gun and, in the same fluid motion, releases a pair of handcuffs. Eddie, for once in his life, has the decency to look scared. My mom cuffs him, Mirandizes him, gets him to his feet. Shoots a glower at me.

"You stay right there," she tells me in the same tone that she used to Mirandize Eddie.

I nod meekly.

My mom leads Eddie to the curb and sits him down, then

speaks into her radio for backup; sirens whine in the near distance. My shoulders start to get sore.

Across the street, Mercedes' door swings open. She's in rumpled clothes—she must have heard us—but before she can come over, my mom thrusts her hand out in a halting motion.

"Go back inside." Loud and enunciated, no way for anyone to misunderstand.

Mercedes tenses as if taken aback and looks at me. I do my best to let her know that I'm fine, though that's hard to do from here. She disappears back inside her door, following my mom's instructions. The way we all did when Damien died. We know who she is. And we know that, for her to protect us, we have to listen.

By the time backup arrives, my shoulder muscles are flaming from keeping my hands in this position. The new police car brings two officers, a lady and a man. They take over dealing with Eddie.

My mother pivots and strides up to me. "Get your hands off your head."

I gratefully let them drop, but inside, I squirm. It's been a long time since I've heard her this angry. The last time may have been when I was four, when Tristan was hit by the car and I ran out on my own, but I was young then—she couldn't expect more common sense from me. "I'm sorry, Mom."

"Don't apologize." My mom takes a knee. "What were you thinking?"

I crisscross my legs. My feet sting—they're raw. I must have scraped them when I was trying to get out from under Eddie.

"*Paityn*," my mom says. "What were you doing outside?"

I sigh, my eyes burning. Don't cry. Not now. "I saw Tristan."

At that, her stolidness falters; she wavers from skeptical to hopeful and back. "Where? When?"

I describe the spot where I saw him and everything that happened, trying to tamp down the emotions writhing inside me. We missed him again, but he's alive, and he's close. If they hurry...

My mother's jaw flexes. She takes a cleansing breath, and for a moment, she is an officer and my mom all at once.

She cups her hand around my head, each bend of her finger bones massaging my scalp. "We'll find him. But you cannot run out of nowhere like that. You have to think." She lowers her voice to a whisper and leans in closer. "They"—she subtly jerks her head toward where Eddie is sitting—"are counting on you to make decisions like that. Don't give it to them."

I drop my gaze. "I'm sorry."

"Stop apologizing." She kisses my forehead, then stands. Back to business. "Go get some clothes on. We'll come in to ask you questions in a few minutes."

I sit cross-legged on the couch, downing a hot mug of chamomile tea. Orangish light peers through the curtains. Mercedes sits backward on a chair in the kitchen, wearing a baggy sweatshirt. Elijah sits in a second chair. His elbow rests on the table, and his knuckles slide over his mouth ponderingly.

"You're sure it was Tristan?" Mercedes says.

"I'm sure."

She sighs. She's hiding it nicely, but I know her too well: I see the betrayal underneath. He was so close, almost teasing us, and gone the next moment.

"Maybe they'll find him," Elijah says. "He can't have gotten that far."

"Maybe," Mercedes says in a monotone.

And if they do? It won't be a reunion. He'll be in cuffs for murder. Still, I'd rather know he's in jail while we figure this out. It's better than him being out there doing who knows what. Than not knowing if he'll be alive in the next minute.

"At least Eddie's off the streets," I say after a pause.

Elijah scowls at the mention of the name and makes a disgusted sound in the back of his throat. Mercedes shudders.

"He is such a creep," she says.

My skin crawls with the ghost of Eddie's fingers, of the knife so close to my body. I swig the chamomile. It's bitter but soothing when it coats my throat. I'm in for a nasty flare. "That's three."

Elijah raises an eyebrow. "What?"

"Three arrested. Eddie and those other two."

Mercedes snorts. "Don't be so sure."

"Why?" I frown.

She rubs the pads of her index finger and thumb together. "His daddy's got ways."

I groan and slam back another swig. After I swallow, I say, "He's not the one we needed anyway."

Mercedes rubs her eyes exaggeratedly. Elijah props his elbows on his knees. "So now what?" he says.

Now what?

Now they know I'm alive. Or, Eddie does, at least, and it's only a matter of time until Tony finds out. So that semblance of safety my family and I had? Gone. They'll want my mom for arresting Eddie. They'll want me for just being alive. And Venus—I have to warn her. She saved me, and now she's in danger too because of one rash decision.

I tilt my head back until it lolls heavily against the back cushion, my throat pushed outward the way it was when Eddie held his knife to it.

"I don't know," I answer. Neither of them responds.

Even though the chamomile tea steams, a chill shakes me. I don't know what will happen, but I won't have to wait long. I have no doubt about that.

———

I leave Mercedes and Elijah, and call the number Venus messaged me from. The dulled floral aroma from my tea has followed me all the way up here.

Venus answers despite how early it is, and I tell her what happened.

I pick at a baby blue thread on my comforter for every second she doesn't respond, guilt corroding my stomach. She helped me when she didn't even know me. She warned me to be careful. Now they'll kill her.

When she does speak, her voice is calm. "They would have figured it out anyway."

Is she being strong for my benefit or her own?

The silky thread comes free, frayed at the end. I smooth it between my index finger and thumb. "What are you going to do?"

There's a bitter but defiant scoff on the other end. "Not run." Does she have a family that she's worried about? Is her fight the same as mine? She must know what she's doing; she's survived this long. "Just be careful. He'll be madder at you and your mom."

"We are."

"Hey, Paityn?"

"Yeah?"

"How did you stop that freak from killing you?"

I fail to block out the image of Eddie's slimy touch. "I broke his finger."

There's a smile in her voice. "Good."

The flareup comes hard.

Tristan was so close.

Nothing. He's gone. As lost as if I'd never seen him.

I go to bed.

I dream I'm at the hospital less than a year ago. My fever's down since Tristan brought me yesterday, carried my slack body when I couldn't walk, but I'm soaked in chills and muscle aches. My throat is swollen, and each heartbeat is a stab.

They'll drain me once the morning comes. I wish they'd stick a needle in me now.

Tristan's cot is parallel to my bed. His chest rises and sinks peacefully as he sleeps. I breathe like he told me to before he brought me here; I just have to get through the night.

My airway gets irritated, and I cough listlessly. Tristan's eyes flicker open. I cough again, and he sits up. Places his hand on my forehead.

"You're awake?" he whispers.

I grimace through a swallow. "I'm always awake around now."

His forehead furrows. "Every morning?"

"Yeah."

I'm not crying. I'm not, but I'm sick, and I have a fever, and it's early in the morning, so hot saline runs down my temple. His thumb brushes it away.

The corner of my vision bends: the same stranger my brain insists on bringing back.

It's his shoulder. Red is pasted over it and drips onto his palm, but strangely, there's also a wet patch on the outer thigh of his pants. His unfurled hand mostly hides it, but it's there.

Tristan absorbs cold sweat from my forehead with his sleeve, which brings me back. Just like that, my peripheral vision is empty.

Tristan gazes at me. His hand against my cheek is soothing, so soothing.

"Will you stay with me? Until I can fall asleep?" I rasp.

He's on the verge of tears. "Of course."

———

Pops.

Rapid. Loud. Close. On my street. In front of my house.

I throw myself into a sitting position and wrench my curtains open. The screws to the rod brackets come halfway out of the wall.

Tires squeal, and a black sedan, an old model, no license plates, zips across the intersection toward us, disappearing when my own house obstructs my view.

And in the middle of the intersection is a different car. The window shattered. Holes shot through the door. Parked where she was when Eddie found me.

Mom.

30

MY HEART FREEZES.

No. No, no, no, please, God, no.

The door to my room flies open. Mercedes storms in and throws the light on, blinding me. Her hands rip her hair into a ponytail as she thunders to my bed.

"*What was that?*" Then she must see my face. "Paityn, what—"

"It's Mom." The words choke me on their way out.

Mercedes blanches and claps a hand over her mouth. I jam my hand up against the window. There's no motion inside her police cruiser, none that I can see, but the window's shattered, and it's pitch black out, so she could be moving in there. She could be alive. She could be—

Please, God.

My blood vessels sting against the icy glass. She has to be alive. She's alive—she's not dead unless I see it with my own eyes.

I snatch my phone so fiercely that Mercedes jumps back; the crucifix and my knife rattle on the nightstand.

Mercedes pivots and strides back toward my door.

"Where are you going?" My voice is severe in a way I've never heard it.

She spins to face me, the same severity on her face. "If she's alive, she's bleeding. We have to help her."

I stand. My knees are shuddering underneath me, ready to buckle. My whole body is. "No. Someone's driving around with a gun. You'll get shot."

"I don't care."

Both of us stare each other down, determined, unyielding. The phone's ring wavers next to my ear. My hand is shaking. Come on, *pick up.*

I want to go with Mercedes. I want to sprint out, find my mom, save her if I can.

You have to think, my mom told me. This is my fault. I made one thoughtless decision, and now I don't know what's happened to her. I won't let the same thing happen to Mercedes.

"You'll do her no good if you're dead," I say.

Frustration bubbles up in Mercedes' flashing eyes. She groans and swipes at them. "I can't just sit here."

I hand her the phone. "Then take care of this."

She's about to protest, but dispatch picks up, and it forces her, forces her to think calmly, to tame the fear that I know is raging through her, because it's also raging through me. I swallow tears; it's harder than swallowing stone. Keep your head. The way she taught you.

Time it. Twelve-minute response or less.

Two minutes. Mercedes' voice is firm as she speaks to dispatch.

Three. Still no motion from the car.

Five. Mercedes isn't speaking anymore, but someone's on the other end of the line.

Six. Sirens wail. Red and blue dots in the distance.

Seven. Onto my street. They're early.

They park and surround my mom's car. Open it. Mercedes crowds against the window beside me. Police lights waver over her pale face.

They pull my mom from the driver's seat.

I cup my hands over my nose and mouth. A torn exhale aches as it rushes out of me. A tear traces Mercedes' nose.

My mom emerges on her feet. She's alive.

31

I KNOW EXACTLY WHO DID IT.

Tony's the only one. Eddie and the two I didn't know have been arrested. Venus saved me. I don't think Luiz has it in him. And no matter what Tristan's done, I refuse to believe that he would shoot at our mom. I refuse to believe he even knew about it.

But my word isn't proof. No one saw. It was dark, and he was fast, and there were no plates. He was there, and he was gone. I answer the officers' questions, knowing it's nothing they can use.

We finish soon. Mercedes slumps onto the bottom step next to the door and kicks off her tennis shoes, which thump gently as they roll away from her. They could stand being thrown in the washing machine—a grayish layer of dirt is stuck to the white laces and teal canvas.

The homey light in our hall falls over her, showing me every place she's shaking as she grips the edge of the stair. "Do you know where she was hurt?"

"Her thigh and the front of her shoulder. If it's as good as they're saying, she might be out of surgery by now."

Loose hairs that have slipped from Mercedes' bun hang by her face and catch in her eyelashes. She suddenly winces and releases the overhang of the step. Red squeezes under the tip of her nail—she must have been gripping so hard that she bent it backward. She sucks away the blood, then stanches the small wound against her pant leg.

"He could have killed her. And the baby," she whispers hoarsely.

I know he could've.

An ugly pressure simmers inside my arteries. Tony shot my mother. And I can't do anything, all because I have no proof of everything he's done.

With nothing better to do while Mercedes finishes getting ready to go see my mom, I slip into Tristan's room—even though it's not going to change, no clue is going to magically reveal itself just because I've walked in here again. His bed is tucked in the corner, his laptop and phone in neat squares on top. His dresser stands guard to my right.

We ransacked this place. Emptied drawers, took off the mattress, went through every pocket and document and contact. And there was nothing, not even in some deep, dark memory on the computer. So where is he?

I flip on the light, and a pale sparkle glints in my peripheral vision: Tristan's metal crucifix.

"Where's my brother?" I ask. The statue doesn't answer.

I close the door behind me and rest against it. Tristan's the key to this. He has as much information as Luiz, and I don't care what I saw—Tristan's not *loyal* to Tony. He's been doing it for some other reason. And now that everybody knows what Tristan did, he has an incentive to talk. I just have to find him.

What haven't I thought of? Where would he go?

I plant myself on the corner of his bed. The cedar scent is

long gone. I pick at splinters on a rough patch on the corner of his nightstand.

Maybe we shouldn't have been ransacking *for* something. Maybe we should have paid attention to what *wasn't* there.

I replay the moments just before Tristan ran. He took his keys, which we now have. I saw him take his knife. What else?

I manage to scratch out a splinter with my thumbnail, but thankfully, I don't get stabbed. I scrape the sliver of wood out and place it on Tristan's nightstand.

The nightstand.

When Tristan was crying, the night he killed Garrett Martin, there was a picture on it. We never found that picture.

I strain my memory for what was in it. The three of us. Trees. A strip of gray on the side.

We'd all gone hiking or visited parks together, so the trees could be from anywhere, but that gray part—cement gray, like a sewer drain.

The underpass.

I jump when Mercedes makes a strange sound from the other room like she suddenly remembered something she's annoyed about. Not to mention the smack of skin against skin, which I have a feeling was her facepalming herself. I leave the room, my heart jittering. I have an idea, but it's reaching.

Mercedes comes out of my room with the middle of her forehead flushed pink.

"What?" I ask.

"My dad took his car to the airport, and the other car's still in the shop."

I stop just shy of smacking my own forehead—I'd forgotten she'd mentioned something was wrong with, what, the ignition?—

and begin considering solutions. We can't take each other as passengers because of the underage restriction on our licenses, but Mercedes has to be able to go. It was her mom who got shot as much as mine. "Let me think."

"You go," she says. "I'll stay."

"Don't give me that."

"No, really." She shakes her head, and the bottom of her ponytail flicks like the tip of a cat's tail. "I can get a ride with Elijah tomorrow. I'll stay just in case"—her voice tightens—"Tristan comes home."

I'm about to object when I realize that maybe she's right. Maybe this is for the best. Just not in the way she's thinking.

"Thank you," I say.

I give her a hug before I go. And as I do, I peer over her shoulder into Tristan's room.

I might know how to end this. Tonight.

When I enter my mom's room at the hospital, she's asleep.

Her thigh and the front of her shoulder are bandaged, ointment glistening at the edges. Bags from a lost adrenaline rush bulge under her eyes, but when the door clicks shut behind me, she wakes up.

When I get to her bed, I cautiously wrap my arms around her, conscious of every place I could inadvertently hurt her. Her cheek is soft and warm against mine, moistened by my leaked tears. She clasps my hand over her stomach. Now I know what it's like to be the one at the bedside. What it's like to see someone I love with her body struggling from trauma it should never have been put through.

My mother can't fix me, but I can make it right for her.

I release myself from her embrace. "Mom, I have to go."

She frowns. "Why?"

I can't tell her. She's a police officer. As far as I know, if I tell her what I have planned and she gives me her permission, any decent lawyer could say she, as law enforcement, sent me. And depending on what happens, it might make anything I get obsolete in court.

"I have to do this," I say.

She catches enough of the hint. Her eyebrows slant. Decisive. Final. "Whatever you're thinking, no."

Not an answer I'll take.

I lower my voice. Lower it until I know she has to strain to hear what comes out of my mouth. In that quietness, I enunciate. Every. Word. Perfectly.

"What if he hadn't missed? What if he'd shot the baby girl?"

That's all it takes. The stubborn angles of her eyebrows and jaw tip away. Her eyes loosen. And they water. My mother, who rarely cries.

I slide my hands into my pockets. She may not worry about her own safety—she risks her life every day—but now there's someone else's life at stake too.

"If you want to protect her," I say, "you have to let me go."

My mother purses her lips until they're gone. She lowers her head so she can rub her eyes with one hand.

"If anything happens to you," she says, not looking up, "it won't protect anyone."

"Nothing's going to happen to me." My mom raises her head from her hand. I touch her strong arm. "Please. Trust me."

She closes her eyes. Then opens them. Fire burns inside.

"You come home safe," she says.

I nod firmly. "I will."

In the hall outside my mom's clinic, instead of shiny tile, the floor is carpet, patterned with loops of maroon and burnt orange. I exhale. Lower to one knee, tie my bootlaces. A light fever steams at my head.

Get through tonight. Do it for them. Then, if I'm right, if Tristan is where I think he'll be, it'll all be over.

I stand. The walls are a speckled cream and devoid of any signage, and every handful of yards, they're studded with a decorative pillar or an architecturally worthless alcove. I stride up to one and press myself into it, vaguely registering that this would be good protection in a shooting: the sides would block any fire from someone coming down either side of the hall. That's what my mom would say. Damien too.

I don't remember which way I came in—my mind was in a swirl, and I was walking mostly on instinct—so I just have to pick one, I guess. I choose the right-hand side, and as I walk, I pass a janitor, a lady with brown skin and a smile ready at her mouth. She greets me, and I return it, then continue until I arrive at the elevators.

Butterfly wings beat in my stomach. The elevator spits me out on the ground floor, but when I exit the bank, it's on a different side of the building than I came in. I don't think I've ever been in this half.

Great.

I shove my hands in my pockets and traipse down the hall, past a drinking fountain and a pharmacy with its counter barred by an aluminum slatwall. More decorative alcoves with absolutely nothing in them.

And, so obscure I almost pass it without realizing, a chapel.

The door is plain, faded wood with a sliding metal label. There's a strip of glass in it, and I peer through to verify it isn't a misnamed closet. Two stained glass windows color the back, and a simple wooden altar with a linen cloth is shrouded in shadows toward the back.

Please, God, let this work. Or people will die.

A shudder ripples across me. I continue down the hall.

The main exit comes into view. I speed to a near-jog, clenching my teeth through the ache in my bones, and maintain it until I break into the entryway.

"Is something wrong?" a voice demands. I do my best to hide the fact that I jump.

A security guard is on the other side of the entry hall. She has thin eyes, pretty and severe at the same time, and a taser is hooked to her belt. She's sitting in a chair near the wall, her knee in a brace.

I swipe my tongue across my dry lips. I'm not going to shout across the space to talk to her, but I'm also not going to make her walk over here, so I cross the lobby. She stands and seems to be decently mobile, but when she's up, she doesn't put as much weight on the braced knee.

"Sorry. Nothing's wrong," I say. There's a large square button encased in glass or plastic on the wall a few feet from where we're standing. It's not a regular fire alarm—it's burgundy, not the typical bright red, and for that matter, the word "fire" is nowhere on it—but it doesn't say what it is. "My mom's upstairs, and I'm going home. Antsy to get out."

One of her eyebrows raises, and she scrutinizes me for a moment, her sable irises darting across me. My fingers itch to nervously tap against my thigh, but I keep them still. If she suspects something awry, I'll never get out of here.

Eventually, she nods. "Be careful."

"I will."

I force myself not to bolt off; instead, I take another look at that odd button.

The guard follows my line of sight to it. "That's a security lock. In case of a violent emergency."

"Violent?"

"Like a shooting. It alerts the police department and locks all the doors in the building so that patients can get out, but the attacker can't go farther in."

"That's handy."

She remains stolid. "I've never had to use it, and I don't plan to. Now, if you want to go home, you might want to get moving." It's gruff, but there's an amount of kindness underneath.

Plowing through my aches, I exit through a door that I assume will lock behind me.

I let it swing shut. No turning back.

The sidewalk is relatively well lit thanks to the bright windows of the inpatient building, but farther out in any direction, it's black. The parking lot is in front of me. The closed outpatient building is to my left, past some sort of garden in between. The void that leads to the city is to my right, hiding everything that shouldn't be hiding.

I wrap my jacket tighter around my neck. Everything inside me screams not to do this.

My mother screamed when she got shot. Mercedes screamed when they cut into her.

I click the fob. Out in the lot, my car chirps and blinks bloodred.

I park at the underpass and shut off the engine. This place—the trees, the dusty ground, the stream of water trickling into the culvert. So familiar. So safe. Which, if I know Tristan—and I do; despite everything, I *know* him—is something he'll seek out if he discovers what Eddie did to me. If he discovers what happened to our mother.

Shadows dance around me. I wait.

32

THE MOISTURE ON THE CAR WINDOWS crystalizes into frost. When I exhale, the warmth is a thin cloud. In the fogging rearview mirror, a car approaches, its headlights bright, and when it cruises up behind me, it sheds an eerie light across the small open space, across the trees.

And a reflective surface tucked among them.

The car passes me and is gone the next moment, but I keep track of the reflective spot in the trees as I rerun the glimpse in my mind. It seemed like two surfaces. One, glass. The other, metal.

Glass and metal. An abandoned vehicle.

Maybe I'm jumping to conclusions, reaching for a connection that isn't there—but those trees would be a perfect place to ditch a getaway car. As well as any other evidence.

I bite my lower lip until the dry skin splits, and warm, metallic fluid creeps out from the sting. My mother told me to be smart, and I promised her that nothing would happen to me, that I'd come home safe. Is it worth the risk?

I search the thicket for any motion. There's none.

My mom's in the hospital for two gunshot wounds. This is how I keep her safe. Her. And Mercedes. And the baby.

I grip my folded knife and wrap my spare hand around the door handle. This is how I keep them safe.

Night air rushes into the cabin, freezing until it hurts my nose, my lips, my ears. My hand aches through the gloves where the edges of the knife hilt bite into it.

I swing my leg out. My exposed cheeks practically crackle in the cold. When my whole frame is out in the open, I set the door shut behind me without making a sound, my shoes falling noiselessly on the dust.

That's maybe a hundred yards to the trees. One hundred yards for someone to spot me. Can I outrun someone for that long if I need to get back to the car? Probably not. And certainly not a bullet. I pocket my knife.

I exhale far too loudly and sweep through the cloud it makes. Goosebumps ridge my skin. Behind me, the street glistens like obsidian from the moonlit ice; there's no sign of the upcoming daylight. To my left is the underpass and the hill it runs beneath. A trickle of water burbles from it. I step over and creep forward, flinching every time my boot crunches on a patch of gravel. My ears ring.

There are no commuting vehicles behind me, only my parked one. No people. At the top of the hill, an owl lands on a dim lamppost. I cross fifty yards and approach the edge of the hill; at the base, its prickly, dormant crabgrass gives way to the dust I'm walking on.

I grit my teeth to keep them from chattering and lean forward to see as far as I can around the hill's bend.

Wild grass, half dead, bows beneath an iced breeze. That's it.

My muscles itch to burst forward, to cover the last fifty yards and get it over with, but I force myself to be slow, silent, unseeable.

At twenty-five yards, the hidden car edges into unobstructed view. The door's wide open.

I stop. There's no hillside next to me now, nothing but open space and moonlight gleaming on me. If that door's open, does that mean the driver was careless? Or does it mean he's still here?

I take another step, and there's no gunshot. I only hope that doesn't mean he's aiming.

I make it to the trees, and the dense needles surround me. I'm hidden. And the car's right there, a dozen yards away.

I rest my gloved hand on a bumpy trunk. This is exactly how I remember. The prickly canopy of bottle green. The sweet pungency of pine pitch. All except for that car and the smell of exhaust.

I nudge a pinecone aside with the toe of my boot, then set my foot onto the dry carpet of fallen needles. The car has no back plate. I ease to one knee, cringing at the pain in my joints, and curve my hand around the exhaust pipe. Warmth runs through my gloves.

I stifle a shudder and, keeping as low as I can, creep forward until I'm at the open door. My back is to the thicket.

There's a handgun sitting on the passenger's seat.

I inhale to steady myself. I get a lungful of sickly sweet liquor. And of spearmint.

My heart drops like lead. I lean in and take another, closer look. An empty skinny-necked bottle sits in the cupholder.

I stare at it. Blood flows away from my head until I'm dizzy. I crouch and put my head between my knees. My jaw burns. I stretch it and swallow to clear the hard knot in my throat.

What now? If Luiz shot my mother, this is moot: getting Luiz arrested will only give Tony another reason to have us killed, and all of his lackeys would be gone, so he'd have to come for us himself. And he wouldn't come drunk enough to miss.

Do I walk away now? There's still the chance that I'm right about Tristan.

I warily rise from my crouch, my ears cocked for any sound. As I do, a rectangular bulge on the dashboard, tucked near the frost-covered windshield, catches my eye. A small camera lens stares at me from the rubbery phone case.

What are the odds he has a password?

I reach in and take it out. The time pops up like it does on my phone. It's not even one in the morning yet. Moonlight slithers through the branches above me. A chill snakes down my exposed back. My skin tingles.

I knuckle the home button. It asks for a code.

My canines snag my inner lip. Great.

I bite down on the fabric fingertip of one of my gloves and wrestle my hand out. An ice-laced breeze flowers up my jacket and cools the sweat in my shirt. His birthday's December 8th. What's that in four digits?

I enter *1208*.

Fail.

I rock back onto my heels; my weight's been on my toes, and my calf muscles are smoldering. Pine needles crackle under me.

It could be anything. He could've put the date before the month or added the year or done the month and year, or he could have chosen a string of numbers with a completely different significance. Or they could be completely random. I can't guess.

Think. I know him well enough to find the answer; I'm sure of it.

The lining of my nose burns from inhaling the arid winter. A few lost, gray-rimmed feathers on the ground somersault when the air moves. I stare at the numbers as they begin to quiver in my hold.

My shoulder is so swollen, so weak; I'm almost afraid the heft of this tiny thing will dislocate it.

Dislocate it.

I race through my memory to when Luiz came to my house with his shoulder a mess. I recreate the way his thumb moved.

Dead center and near the bottom. *0*

Then to the left. *7*

Stretches straight up. *1*

Finishes on the opposite diagonal. *9*

My shoulder blades crawl toward each other as I submit.

It unlocks.

The last app open was his text messages. To Tony.

My pulse thuds in my temples. Five messages in the thread are visible.

From Tony: u shot her mom yet?

Luiz: Done.

Tony: u better b right

Luiz: Paityn's not that stubborn. Or stupid. We won't have any more issues.

Tony's latest message from about an hour ago: good work.

I can't tell what's betrayal and what's anger. They both feel the same, hot and thick and leaving my muscles curled.

Defiance doesn't—that's its own sensation, crisp and sweet.

I tamp that for now and command myself to think logically. If he left his phone, that means one of two things. He's wasted nearby. Or he's on his way back. I grab my own phone from my jacket pocket and pull up the camera.

I think my pacemaker nearly blips when a sharp inhale slices the silence.

I go as still as a rabbit sensing a coyote. The light of the two phones glares condemningly on my face. Two minutes ago, I would have told anyone that he would never hurt me, not with his own hands. Now the text messages on the screen mock me.

His gun's in the passenger's seat.

Please, Luiz, do not make me go for that. Do not make me hurt you.

I don't find him, but I heard that breath. I heard it.

I lower to one knee to cloak the phone's light. I wish I didn't have to get my fingerprints on the screen, but I scroll to the beginning of the conversation that Luiz left. The earliest message is from months ago.

He hasn't deleted one. It's everything I need.

Within twenty seconds, the entire conversation is in my photo gallery.

I tuck my phone back into my pocket and close the zipper. This is my mother's life. The baby's, Mercedes'. They're protected. If I can make it out.

I stretch forward, my bones and muscles and joints screaming, but I manage to slide Luiz's phone back where I found it. I hope it's exactly the same.

Not that he'd notice anything askew. I steal a glance at the liquor bottle.

I don't dare stand up; instead, I crawl backward with my face toward the thicket. Dust cakes the knees of my jeans. Then I'm far enough away that being low serves no purpose.

I get to my feet painfully. Now, wherever Luiz is, he's closer to his gun than I am.

Even if I were closer, would I really be able to use it? Maybe to give him a flesh wound, to delay him enough for me to escape. Maybe, but that would mean I'd have to see him bleeding again.

I keep backing up until I realize I'm at a different angle than I came in at—I'm closer to the hill than I was before. And when I search the trees, a black tennis shoe and a copper ankle stick out from behind a rough, brown trunk and a prickly bush. Not fifteen feet from his car.

How drunk is he?

I stop when I've crept back to the underpass. The phone weighs heavily in my pocket. I have to call the police, but when they come, they might stay. Which means Tristan will steer clear.

I'm so sure he'll come—but that's not as certain as the pictures on my phone. Not as certain as the fingerprints, the saliva, the *person* less than a football field's length away from me.

The burbling of the water in the drain flows into my ears. I'll find Tristan. I will. Just not tonight. Tonight, I keep us all safe.

My ears throb in the merciless temperature. No, not just my ears, my whole body. My muscles are spent from containing a fit of shivering. I step over the tiny brook.

I can spare one minute.

I dip one boot in the water and duck into the culvert. This is exactly how I remember it too. I savor the wet smell of algae, the sand beneath my boots, the odd comfort of the tunnel offering me no way but forward or back.

I shove my gloves into my pocket and run my fingertips against the slick wall. With the other hand, I start the flashlight on my phone. It shocks me so that when I close my eyes, bright dots wink on my corneas, but after a few seconds of blinking, I adjust.

I'm not sure what I expect. A thread from a sweatshirt? A wrapper? Idle scratches on the wall? He's too smart to leave any of that unless he wants to be caught.

I comb the area, every fissure in the cement, every patch of sopping moss, every square inch of the water-covered floor and the low ceiling. The stream soaks into my boots. Its gurgling becomes white noise.

Cutting through the white noise, footsteps approach.

33

I DOUSE THE FLASHLIGHT on my phone and jam my hand in my knife pocket in the same motion. I close my lips to hide plumes of hot breath, and conceal my nose behind my hand. The other hand slides the knife out of my pocket and unfolds it.

The tread outside has the distinct crunch of shoes on dirt, coming from the direction of the trees. It's sluggish with a drag interspersed.

Did he see me come in here? What was I thinking, using the flashlight?

Outside, Luiz coughs. The tip of my knife quivers—I'm already sick at the thought of having to use it. I should be far enough into the tunnel that he won't be able to see me in the dark, especially if he's so drunk.

But what if he does come in? He's got a gun. I'll be trapped.

I could run. I could bolt for my car and hope I make it.

He's got a gun.

My nasal passage stings from the cold, dry air. A foot crunches just outside the tunnel mouth. If I move now, he'll hear the splash.

A hand.

My teeth seize my lip. Five skeletal fingers, black as onyx, creep over the rim of the man-sized pipe. Not violent. Not even sinister. A distracted touch. And from the way his knuckles are facing, it's his right side.

He's right-handed. Which means the hand that I assume he'd shoot with is empty.

A tired exhale and a wave of steam sweep past the mouth of the pipe. I press myself against the concrete wall until I imagine hairline fractures on my skull. The hilt of my knife is slippery with my sweat.

The toe of a tennis shoe rocks into the bank of the rivulet. His body follows.

How dark is it? How drunk is he?

His eyes shift.

His black mass spasms so fast I can't react in time. The collar of my jacket bunches in his fist. My knife hand twitches up, stopping millimeters from his neck.

He freezes with his chin withdrawn from the edge of my knife, eyes wide. His clutch around my collar drops away, and his hand falls. The other holds the trademark glass bottle.

I lower my knife, exhaling unsteadily. His narrow eyes have slackened. They run across me, over and over, as if he's seeing someone he thought he'd never see again.

"Paityn?" He poises his knuckles over my jawline. "What are you doing here?"

The skin in my throat is so dry it sticks when I swallow. So he doesn't know what I was doing.

I smack his hand away from my face. Or, rather, he lets me. "I was hoping Tristan was here."

He chuckles, giving me a whiff of alcohol. "In the dark?"

"I had a light."

"And?"

I pull out my phone to restart the flashlight; my gut is sour and churning as if he already knows what's on here. My fingers are so cold it makes the touchscreen difficult. As I work it, Luiz downs what's left of the drink. When he's done, he wipes his mouth and tosses the bottle to the ground. It breaks.

"Your mom," he says.

I stall. "What?"

"How is she?" His words slump against each other, like they're too intoxicated to stand on their own.

I imagine the ruby stains on her bandages, and my neck heats with fury. "You're drunk, Luiz."

He chuckles again and leans against the wall. "Aren't you observant." Still smirking, he kicks a shard of glass, and it hits the bottom of my jeans. His teeth are bright even in the void of the tunnel, but that grin falls away, and he becomes solemn. "You didn't answer my question. Is she all right?"

I hate when his speech sounds like that, with his lips and tongue sluggish. I always have, but I've never heard it this bad. Yet, somehow, the rest of him seems sniper steady. It always does.

I almost answer that my mom's fine, just to appease him, but that would be more suspicious than anything.

"No thanks to you," I say, still working the phone. I switch on the flashlight, and it blinds both of us. Luiz angles his head away.

When that passes, the sweet shade of his face is gone. Something forbidding replaces it. He wades forward so that I'm between him and the wall.

"Back up," I tell him.

"Let me explain something to you."

"I said back—"

Luiz slams his palm against the concrete next to my head. I wish I didn't flinch.

His face is within inches of mine. I inhale his exhales, alcohol on his breath until I'm ready to gag. And, underneath, spearmint, as if he secretes the stuff.

I once would have let him get closer. I once held him on my shoulder. When he speaks, I can almost feel the motion of his lips against mine. "I'm the reason your mother is alive."

"What are you talking about?" A hot tremor rattles my voice.

Luiz stands to his full height—his head almost skims the top of the culvert. His eyes have to shift down to meet mine; a vicious smile curls onto his face.

"If I had wanted to kill her," he says, "I would have killed her. Tony was going to." He snaps his fingers effortlessly. "Quick as your stepdad."

I knew it. I was right. I knew it.

I beat back the fierce stinging in my eyes. Don't cry. Do not let him see you cry.

"What about when Eddie came to kill me?" I say, my voice somehow cool. "Was that you too?"

His smirk slips. So does his arrogant posture. Weight on one hip, shoulders loose, head halfway dipped. "No."

"But you knew."

He looks away. "I knew."

I lost my father trying to save him. And he was willing to let me die.

When I don't say anything, Luiz pivots and makes his way back to the opening of the tunnel.

"Why did you protect her?" I say far too loudly, so loudly my senses hiccup.

Luiz pauses. Turns to the side so his scar faces me. "I wasn't going to kill a baby, Paityn."

My jaw slackens.

I never told him. How did he—

Tristan. Tristan must have.

He circles farther around as if waiting for a reaction I won't give. Then he says, "Go home, Paityn. Nobody has to die."

Again, he means. Nobody has to die *again*.

And he's gone.

I stand for a minute as the cold throbs in my ears. I'm shaking by the time I remember my phone.

I end the video recording.

34

THERE'S NO GOOD REASON for me to sweep my light across the walls one last time, but I do. And I catch a small white corner of paper jutting out of a crack farther down the tunnel.

Now that my muscles aren't so tense, the uncontrollable shivering comes on, but I stoop in front of the crack and free the paper. When I unfold it, it's the picture of Mercedes, Tristan, and me, the one that led me here.

I check the back for any clue, but it's blank. Still, a tear slips away. Maybe he does want to be found.

———

I don't bother being quiet as I hike back up to my car. I get in and blast the heating and swallow the hot pain in my throat.

I call the police station and send both the pictures and the recording. Maybe that part about him protecting my mom will help Luiz. Maybe it won't. It's out of my hands.

They won't hurt my family. Ever again.

———

Luiz watches me at the edge of the thicket. I'm sure he's waiting for me to leave so he can get the car and go.

I wait until the sirens sound in the distance. And he must hear them too because he bolts into the trees, and I don't see him come back out after that.

―――――

I pull up in front of the hospital and park a few feet from the corner of the inpatient building. Surrounded by a sidewalk perimeter, the serenity garden spans the area between inpatient and outpatient. Inpatient's concrete walls are unforgiving and black; outpatient's are bluish-green glass.

I could go inside, but I'm getting warm, and I don't want to figure out how to get back in when the building's locked. I send my mom a text message to let her know that I'm safe and I'm just outside the door, then send one to Mercedes, telling her where to meet me when she and Elijah come.

I toss the phone onto the passenger's seat. Tilt my seat back and relax into it.

Now I can rest.

―――――

Mid-September, warm for the night. The nighttime is so silky it slips around me like water. Crickets trill. My stepbrother is down the hall. And everything is right in the world.

Two rapid, harsh pops.

I bolt upright, heart rate flaming, but as my feet touch the cool laminate, it sinks in: I've been here before. I know what will happen. There's no way for me to stop it.

The shock, the fear, drain away, leaving me hollow. I nudge back my curtain.

Three figures are on the sidewalk, draped in inky darkness. One is unmoving on the ground. The other two stand over him, leaning toward each other as if exchanging words. Then they run. Figures I recognize.

The front door flies open. Tristan tears out, screams for his father, skids to his knees on the concrete.

I stand. I remember the first time this happened, when it was real. I remember running, sprinting. Now I stagger down the hall, the stairs, onto my front porch. My mom's already there, on one knee next to Damien, telling Tristan to back away.

I drop to my knees. And I pray now like I prayed then.

My mother sends Tristan over to me. He stumbles, practically drags himself up our driveway. When he gets to me, he falls to his hands and knees. His heart breaks before my eyes.

I wrap my arms around him, try to gather every inch of him into myself as if that could protect him, even though it's too late, it's far too late. He does the same to me.

Mercedes' door bursts open. She rushes across the street, and forces us into the house, out of harm's way. And then she's on her knees with us. My mother rocks Damien, and all I can think is that there's nothing she can do.

We hold each other. Tears seep from my eyes as my mother cradles my father.

And then, past them, on the other side of the street, is the man from the cemetery. He's on one knee, and his head is bowed in pain—or grief. The side of his face drips red.

I bury myself in Tristan's shoulder.

I flutter awake.

There's a shadow outside my window before it shatters.

I

35

SHARDS SPRAY.

A thick hand jolts in from out of the twilight. It pops the lock, wrenches open the door, wraps around my throat, and tears me out of my seat faster than I can blink. My head slams into the glass of the backseat window. My lungs convulse for a gasp, but muscular knuckles dig under my chin and grind my teeth against each other.

Tony.

My head drains. Luiz must have gotten away. And let his drunk mouth run.

"You're coming with me," Tony purrs. He smiles. My skull jams into the window again. Stars blink in my vision. My ribs spasm, in, out, anything.

A tighter squeeze traps blood in my head. Then I jerk forward, away from the metal of the car, and he torques me around so that my back is to him. His arm is around my neck, loose enough that I can get oxygen but locked so that he can take me wherever he wants. His hand clamps over my mouth. He drags me.

I drop to dead weight, thrash in his chokehold, and scream through his burly fingers. I try to sink my teeth into him, but my jaw is vised shut by his arm.

My shoes scrape against asphalt and glass. The hospital's twin buildings loom over me in shadows. I claw at Tony's arm, thrash again. I try to get my footing so I can ram my heel into his kneecap, but before I have the chance, my ankle bangs against the curb, clubbing my feet out from under me.

Tony hauls me the last few feet until we're on a strip of sidewalk between the inpatient building and the serenity garden—around the corner where no one will find us. Where no one will find my body until much, much later.

He spins me again. Hot liquid trickles down my neck from where my scalp slams into the rough wall, and I'm back where I started with his powerful hand slithered around my neck.

My ears ring. I jerk my shoulder against his forearm and writhe, searching for a pocket to breathe.

He squeezes. And then there's no air at all. No air, no blood. My vision dims. The ringing in my ears fades, mutes. I go limp.

As I do, when I stop fighting, the choke loosens. Blood and oxygen crawl back, enough for my vision to merge, for my hearing and that ringing to return. And now, muffled, an engine rumbling. I think. Or maybe it's my own heartbeat in my ears.

Tony's free hand disappears behind his back. He leans in until his face is inches from mine.

"I gave you a chance." His breath is warm and humid, appearing as a thin white cloud before it coats my skin. It smells clean, not as much as his brother's, but still clean. A handgun cocks. "This ought to do the trick."

The engine, or my heartbeat, I can't tell, roars harder. Tony's attention slides away from me.

The rumble's not in my imagination. It's not my pulse. It's a car, so close, so fast it buzzes in the soles of my feet and shakes the scattered shards of the annihilated car window. High beams glare. Tires squeal and smoke to a stop with an acrid smell.

Tony's distracted.

I take anything my mother and Damien ever taught me: fast, strike the joints, thrust your hips into it. Get out alive, come home, make it hurt if I can't. On my terms.

I slam my forearm into Tony's wrist. The joint bends backward. Bruising swells in my arm at the impact, but his grip comes away. I crash onto my knees, biting through my tongue, and wrench open my ribs for air.

"Tony, don't!" A blur of black comes at me. I recognize Luiz just before his body slams into mine.

The world spins as he shoves me to the ground. Lightning rips across my vision, black and white at the same time. My solar plexus freezes from the impact. My nose splinters; my cheek is raw.

A few of his thin fingers are caught between the ground and my temple. He broke the fall.

He withdraws them, and the last of my skin meets the cement. One of Luiz's hands presses between my shoulder blades. The other fixes my head against the ground, as if warning me not to move.

"Tony, stop it," he says. "The cops are already on us. This is more trouble than it's worth."

The smoothness vanishes from Tony's voice. Hatred for me from all these years takes its place. "Get out of the way."

Blood spills out of my nose. My right hand is trapped under my stomach. Luiz has me at an angle so that all I can see are Tony's ankles and the vast, empty parking lot, lit violet as the sun struggles to rise.

No one. No help.

Luiz's tone changes. Becomes demanding. Threatening. "I said back off." His hand tightens around my skull as he speaks. A moan drags out of me before I can prevent it.

Tony scoffs. "Can't ever take the shot."

What?

Luiz's hand stiffens between my shoulder blades.

Damien. Luiz was supposed to kill him.

He knew. He knew the whole time.

Tony's voice again. "Make a choice, Luiz."

No response. Above me, an exhale clatters out of him. A thorn—at least, it feels like a thorn—is trapped beneath my cheek, stuck deep in the skin, sending a thin spine of pain up my nerve. The cloth of my scarf is cold against my scalp, except where Luiz's hand cloaks it. His touch has become so light it's almost tender, caressing.

Hesitating. Considering.

"Hurry up. Or are you going to run again? Get us arrested like you did with Dad."

I pivot my face on the ground so I can see, leaving skin behind. Luiz doesn't stop me.

Tony has the gun aimed at Luiz. Loosely. As if he's threatening to shoot him—but also offering the gun for him to take.

"Be a man for once," Tony says.

A breath. Two.

Luiz's weight lifts off me. Reaching out.

The gun transfers possession. My fingertips scratch the ground. He'll shoot. But I won't have been lying still.

I twist underneath Luiz, get on my back, snatch the lapels of his aviator jacket, and yank him toward me. The cloth rips, but he lurches forward enough for me to grab hold of him and throw us both sideways. We crash to the concrete, all our weight on his firing arm. Luiz groans in frustration, his breath on my neck. It tickles the same way it did when he cried on my shoulder.

The heel of his palm cracks under my chin. My teeth hit each other before his hand snakes over my mouth. A metal circle brands my neck—it's still heated from when the gun was fired into my car. It's almost hot enough to blister the skin.

It digs under my chin, bruising my throat, and I can't contain a gag reflex. Luiz hauls us to our knees, then to our feet. I'm trapped against his collarbone. His hand is sticky over my mouth, covered in sweat or blood or both. Spearmint fills my nose.

Tony has his arms crossed.

The gun's front sights burrow under my jawbone. An exhale shudders by my ear. Luiz's voice is hushed. "What the…"

Tony frowns and shifts his attention from us to the street where Luiz's car idles. My back arches to distance my neck from the barrel. Luiz clinches me harder. Somewhere, an engine throbs. Not Luiz's. A new one.

A car door opens around the corner, two, then both shut. A voice I know. "Oh my—*Paityn, where are you?*"

Mercedes. My text message for her and Elijah to meet me.

No, no, no. Don't come over here. Do not come over here.

But she is, and so is a second pair of strides, both of them running closer, running to my broken window, Luiz's idling car, the trail of blood I left.

Tony slides his hand into his front pocket. Raises his eyebrows, almost entertained. He glances at Luiz as if to say, *And? What are you going to do?*

Luiz could shoot me. He could shoot me right now. All he'd have to do is pull the trigger, a tiny motion, and I'd be gone by the time they get here. They'd see my broken body, and then he'd shoot them too. We'd all be dead, and there would be nothing I could do about it. Nothing. He could finish this right now.

They're sprinting closer. The muzzle eases from my chin, my skin going from burning to freezing as it's exposed to the early morning air.

His arm extends like a bronze spear with a lead point. I can taste the salty sweat from his hand, the minerals from dust on his palm. I can taste my own blood. He's warm. His heartbeat slams against my back, as if desperately trying to break me free.

He aims.

Fires.

36

THE SHOT RIPS INTO THE SIDEWALK by Mercedes' feet.

For a split second, Tony and Luiz stare at me dumbfounded, Luiz's hand still pinned over my mouth. They stare at my weight thrown into Luiz's firing arm, grinding it into the wall, shoving the tip of the barrel down.

That split second ends.

Luiz's finger is poised over the trigger. He yanks back to regain control, but I hurl my shoulder into him, and his arm scrapes red stains across the rough brick. I wrestle my mouth from his hand, jam the heel of my palm against his firing wrist, securing the gun against the wall.

Tony lunges toward Mercedes and Elijah, but Elijah blocks him from Mercedes, who thrusts toward me.

Luiz makes a vicious noise that buzzes in my jaw and sickens my gut. He jerks his hand back again. My wrist and elbow buckle like they're nothing. He grabs the back of my neck and levers me over his knee onto the ground headfirst.

Mercedes collides with him. There's a bang, but no cry of pain. My hands smack into the ground. My shoulder follows, the side of my face. I roll. Pain fractures across me.

Who has the gun?

Concrete stabs into my temple. I blink blood out of my eyes.

Mercedes is close enough to Luiz that her body is almost up against his, so the extended barrel is behind her, but Luiz looks prepared to jab it under her arm. Neither of them are bleeding—that shot I heard must have been accidental.

Elijah is at the wall past them, the only thing standing between us and Tony. Tony's thick arm twitches forward, and Elijah dodges his fist. He returns the blow and clips Tony in the chin before Tony can completely slip the punch.

Luiz draws the barrel toward Mercedes' torso. I gasp, and the air scrapes over my vocal cords, but Mercedes hooks her arm around his and clamps down with a yell of effort, of drive. She pins his elbow against her ribs and traps the gun behind her.

Tony's knuckles drill into Elijah's side so hard I feel it in my own body. Elijah groans but holds his ground.

Raise your head, Paityn. Get off the ground. Stand. Up.

Luiz's breathing is like an animal's. He clutches a fistful of Mercedes' hair, ready to tear her off, but she throws all her weight into an elbow to his jaw. His temple cracks against the wall, and he drops like a corpse. A heavy object clatters to the cement.

Tony's attention jerks to Mercedes. His eyes are wide, shocked.

I push myself to my elbow.

Elijah torques through his injured side, throws a hook, and lands his knuckles on Tony's jaw, but Tony doesn't collapse like Luiz did. He swings his arm like a club. His full momentum slams into Elijah's mouth.

The blow brings Elijah to his knees.

Mercedes screams his name. Her weight plunges into a crouch, and she reaches forward for something. I try to call for him too, but my lip is swollen, and I'm too dizzy to get the sound out. Tony grabs the back of his jacket and throws him into the wall. His temple slams against the brick and leaves a bloodstain. The light leaves Elijah's eyes.

I try again to call his name, try to push myself to my hands, but my vision crosses. I cough. There's blood in my mouth, dripping down my chin.

Tony is on one knee, his hand on Elijah's collar, ready to slam him again. The other bores into his pocket and emerges with something that flips open and doubles in size, metal and glinting.

Mercedes stands from her crouch, arms extended. "Drop it."

Tony looks up to find himself downrange of the gun.

Elijah's eyes flutter open, then roam. Luiz is inert. A bruise is surfacing on his face. Everything around me seems to double, then halve, then come back to a single image.

Tony stares Mercedes down. Her hands are dead steady. "I said drop it."

Tony's eyes narrow, searing with spite. They flick to the left. To Elijah.

He wrenches Elijah in front of him and levels the knife over his throat. "You first."

Mercedes' stance stiffens. "Let him go."

"You think I'm kidding? Drop the gun."

My heartbeat rushes in my ears. She can't shoot Tony without killing Elijah.

Elijah moans and stirs. Tony tightens the knife so blood begins to drain from it. The blood is blurred, but it remains a single red line—my vision doesn't double it as it carves down Elijah's neck, disappearing into his shirt.

"No, stop," Mercedes says. She lowers the pistol.

Tony will kill Elijah even if she disarms herself. He'll kill us all. She knows that.

Luiz stirs. My head is helium; I duck it down, hoping to get more blood flow to it. I need to see clearly.

Mercedes exhales raggedly. Stifled defiance blazes in her eyes. "Let him go."

Another clatter on the concrete. It skids near me.

My vision stays straight.

Don't look. He'll see it.

Tony smirks. Drops Elijah mercilessly. Stands, knife in hand, and looks down at him. "Why don't you watch this."

Elijah groans and begins to push himself up, but Tony kicks him back down. Mercedes stands rigid, chin high. Luiz's eyes open.

Tony crosses the distance faster than I ever thought he could move. Faster than Mercedes can react.

She hits the wall like I did.

Luiz staggers to his feet, dizzy, and supports himself against the brick building. Elijah drags himself to his elbows. He weakly calls Mercedes' name.

Her turquoise hair absorbs deep red at the back; her face flushes to near purple. She claws at Tony's hand around her neck, kicks, but his arms are too long for her to do much damage.

Tony smiles. He plants the tip of his knife into the skin on her throat. A dark bead of fluid leaks out. "I'll make this quick."

I throw myself forward. Grab the gun.

Pull the trigger.

37

I PULL IT AGAIN. And a third time.

A convulsion racks Luiz's body and a choked sound leaves him—all in the time it takes Tony to fall to the ground.

Mercedes sucks in air desperately and scrabbles at the brick behind her. Tony's blood is splattered on her face. Elijah gapes at me, then at the body laid out on the ground.

Adrenaline pushes me through the dizziness, to my feet. Luiz's hand is bloodless, crushing against the wall. He turns his eyes to me.

And in them, I'm sure I can see my bleeding, dead body.

"You killed him." His voice sounds like a brand new blade, cold, waiting for its first task, so sharp you'll be killed before you even realize you've been cut.

"Don't make me do this." The words tremble as I level the sights at his chest.

Muscles bulge in his jaw and forearms. Sunrise has stained the sky and the shards of glass on the ground blood orange. Luiz's car hums a few yards from us.

Mercedes and Elijah both recoil from me, as if to make sure they are completely out of range, but there's no way I'll miss—it's practically point-blank.

Blood flows down the side of my eye. Please, Luiz, don't make me do this. "Get down."

Luiz's knees bend, but not like he's lowering himself to the ground. He's getting ready to spring.

"Don't," I warn.

Luiz is unmoving. Long enough that sweat drips into my wounds and burns. Then he lowers himself to one knee. A bruise blossoms black across his cheek, under his eye, up his forehead. His scar stays as white as chalk. Tony's hand, limp around the knife, is less than a foot from Luiz's.

I see it too late.

His arm swings, and the open blade hurtles toward me.

I fire. Recoil jams my shoulders, and the knife smacks into my arm, hilt or blade—I'm not sure. I feel nothing. Luiz moans so sharply that I know I got him, but I don't see where. He bolts for his idling car.

Mercedes and Elijah both jerk forward to stop him but throw themselves backward when I train the muzzle back on target. I go low, aiming for his leg, but the round buries itself into his door as he closes it behind him. The engine revs and tires squeal, and he's gone, a trail of garnet marring the sidewalk where he used to be.

The gun is extended in my shaking arms. I ease it down. And turn to Tony.

He's bleeding. Split open. His eyes are the same shade of brown as mine. Wide. Unseeing. Lost.

Mercedes hauls Elijah to his feet. They both stare at me.

Everything rushes out of me, and I collapse to my knees. Pebbles drive into my skin like spikes, and the pain registers through every nerve inside me, but I don't react to it. I can't bring myself to.

Tony's body never leaves my sight.

Elijah and Mercedes rush to me. Mercedes drops to one knee next to me so quickly she tears her jeans. The pale frayed threads quickly soak in red; I'm not sure whose blood it is. It must be Tony's—that's the only blood I can see.

Elijah removes the gun from my hand and sets it off to the side. It clacks heavily when its metal balances on the sidewalk. It's tinted orange by the rising sun, just like the sky and the glass.

I think they're speaking to me. Shaking me when I don't respond. I double over and dry heave until my sides ache. Supportive hands are on my shoulders.

When the dry heaving stops, I raise my head, and Tony's still there.

I did this. I did this to him. I killed him.

38

THEY CLEAN MY WOUNDS. It burns, but I don't make a sound. They're asking me questions that I'm barely able to answer.

Elijah was holding Mercedes' face in his hands. I haven't seen him since.

Mercedes sits shellshocked at my bedside in the hospital. There's suture tape over her neck, where Tony's knife bit into her. Where it came so close to taking her away from me forever. A small bandage pads the back of her head at her hairline.

The door is pushed open, and there's a voice I know, a voice I love, saying my name, calling it again when I don't respond.

I shift my head listlessly to my mother. She limps over her bullet wound and bundles Mercedes against herself first, then approaches me. She cups my cheek in her hand.

I shot him.

My mother looks into my eyes, and I know she knows.

I cry.

Mercedes sits in the desk chair across from my bed at home. Her pencil makes gentle scratching sounds as she journals or sketches in a notebook that has orchids printed on the cover.

She closes the notebook with a quiet snap and looks up. "You saved me."

How long ago was that? Four days? I don't know. I witness Tony die as often as my eyes close.

"You saved me first," I say. Mercedes gets a chill. I remember the spray of blood. That's all I remember. "Luiz is still out there."

"They'll get him."

Yeah. That's what I thought before. "How did you get there? Usually you're out running at that time."

"I saw your text, and I thought something was wrong, so I got Elijah to bring us over."

In my mind, Elijah slams into the hospital wall. "Have you heard from him at all?"

Mercedes nods. Her line of sight is elsewhere, but not like she can't handle eye contact—just that she's thinking.

"You have?" I say. "When?"

"When you were in the hospital."

I'm quiet. I don't know what to say. He's not distancing himself from everyone. He's avoiding me.

It aches. Aches that my choice—the only choice I could have made, the only choice that would save their lives—cost me him.

Mercedes inhales suddenly. "Paityn, he came to me and cried."

My lips part. It is a few seconds before I can get them to move. "What?"

She doesn't speak until she blinks her eyes clear, and when she does, her voice is quieter. "He's scared for you. We all are."

I know. And I would give anything to take that fear from them.

Grief wells up inside me. From releasing. From losing something beautiful.

I haven't lost everything, though.

"Thank you," I tell Mercedes. "For being here."

She does her best to smile. "Always."

Several nights later, I lie awake so I don't have to see Tony die again. So I don't have to kill him.

My blankets, made of flannel and fleece, surround me protectively. Sweat flushes out a light fever. My eyes are heavy.

I keep them open, fixed on my nightstand—on the crucifix.

"Why did You let this happen?" I whisper. Anger cracks the words down the middle.

And as always, He's silent.

Hours. I wait for hours, until dawn dips the sky in denim blue, gazing out that window, waiting for Tristan to come home, searching for any shadow that could be him.

There's motion at the corner of a fence across the street. The tiredness suddenly rushes away.

That wasn't Tristan. The shadow was too angular, a bit too tall and thin. It seemed like another silhouette I could recognize anywhere.

I shake my head. My imagination's overreacting. I didn't see him. I didn't see anything.

I lie down and turn over. I'm not going to miss Tristan. He's not coming.

39

I FINISH TYING MY HEADSCARF, standing in front of the bathroom mirror. My shoulders sting from the brief exertion.

I hazard a closer glimpse at my reflection. My skin is so thin that a few veins emerge, light traces of blue and green braiding and branching across my forehead and jawline. The bruises across my cheekbones are a diluted yellow. A white film of skin coats the scabs on the side of my face.

I turn away.

I gingerly trek from my shower to my bed and collapse onto it. A late-February snow falls outside my window, but the sun pierces through breaks in the clouds. Once the snow stops, there will be a downy covering on the ground, and the air will be clean and crisp. Mercedes' driveway is already covered. Hopefully, she's catching up on sleep over there; I'm not sure how much she's gotten here.

I read the date on my phone. Saturday. Two weeks until I'm shipped off for my procedure. I exhale through puffed cheeks; I don't want to think about that right now.

My phone dings. I open the screen, hoping it's my mom telling me the doctor said everything's all right with the baby. And a twinge inside me prays it's from Tristan. If he's alive.

It's Elijah.

Can I come talk to you?

I surprise myself. My eyes well up when I see his name. They still haven't cleared by the time I reply. Of course.

An answer pops up within seconds. Thanks.

I stretch my ribs in an inhale. How long has it been since I saw him last? Since he saw me kill Tony. Since he saw the one side of me he had never seen, the side I never knew I had.

I close my eyes to cut off a flashback. And I almost fall asleep before a series of pleasant digital tones tugs me back. My doorbell. Outside, a path of footprints leads up to my porch.

I grab the keys from my desk, hurry downstairs, and open up the first door.

He stands on the other side of the storm door, wearing his black leather jacket, his hands tucked in his zippered pockets. His eyes were on the step until I came. I open the glass so there's nothing but winter air between us.

I shiver. "Come inside."

He gives me a glimpse of that old smile that fills me with so much warmth, with peace.

His hair is wet, and his shoes bring in a dusting of white flakes. I inspect the yard behind him—it's covered in spotless snow except for his footprints and a different set on the sidewalk that leads behind the fence.

Unease creeps up in me. I'm not sure why.

Elijah closes the storm door behind him and turns the lock with a clack, bringing me back to the present. I shut and fasten the inner door with the two deadbolts. "Let's go upstairs."

I lead him to my room, where I take a seat on my bed and have him sit where Tristan used to. He lithely sets himself down.

"How are you feeling?" he says.

"Well as I can."

His only response is a nod. His gaze slips out the window.

As far as I can tell, he watches nothing in particular. Both of us do, except I glance back to him every so often. At first his eyes are steady. Then they water.

I wait until they've dried again. His footprints outside are filling up with a fresh layer of powder.

"What did you want to talk about?" I say softly, even though I'm sure I know.

He opens his mouth, then stops. Clamps his jaw shut and swallows. He doesn't move until the footprints are almost gone.

Finally, he meets my eyes.

"I'm sorry I haven't come to see you," he says. "I just—" He exhales so painfully I can feel it in my own heart. "Every time I look at you, I see Cynthia."

He rests his hand on top of mine. It's warm and smooth and strong, but careful, so delicate with mine, like he's handling something fragile. And priceless. His skin is bronze against my ivory.

"I lost her," he whispers. His eyes…so intense, so deep, an ocean that I let take me. "I can't lose you too."

A wet streak carves a warm path down my face.

"Hey." I wrap my hand around his and squeeze. "You're not going to lose me."

His eyes well up. He smiles at me in a way that makes me think his sister told him that every day.

We sit there for a long while. His hand warms mine. Mine cools his. His eyes never leave me. Slowly, the grief in them bleeds away, and it's just him and me again.

Our gazes trail off, and we both wind up looking out the window at the thin layer of snow on the ground. When there's the unmistakable swish of the front door opening downstairs.

Elijah's eyes dart to me, his brows low.

I locked it. I always lock it, and I know I did this time. Mercedes and my mother are the only other ones with the keys.

Strides hammer upstairs. Elijah stands and steps between me and the door. Unzips his jacket and throws it to the side, leaving him in a long-sleeved royal-blue shirt. I snatch my knife from my nightstand.

The footfalls stop outside my room. Muffled breathing.

The knob turns. The door swings open.

Luiz holds a knife.

40

HE STANDS IN TORN BLACK JEANS and a baggy jacket. His brown eyes are so devoid of light they're black.

My line of sight flicks to the side, to my phone.

"Don't even think about it," Luiz says. He adjusts the knife in his grip.

I hide my own knife against the side of my thigh, behind Elijah's frame.

"Don't do this," I tell Luiz. "Please."

He watches me for a moment. Then he laughs, an ominous, ugly sound that sends a shiver down my spine. "You should have thought about that before you shot my brother."

I used to know this boy. I knew him and would have done anything for him, anything to get him out of the pain he was in.

My thumb brushes the blade. I don't want to hurt him, but he's not giving me a choice.

Sweat lines Elijah's hair. This is my fault. I have to face it.

I can't win this. I'm weaker than Luiz.

"I didn't want to kill Tony." My mind races. Elijah could use the knife, but I can't let him take this fight, let him risk his life again. I can't. "I would never do that to you."

Luiz tilts his head back a little. "And yet you did."

But giving it to Elijah might be our only chance. Elijah's only chance. I inch the blade open.

As I do, Elijah, so slightly it's almost imperceptible, shifts his chin down and to the side. I realize the knife's in his peripheral vision. He saw me take it.

Elijah exhales steadily. "She wouldn't have shot him if you hadn't tried to kill her."

Luiz is ice. "Get out of my way."

"Over my dead body."

Not if I have anything to say about it.

I watch the last of Luiz's coolness dissipate. I whip my blade open and thrust it into Elijah's palm.

He hooks the hilt just as Luiz throws his arm in an arc.

I hurl myself to the side, my hip clipping my glass nightstand, and it falls, shatters, shards beneath my unprotected feet. Adrenaline numbs me. My back and shoulders plow into drywall; my elbow goes straight through. Flakes and chips shower on my neck and into my shirt, and a wave of unheated air sweeps in from the gap.

Elijah dodges unscathed.

Luiz adjusts his stance and throws his eyes between the two of us as if debating whether or not he can beat Elijah to me. Decides he can't.

His strike isn't an arc this time. Luiz stabs the blade toward Elijah's abdomen, but Elijah sidesteps and slams my knife into Luiz's biceps. A sickening scrape of metal through skin and muscle and tendon slices into my ears.

Luiz gasps, the knife falters in his hand, and for a split second, I think this might be over, but he regains control, blood streaming down his arm and onto the floor. He stabs up, and this time Elijah doesn't evade fast enough. The knife sinks three inches into his shoulder, half the blade.

Elijah locks eyes with me.

I propel myself off the wall, over glass, and ram my shoulder into Luiz. The sudden force catches him off guard, and his weight pitches to the side, but he keeps his grip on the knife and yanks it out of Elijah's shoulder. Elijah cries out.

I catch my footing. So does Luiz. He's breathing through his teeth, his knife dripping with blood, Elijah's blood. I stand with nothing but my own body between them.

Through the pounding in my ears, Elijah calls my name. A royal-blue bar—his arm—swings against my chest and throws me out of the way of Luiz's next strike. I slip on the glass, and my skull knocks against the wall. The breath is shocked out of me. Whiteness dots my vision.

There are sounds before the pale spots recede. Metal on metal once, metal on flesh twice, all within a heartbeat.

Get up, *get up.* To my feet.

My vision clears. They've maneuvered away, closer to the door, Elijah nearest me. Blood pours from them both.

Luiz inhales sharply. He lunges.

And buries the blade to the hilt.

41

A CHOKED, SHOCKED GASP. A caught inhale, cut short by the knife piercing through his abdomen.

Elijah's stunned eyes drift from the knife to the hand that holds it. To Luiz's face. To me.

His knees give out. Luiz rips out the blade as he falls.

Every muscle in my body strains to go to him, to break his fall, but I'm paralyzed.

My knife slips from Elijah's grasp and skids across the floor, clinking against the shards of my nightstand as the blade spins and slides.

Elijah collapses to the ground, his black hair in the glass. An agonized groan tears out of him. He curls in on himself, clutching at his stomach.

My knife lies harmless near the foot of my bed.

Luiz stands over him. His eyes, so narrow, so hard, falter. His throat bobs once as blood rushes through Elijah's fingers.

Then he sets his jaw. And I forget fear.

I throw myself toward Elijah, but rather than protecting his body with mine, like every fiber inside me screams to do, I scrape my knife from the floor.

I square off. Luiz's muscles are coiled, his knuckles white around the hilt of his knife. Elijah pulls a blood-coated hand from his stomach and reaches out to me.

Luiz steps over him.

He thrusts. I lunge.

Luiz sees my strike at the last minute and shifts his momentum. The tip of my knife snags the soft skin over his ribs, hooking it and tearing it open. Bright red blood floods over the blade and into his shirt, a hole slashed into the fabric.

His knife finds my side. My skin splits, the thin metal wedging in between, and I gasp, but only because it's a reflex. The pain barely registers—there's only adrenaline. I don't know how deep the cut went, and I don't care. Blood runs down my hip. I stab my knife up and slice under his arm.

I don't retract it in time. Luiz grabs my wrist, wrenches it in front of us, and slits the back of my hand. It feels like nothing more than a cold line. The cut isn't deep, but my fingers unfurl. My knife clatters to the floor.

Luiz's hand claps on my throat, and I slam into drywall. My vision crosses. A hard, heartless point presses on my stomach. The metal should be cold, but it's not—it's warm. It's warm from Elijah's blood. Luiz is close enough that his breath brushes my face. Spearmint. A slash races across his cheek.

No fear in your eyes.

There's none.

The point presses farther into me, registering as heat, as a shock that steals my breath. I don't cry out. I force a shaky exhale.

Luiz's jaw is clenched. His eyes are hard, eyes I once would have sworn belonged to a gentle spirit. His bony joints stab into my neck.

Elijah has gone silent.

Luiz keeps me pinned. I wait for the knife to disappear into me. I wait to feel what Elijah feels.

Seconds pass. Seconds where I listen for Elijah's breathing, but I can't find it. It's so silent. My heart has slowed, as if easing itself to a stop, and Luiz's chest minutely expands and contracts, but he makes no sound. My ears aren't even ringing. I can't hear anything.

Luiz looks at me as I look at him. I beat time with my heart—slower, slower, a steady, fading pace.

Luiz's hold under my chin loosens. Barely, not enough for me to fight back, but it's there.

His eyes are on mine. To anyone else, they'd be lost—soulless—but I've learned to read them. He taught me. And there's something else under there. A falter. A faint sheen.

They shift to the side where Elijah is lying. Then they come back to me. The sheen grows.

And his shoulder jerks.

It jerks back. His palm crushes my collarbone, shoving me against the wall, as he tears the tip of the blade out.

I drop to the ground. My knees crash against the hard floor, the glass, and I cough away the pressure of Luiz's fingers. Bruises break out on my throat, my kneecaps, my shins—I can feel the dark blood blooming under my skin, growing with each heartbeat.

It's a few seconds before I'm able to raise my head. When I do, Luiz is fixed on Elijah's body.

He's shaking, shaking so badly that the knife's blade taps the side of his leg. He looks down at it just as a burgundy droplet falls off the tip and splashes on the floor.

My next inhale is torn. Luiz's attention jolts to me.

I hold his gaze until he tears it away. He runs.

In a pool of blood, Elijah's stopped moving.

Please, God, no.

I drag myself to him. Touch the side of his face.

Please.

"Elijah?" I whisper.

He coughs weakly, and blood spills over the side of his mouth.

I stretch out, my face inches from his, and slide my left hand under his head to prop it up. His face is slack. His whole body is.

Please.

"Elijah. Elijah, wake up."

His blood flow ebbs. I cover his wound with my hand, as if that will stanch the bleeding, as if that can save him.

God, You can save him.

He finally winces. His eyes struggle open, and I sink into them the way I did when we first met. Dark brown. Long black lashes. Soft and kind and brave and strong.

Please, save him.

My hand over his wound is slick.

Don't take him. I'm begging You.

I wipe my hand on my jeans and press his hair back from his forehead. Sweat soaks it.

His body tenses under me as he raises his hand to his neck. He gropes for a moment, stamping maroon stains into his shirt and onto his skin, before he gets hold of his necklace. He breaks it off.

He raises his other hand, lifting it past his neck, up until he brushes my wrist next to his face and guides it away. His hair falls forward again, matted with sweat.

He tucks the necklace into my palm. Closes my fingers around it. And smiles.

I press my forehead to his.

God, I'll do anything.

His weak pulse beats against my skin.

Anything.

He exhales.

And his pulse stops.

42

I BURY MYSELF IN ELIJAH'S NECK. Wrap my arms around his shoulders. Crush my heart against his. Like if I hold him close enough, he'll come back for just one more moment. Just one more moment.

His body wash cuts through the blood. He's warm.

I hold him until I memorize his smell, his weight, every curve of his face as I press it against mine.

A voice calls my name, frantic. Someone runs up the stairs.

I trace the backs of my fingernails against Elijah's cheekbone. His eyes are halfway open. I can't bring myself to close them forever.

My door is thrown open. Mercedes bursts in.

She freezes. Except for the horror in her eyes. It spills down her cheeks.

She hits her knees.

Mercedes closes his eyes. Cradles his face.

She must call my mom. Or my mom comes home from her appointment. Either way, she finds us.

This isn't a police officer, stoic, analytical, and vigilant—this is a mother.

She kneels next to us. Holds Mercedes, who weeps until she can't anymore. Then gathers me in her arms, but I won't let go of Elijah, so she supports both of us, our limp weight, only one of us with a heartbeat.

She cries.

———

The police arrive. They take me from him. He lies limp. The center of his shirt is torn.

I think I answer some questions. I think I hear some of Mercedes' answers. That she was just waking up when she heard us across the way.

They contact Elijah's mother.

I go to the hospital. I get stitches. My side, my stomach, my glass-shredded feet.

The necklace never leaves my hand.

43

MY MOM AND DR. TAHAN are out in the hall. The door is propped open, and a chest of medical drawers sits next to my vitals monitor. Stitches are like nettles on my stomach and the back of my hand. Heavy pain medication has drowned the panic. Not the grief.

"Her heart has taken serious damage." Dr. Tahan.

A solid silence is followed by my mother's raw, hoarse voice. "Will she be able to get the transplant with these new injuries?"

"The injuries are less concerning than the risk of infection, but we have no choice." Dr. Tahan hesitates. When she speaks again, her voice is lower. "If this damage keeps up, she won't last long. Not with so much scar tissue building up."

I can't lose you too. He told me that moments before he died. Moments before he gave his life for mine.

I hold Elijah's necklace to my heart so hard that the points bury into my palm. Tears drain down my face. I'm quiet, so quiet, but not enough to escape the notice of Dr. Tahan and my mother.

My mother strides past the chest of drawers to my side and strokes my face with the backs of her knuckles. Her touch is cold, and her eyes are swollen, her eyelids heavy until I can only see a thin line of her brown irises between them.

Dr. Tahan examines my vitals. She wears a dove-gray hijab. She's pale. I've never seen her like that. Is it because of what happened? Does she know?

She can't. Not the same way I do.

Sticky warmth seeps in between my fingers. I shudder, and Dr. Tahan notices. Gloved, she firmly guides my hand from my chest and inverts it wrist up, as if taking my pulse. In the new position, my grasp unfolds, and she eases it open.

I flinch away, clutching the necklace. Both my mother and Dr. Tahan jump at my sudden move.

"Don't take it," I whisper. "Please."

For a split second, Dr. Tahan's eyes water. "May I see it?"

My fingers refuse. They refuse to open, to let go, until my mother strokes my scalp. "It's okay. Let her see."

Blood weeps from my palm. I unfurl my fingers. Unfurl them as I remember how his hands eased them closed.

The skin inside is smeared from a couple of nicks. The crucifix is wet with blood. Elijah's or mine. Or both.

Dr. Tahan examines the necklace the way she would a wound. "This was his?"

I nod. My mom turns her head painfully.

Dr. Tahan considers me before she opens one of the drawers and chooses an alcohol wipe packet. She tears it open, releasing sharp fumes, opens my hand again, and tenderly brushes the wipe over the punctures, the crucifix, and the broken chain. My hand stings with disinfectant. Eventually, the metal and my skin are clean.

She crumples the red-stained wipe, reaches for my other hand—the gauzed-covered one—and draws it closer, careful of the IV needle in the front of my elbow. I let her slide the necklace from the hand she cleaned and replace it in the injured one.

"Don't hurt yourself," she says.

I want to thank her, but I can't get the words out, so instead, I hold it delicately for her to see.

Dr. Tahan nods. Her eyes glisten as she tells me she'll check on me soon and leaves.

Elijah's crucifix, tucked into my hand. The last piece of him I'll ever have.

I'll never be able to tell him. How sorry I am. How I would do anything to bring him back. How much I miss him.

And he'll never be able to answer me.

———

I don't know how long it's been. All I know is that I'm on enough pain medication that I don't dream. I don't think. I don't feel. I sleep, keeping Elijah's necklace twined around my fingers so that I don't lose it too.

There's a knock on the door, and Mercedes slips in. Her eyes are glassy and drained and swollen. Her turquoise hair is tucked in a low bun and hidden under a black fedora. Her boots, also black, are coated in a thin layer of frost. Actually, she wears all black.

It takes a moment for me to realize through the painkillers.

"You went to the funeral." My drugged lips almost can't form the words.

She opens her mouth but then stops as if her throat suddenly closed off. She nods. My hand tightens around Elijah's necklace, the way his used to whenever he spoke to me.

"What's that?" Mercedes asks.

Outside, the sky is slate. I unlock my fingers one by one, inhaling the medicinal smell of this room. My palm is printed with indentations from the chain and pendant.

A tear slips out of each of her eyes, streaming down her hollow cheeks as she extends a shaking hand, and I let her take necklace. She deserves it as much as I do. The broken clasp hangs over the backs of her fingers. "He gave this to you?"

I nod. She's silent while she turns it over and over as carefully as if she held her whole world in her hands. Then she sighs, a heavy sound like tears with no strength to be released.

"I have a chain you can use." She tries to smile. The effort breaks her.

She covers her mouth with her hand as if she can barely breathe. Half drugged, I stretch my arms out to her. She leans forward and wraps her arms around me, and I hold her as tightly as I can, hold her like I'll lose her too if I let go. Her shoulders shake underneath me.

My vision blurs, and I see Elijah one last time. His smile. His brown eyes. His tall frame that never let anything hurt me.

It's a stabbing, ripping pain. The same as when Damien died, a piece of my heart being torn off with bare hands.

It's so harsh, so painful, that it goes numb. The wound is covered with a scar, which may as well be stone.

I drift into a half sleep. Just enough for Elijah to die again.

His forehead is against mine. His pulse softens until it's gone.

There's no ripping pain this time. Not in the dream. Not anymore. Only the knowledge that a place inside me is empty where it should be full.

I rest him on the floor and close his eyes. His hair flows in waves over the dark laminate slats.

A dim motion reflects in the scattered shards of glass, in the blood spreading away from us. I expect the man from the cemetery.

It's not. It's Tristan.

He's sitting in my desk chair with the same blank, controlled expression that he's had ever since Damien died.

A muscle spasm snatches me out of the half sleep. I can almost feel Elijah's skin against mine. I can almost see Tristan, finally realizing what he's done.

How did it come to this?

44

ABOUT TWO WEEKS LATER, I'm still in the hospital. They won't let me go home. Too much of a risk, they say.

I squeeze the hand that Luiz cut, stretching the wound under the bandage. I must have yanked my hand away at the last minute; otherwise, Luiz would've sliced right through my tendons and left my fingers worthless.

And he was going to—I can picture his grip, the ferocious jerk of his arm. He wanted to end it all.

An IV needle is stuck in my other hand. I draw my legs closer to me and try to focus on the warmth and spongy softness of my thick cardigan. It's not helpful.

There's a knock at my door, business-like and almost urgent. "Who's there?"

Instead of a name for an answer, the door opens.

My only reaction is to look at her. "Venus."

I wouldn't recognize her if I didn't know her. Her hair is in her natural coils, thick and tight, much better than the flat-ironed version. The lipstick and the eyelash extensions are gone. Her clothes are flattering but looser, covering more. They suit her.

She seems tired. I think this is the first time I've seen her like this: her shoulders are slumped and the skin underneath her eyes is puffy. Her movements, while precise, are slow and dragging.

"What's wrong? What are you doing here?" I ask her.

Her round eyes lower. "I heard about your friend. Elijah."

Something inside me switches off. Scars up to protect me.

"Yeah." My voice doesn't sound like mine. It sounds like a recording, all the life bled out of it. "You watch the news."

There was hype across the city over someone they didn't even know. They'd never heard his heartbeat as he carried them to safety. They didn't hold him as he died.

Venus shakes her head. "Tristan had no idea."

I don't move. That scar hardens. She waits a long time for me to respond.

"You talked to him?" I finally ask.

"He found a phone."

Found a phone and talked to Venus about Elijah. Not to me. Not to his family. "Did he tell you more?"

That tiredness clouds her face again. "He wants you to know he loves you. All of you."

Those words. Through a phone and another mouth while he's on the run. After he betrayed us. Got Elijah killed.

"He needs to tell us that himself," I say.

She nods. "That's what I told him."

I wonder if there's something more underneath her stoic shell. "Is there anything else I need to know?"

"No."

"Then thank you." I mean it. I shouldn't take this out on her, not after she risked so much to help my family.

She begins to leave, but when she's at the door, she stops and turns back. "I really am sorry. I know you two were close."

Close to Elijah? Or Tristan.

It's not worth the waste of oxygen to ask. They're both gone.

"Thank you," I say again with no emotion.

Venus leaves.

The outside of the hospital campus is well kept, snow dusted, and nicely populated. There are a few people, so it's not crowded, but I'm not walking alone either. I'm not ready for that yet.

I tread gingerly on the glass-wounds on my feet. A hood shields my face from the cold. My arms are cradled around me to protect the healing knife cuts in my abdomen.

As I walk, my muscles slowly tighten under my clothes, threatening to seize up. This is too close to where Tony and Luiz jumped me. Pedestrians shuffle back and forth between inpatient and outpatient, so close to the area where it happened. It's clean. No glass. No blood. No body, dead by my hands.

Stop it, Paityn. I can't hide forever. That's not what they would have wanted for me. Elijah or Damien. This is how I make sure the girl they knew doesn't die with them. The girl that survives through the pain.

I delicately pace farther down the sidewalk toward outpatient until I'm halfway across the serenity garden between the two buildings. Paths snake between perfectly circular thickets of evergreen bushes, some needly, some broad leafed. A few trees, pines and dormant deciduous, stretch toward the sky. At the far side of the garden, near outpatient, one of each touches the other, their branches nearly reaching a window on one of the higher floors. If you leaned out from the pane, you might be able to touch them.

Gravel crunches beneath my feet as I weave down a path. A clearing with a bench on the rim marks the middle of the garden.

And sitting on that bench, with his head bent low, is the man from the cemetery.

There's no surprise, no curiosity. Not over something like this, not anymore. I don't want to know who he is. I don't care.

His shoulders tremor every so often. He's crying.

I don't want to be out here anyway. I begin to turn to leave when he raises his head.

"Sorry," I say. "I'll go."

His hazel eyes are swollen. His hair is down this time, the curls hiding his cheeks. "Elijah loved you, Paityn."

The ground drops out from under me.

"How do you—"

"I knew him. He talked to me about you all the time."

He knows my name. And he says he knew Elijah.

I wish I could feel the grief, but it's numb.

"He's safe now," I say mechanically. "But—"

Why did I just say that?

A thin tear disappears behind the man's hair. "But what?"

I can end this conversation right now, yet I open my mouth. "Why is that an excuse?"

Why is saying he's in a better place an excuse for someone so innocent being killed? Being taken from the people who loved him more than anything.

The man stands, and when he does, he winces. His hand drifts painfully to his side, and his stance is uneven on his feet, as though he's being gentle on the soles.

"It was never meant to be an excuse," he says.

I shake my head. I'm done. I'm done talking to this man who always seems to know me. Who shows up in my dreams, always bleeding in them. Who knew Elijah before he died.

But his response burrows into me and doesn't let go.

It's something about the words or his tone. Or his eyes. I don't know, and I don't understand, but somehow, I hear more.

It should never have happened. And He never wanted it to happen.

I hear it as clearly as if he'd said it aloud. Clearer.

I back away. The slits on the soles of my feet open, the skin split apart. "I have to go."

Before he can say another word, I retreat to the hospital.

45

THIS DREAM ISN'T A MEMORY.

We're walled in by panes of glass. Beyond them, sickly pale sunlight fights through pollution so thick it clouds anything beyond it. Asphalt, spiky and sticky with blood, is beneath my bare feet.

Elijah lies dead on the ground, but it's not Luiz this time.

Tristan kneels next to him with his hand on the hilt of the blade buried in Elijah's stomach. His head is bowed as if in pain. Or regret. Outside, the pollution churns.

Tristan raises his eyes. They're clear and focused, but gentle. Seeing deeper.

He slides the knife free and stands. Drops of blood land on his feet, which are bare like mine.

The knife in his hand is wrong. Luiz's was longer, wider—this blade is only three inches long, and the hilt is rough black: the pocketknife his father gave him.

He comes closer. I retreat. Not running—there's nowhere to run—just backing away until my spine flattens against the smooth, cool sheet of glass. I close my eyes, waiting with the scent of cedar, until a metal barb presses against my solar plexus.

I reopen them and look into his. Green. Tired. Pained.

"Where did you go?" I ask.

There's no response except for the harsh steel point pushing harder.

I scar over. It doesn't matter where he went. He's never coming back to us.

Tristan's face changes. Skin pale to copper. Hair dark blond to black. Eyes soft to piercing, from green to brown. A pale scar fades onto his forehead.

Luiz has the same regret written on his face.

He looks behind him at Elijah's body. The knife never recedes, only scrapes to the side. "Here we are again."

I'm nothing but scar. "This is a dream."

"Is it?"

"Yes." I curl my hands around his on the knife.

He turns back to me. Our eyes meet.

His wrists twitch toward me. The blade sinks deep.

I curl in on myself, and my IV jams in my arm. A moan scratches the back of my throat.

"Shh, shh," my mother says. She's sitting next to me on the side of the bed with her arm wrapped behind my neck. I had forgotten that she had climbed in before I fell asleep. I inhale her warmth and the smell of her rose perfume. "It was just a dream."

It wasn't, though. Not entirely. Elijah's dead. And Tristan...

The ache in my throat turns bony.

"Elijah again?" My mom's wearing a pair of pale jeans that taper in at her crossed ankles like the khaki pair I'm wearing.

"Yes." I don't feel like explaining more.

My mom's arm wraps protectively around me. The pressure of her leg against mine is comforting. Outside my window, evening lights are already on, and a flag blows on a pole in the hospital's packed parking lot. Gray clouds mist the navy sky. My flight for the procedure leaves tonight.

I snuggle closer to my mother. A small, warm piece of metal tumbles from the center of my collarbone to the side—Elijah's necklace on the new chain Mercedes gave me.

She's with God now, Elijah once said.

That doesn't bring them back.

"Why does He let this happen?" I turn my head to see her face when she responds—it's sad in a way that I haven't seen in a while. Not since Damien died.

"I don't know," she says. And she doesn't try to come up with anything. I'm grateful.

"I wish I could've stopped it," I say.

"Baby." Her voice is an intense, intense whisper. She readjusts the crucifix so that it's centered on my collarbone. "You were there with him."

I almost protest that it wasn't enough, but she's said that to me before. I ransack some distant corner of my memory. That was what she told me after I found Tristan lying on the road. When I couldn't do anything except sit with him.

What happened to the boy I met that day?

My mom stiffens under me, and she gasps through her teeth. I flinch at the suddenness of it, then wait powerlessly as she relaxes. Another false labor pain.

Outside, a plane with red and white beacons trails down the sky. I'll be on one soon. And hopefully on one back.

I wonder where Tristan is. And I wonder if he knows—if he cares—what he's done.

46

THREE HOURS. There are three more hours until they take me to my flight. And since my mom went home to pack and Mercedes hasn't gotten here to say goodbye yet, I'm alone.

I'd better get used to that once the process for my procedure starts.

The irony is that I feel fine. Good, even. Good for me anyway. The pain is mild in my chest and my joints without any medication. I don't have a fever. All my wounds are almost healed.

The treatment could make sure I'm like this—better than this—for the rest of my life. Or it could kill me.

The lights are out. My bed is angled at forty-five degrees, and my knees are bent so they form a tent with the blanket. City lights—cars, streetlamps, lit buildings—blink at me. The odd snowflake, fat and downy, catches in them. Underneath my door, a thin space lets in a bar of fluorescent light. Walking shadows pass.

Then one doesn't. It lingers. Darkens. Approaches. Hesitates just outside.

The tiredness wanes from me. My spine pops as I reposition and sit all the way up, my feet still flat against the mattress. I push off the blanket.

The door opens. He slips in.

I sit blankly. "Tristan."

I should feel something. Relief, joy, confusion, anger, anything. Anything other than what this is.

He doesn't respond except by letting the door ease shut behind him. He wears dark jeans and a gray sweatshirt. He doesn't seem surprised that I'm by myself—as if he planned it that way. As if he waited until he knew our mom and Mercedes were gone, so that there'd be no one to stop him from leaving again.

"Where have you been?" It's a monotone, analytical question requiring a statement of fact for an answer. I'm not even going to attempt to figure out how he got in here.

His eyes stay somewhere on the ground. "Paityn…I—"

"Spit it out."

He doesn't react. I feel nothing.

"I need to talk to you," he says.

"Now that my friend is dead."

He winces as if he were the one who was stabbed.

"I never meant for this to happen," he murmurs.

An acidic scoff exits me. "Neither did I."

Out the window, snowflakes and dots of light speckle the wintry nighttime. Out where my mom and Mercedes are with no idea that Tristan's here. Out where Elijah should be alive, not cut through, hidden beneath the ground forever.

"Paityn, please." Tristan steps to my bed and places his hand on the rail. His closeness raises tears into my eyes. "Look at me."

"It should have been you."

He stops. Everything just stops. And those eyes that he's always been able to control so well, that he's hardened to me for months— raw shock hides behind them.

They water up. I let him see mine spill over.

I gesture at the door. "They're going to be here soon. If you're going to leave, you might want to do it now."

He clamps his eyes shut. I spread salty smears across my cheeks. Nothing replaces them.

Then a warm weight on my foot. A thumb brushing over it.

Something like a slit in my gut aches and bleeds and spreads.

He's gone. Tristan closes the door behind him for the last time. My foot hums from the shape of his hand.

That ache in my gut seeps across me. I try not to feel it, feel anything. Try not to picture his face as I slip into exhaustion.

Months before. Forever ago and forever since.

I sit on my own bed, my forehead against the window. The glass is fogged from my breath and lit pale by the moon and fluorescent porchlights. The grass is green and lush and dark, almost as if I'm seeing it at the deep bottom of a lake of emerald water. It sways weakly in a breeze as though flowing.

I'm cold. Aching. Alone. Me and my crucifix. I breathe in through my nose and out through my mouth. Nice and easy, the way Tristan always tells me.

A chime rings from my phone.

I frown. Who in the world?

I slide the phone off the nightstand and blink at the digital light. A text message. Tristan.

I swallow over a sore throat. Is something wrong?

I open it. Are you still awake?

The better question is, why is he?

Yeah, why?

Brief silence. Another chime.

Do you want me to come in?

I read it five times. He woke up at four in the morning because he knew I'd be awake on my own.

I can' t ask you to do that.

A third chime back. You didn' t ask.

I linger over the message until my vision blurs at the bottom.

Yes. Please.

Instead of a chime, there's rustling down the hall and a doorknob turning. I hold the phone against my chest and let my irregular heart push against it.

A soft knock, and I call him in, my voice timid as it maneuvers out of my sore throat. He strides to my bed. Sits on the edge. Lays his hand over my foot and gives it a gentle squeeze.

He came. He came in the middle of the night to sit up with me so I wouldn't have to brave it alone.

I search for the strange man, but he's not here. No blood. No fear. Just Tristan and me, my crucifix, and a sweet ache I haven't felt in a long time.

"Thank you," I whisper.

He smiles, all moonlight and fall air and soft green eyes. And I smile back.

I don't know if I'll see him again. And I chose what I said.

Tears soak into the hospital pillow, their salt irritating my skin.

"More bad dreams?" my mom whispers from across the room. She must have come back when I was asleep. Something about her voice is off.

I unstick my eyes, but before they're all the way open, I jump at her soft groan.

I'm not the only one. On the other side of the space, Mercedes' turquoise head pops up. Snow drifts outside. My mom's sitting on a cot under the window, her temple propped against the glass. Wonder where I got that habit from.

Her hands are folded over her belly. Her breathing is strained. "Mom?"

She exhales methodically. "I'm fine."

Mercedes and I exchange a sideways look, but we don't argue. She reties her ponytail, and without saying anything, we each nestle back into our spots, energy sapped, waiting for the next thing to come to us. My mom's coming with me to New York; we'll have to say goodbye to Mercedes for a while. She'll be alone. More alone than me.

We all doze.

I'm halfway asleep when my mom groans sharply.

I'm completely awake at the sound of her body hitting the ground. Mercedes is across the room in one stride and slams the light on.

On the floor, my mom is on her side, face contorted, her hand over her tiny baby bump, near writhing in pain. Crimson stains the pale blue of her jeans.

Fear crystallizes around my heart. She's in labor.

47

MERCEDES SCREAMS FOR HELP. My mom curls in on herself, her teeth clenched. I'm frozen, my lungs, my heart, my throat, my thoughts.

Nurses swarm the room, tear Mercedes away, drag my mom to her feet, load her into a wheelchair. I think I'm calling her name, but I'm not sure. Everything's a hum.

Nothing from my mother. She doesn't make a sound.

They take her away with shouts following her.

Can the baby survive so early? Will my mom survive the labor?

Mercedes is quaking as she draws herself to her feet, that same shock as when Damien died plastered on her face.

She staggers forward and clasps my hand in hers. I grip her just as tightly, and as her pulse bangs under her skin, under my fingers, I know we're the only things keeping each other from breaking into a thousand pieces.

Mercedes cries. And in between her jagged sobs are familiar words. A prayer my mom taught her—taught us both—when we were little. A prayer my mom will teach my baby sister. A prayer we'll teach her. If she lives. If they both live.

Please.

The snow has worsened, raging outside the window. Mercedes holds my hand. Water drips out of her eyes once in a while. Her lips keep forming soundless prayers. Mine are dry and bitten through.

Pale, sterile lights bleaching my vision   shiny floor, reflective needle jammed up my arm, reflective IV rack   plastic tubes, plastic saline bag, distorting reflections   distorted blue pleather bench   distorted rolling stool, round black seat, chrome legs   dull chrome doorknob   rough sheets, a drained shade of white   drained green wall paint, drained blue curtains   the only bright colors are my vitals, uniform scribbles, crest, canyon, crest, canyon, crest, canyon—

I punch my head back and pull my hand from Mercedes'. A frustrated groan is sucked out of me. Sick, danger, dying, that's all this room screams.

Claustrophobia sneaks up on me. I need out, need something other than this medical room, but where can I go? I'm stuck in this hospital, and there's nowhere—

The chapel. The one I passed when I went to get evidence against Tony.

"Paityn, are you okay?" Mercedes asks. I think I scared her when I snatched my hand away.

"I need to get out of here."

Mercedes grimaces. "Dr. Tahan's not going to let you."

"She might."

"The plane, Paityn."

"We're not prepping to leave for thirty minutes. I can afford five." Heat rises into my voice. Mercedes gives no indication that she notices—no change from the patience hiding the pain.

I sigh. "I'm sorry. Please just get—"

"What's the matter?"

Dr. Tahan stands in the doorway, wearing a royal-purple hijab, wrapped up to the chin and wrists in black under her white coat. Her brow is snug with worry.

"I have to go downstairs for a minute. I—" I sound pathetic. Focus, Paityn. Keep yourself grounded. Name what you know. A drop of saline releases into the drip chamber. Ripples. "I just—I need a breath."

Mercedes sits quietly, waiting. Waiting for my question, waiting for an answer. Waiting to find out about my mom, waiting for the baby, waiting for them to take me away.

Dr. Tahan's frown compresses further, and I get a flash of my mother, as if I were her own child and she wants more than anything to let me run free.

"I understand you're worried," she says, "but I'm not sure it would be prudent."

Blank white coat. Sanitizer tang. "I only need a few minutes."

I have to get out of here. And for a reason that I'm not going to try to pinpoint, it has to be that chapel.

Dr. Tahan chews on her lower lip, a strangely insecure gesture for her.

The floor gleams where my mom was bleeding less than an hour ago. Cleaned, bleached, the chemicals still burning my nose.

Dr. Tahan considers me. My vitals. My IV. Mercedes. Me again. She advances toward the monitor and shuts it off.

"Ten minutes," she says, her voice low. "If you're not back by then, I will send someone for you."

Mercedes' eyebrows twitch up like she's surprised.

I exhale. "Thank you."

Dr. Tahan nods tersely. She gloves up in pungent blue latex and unhooks the IV tube from the needle. Mercedes stands, her jaw flexed so firmly that a muscular bump has risen over it.

Dr. Tahan slides the needle out, and I bend my elbow. Pain screeches in my joints, but there's a feral satisfaction in the range of motion.

Dr. Tahan leaves as though she's not supposed to see what happens next.

I swing my legs over the bed, and cool air spills over my khakis. Mercedes grabs my socks and shoes for me. Aches spread across my muscles as I tie the laces, but I don't care. Nothing matters.

City lights outside the window. The muffled chatter of nurses. Hollow taps of clogs outside.

I slide off the bed. My back and the bones in my legs throb.

Ten minutes. Five to get to the chapel and back. Five for me to do whatever I need to.

I'm not sure what that is exactly—nothing is straight in my head. All I know is that my mom's bleeding, and the baby's coming, but she isn't ready yet. She won't live, and my mom might not either.

My mother shouldn't have to live without her baby. The baby shouldn't have to live without her mother. I shouldn't have to live without either of them.

Fluorescent lights. A nurse with a long blond braid. Another with diamond studs in his ears.

Mercedes is by my side. I'm stiff and unsteady, but then my circulation starts flowing. We make it to the elevators, and there's a queasy plummet in my stomach as the car we take descends. Past the fourth floor, the maternity floor, where my mom is right now.

Round buttons, dirty with fingerprints. A single one at the bottom glowing orange. Faint shoeprints on the synthetic flooring.

The doors open, we exit, and the hall's empty like it was when

I came here the first time. Mercedes sweeps across her eyes with the heel of her hand.

We arrive at the chapel. Mercedes pulls the door for me and props it open behind us with a wooden wedge, chipped and dirty.

There are no lights. Three rows of wooden pews line either side of the center aisle. The snowstorm outside beats at stained glass windows, which are soothing shades of maroon, scarlet, and cobalt, except for a single crystal strip in one of them. In the center is a depiction of the Crucifixion.

I slide into the front pew first and tuck my hands, which are already chilled, between my thighs. Mercedes settles next to me.

And I sit. I sit, and I don't say anything, just stare at the bleeding face in the stained glass.

Thorns in His forehead. Gray circles for nails in His hands and feet.

God, please.

A thin curve of red glass funnels from the thorns, down the side of His nose. It looks like red tears streaming down His face. Like He's so broken that He's crying blood.

I exhale. I imagine a red tear tracing down my own cheek.

A clock ticks second by second in the back of my mind. I have a total of ten minutes before Dr. Tahan will think something is wrong. I'm guessing it's been about six now.

Another minute passes. We should probably leave.

Wind howls. Snow shavings buzz past the transparent pane in the window.

There's something else.

Two people. When Mercedes' lips stop moving, I know they're not in my imagination.

It's too brief to see much. They're both dressed in black. One with pale hair. The other's spider-black and silken, blown over his forehead in the wind and bejeweled with snow. A fluid gait I'd know anywhere.

And a dark, metal glint in his hand.

48

MY KNUCKLES TURN TO ICE as I grip the edge of the pew. I shift my eyes to Mercedes, too afraid to do anything else. Hers are wide, alert with a shade of that petrified shellshock. She saw him.

"Get down," I say.

Neither of us moves. I sit stone solid, the back of my neck prickling with electricity, waiting, praying we're wrong.

A bang I know too well rips through the hospital. My hands fly to my ears, my spine goes rigid, a gasp slams into my lungs.

Get down.

Mercedes and I hit the tile, flat on our stomachs. Bruises crawl across my ribs. We wedge ourselves under the pews at an angle, shoulder to shoulder, feet toward the wall. There's shouting outside, harsh commands, then a second bang, a third. Dead silence.

What have I done?

There's no sound except a shaky exhale from Mercedes that she stifles before it finishes. Her jaw is gritted. A swallow reveals the tendons in her neck. Then murmurs. Only murmurs, no words, nothing I can make out. What are they doing?

There's no light in the chapel—except for a bright rectangle from the door. Wide open.

I'm paralyzed. A harsh sniff, as if his nose is running from the cold, swings down the hall. Tall strides from long legs echo. Confident. Intentional. Closer. Coming to find me.

The floor smells of dust. If he finds me, then he also finds Mercedes, and we're both done.

A shadow in the rectangle of light stretches across the ground and brushes over my face. My throat is shut.

The shadow passes.

Air crawls into my lungs, and I shift my head enough to see Mercedes.

Where's the other one? she mouths.

Still outside. Luiz is hunting for me. I'm not up there, but others are, innocent, sick, unable to hide.

My heart drops into my sickened stomach. My mom's up there.

Get out. Get out, do something. Set off the alarm, the alarm that alerts the police, that lets people out but not in. The alarm the guard never got to push. Do it, *now*, before Luiz can get anywhere near my mother and the baby.

But there's another one out there, who will shoot me before I can do anything.

We jam against the polished tile at another round of shouts, of bangs. The bones in my face throb. There's a low, harsh yell, a scream, a dozen other sounds I should never have heard, no sense, no words, only violence and pain. Voices I think I should recognize but are too distorted. Silence again. Too long, the silence is too long, and *where is the other one?*

He comes. Flying footsteps, sprinting—nothing like Luiz's arrogant stride—rubber soles slapping and screeching against the floor. Right past us.

Mercedes' eyes take on a dangerous clarity. "Let's go."

I haul myself out into the open. An empty hall greets me. Mercedes is already on her feet as I get to mine, both of us easy targets.

We run. My pacemaker slams. Bright light constricts my pupils as we approach the entry. Mercedes is next to me; her hair bounces with her strides. We tear into the entrance hall.

Four. Four bodies.

A janitor. Black curls haloed around her. Tall body, well-worked hands lifeless.

The security guard. Arms and legs splayed around her, her knee still in a brace, her hair soaked in red.

Eddie Davis. Peppered with spreading garnet stains.

Venus Driver. Shot through the side of her mouth, but she's not dead. She's quivering. There's some light in those eyes.

"There." I point across the room to the bright red alarm. Mercedes will get there faster. "It'll lock him out."

She bolts across the room and hits the button.

The siren shrieks. I can practically feel every door in this building seal shut. Mercedes exhales.

I kneel next to Venus. Her wandering eyes struggle toward me as I try to fathom what on earth she's doing here.

A wave of dizziness hits me. I was right: the few teeth I can see through the gash in her cheek are split, fragmented. I don't know where the broken chips are. Maybe in her mouth. Maybe on the floor around me. Blood collects in her mouth where it can and spills onto the floor when it can't.

I touch her shoulder, then flinch back when she moans. Why is she here? Why is she here *now*?

"Help's coming," I tell her. And though her entire body shakes, her eyes relax.

The police have been alerted. Twelve minutes. Twelve minutes until this is all over.

Twelve minutes for Luiz to kill who he wants. What floor is he on? Maternity's on the fourth. He had enough time to get up there, and I don't care that he said he wouldn't do it before. He's past all that—the scene around me proves it.

He's come to finish this.

Mercedes rushes over to stand near me. "You said that'd lock him out?"

"Yes."

"Does it lock him in?"

"No." Which means he can come for us. Luiz knows someone set off the alarm. "We have to get him down here." Somewhere where there's no one for him to kill.

Mercedes' eyes flit to Eddie's body. She gags, then crouches next to him. Ducks her head like she regrets what she's about to do, and rolls him over onto his back. His head lolls to the side. His glassy eyes are blue, a pretty blue, even.

He was the one who came in with Luiz. So if he's dead, who ran past us? Did someone else come with Venus? Or was there a third one with Luiz?

Mercedes unzips his jacket, folds back the flaps, and searches him. She comes back empty. No gun. No weapon. Nothing to defend ourselves with.

Then an electric note. Mercedes recoils and slaps her hands against the floor behind her to catch herself. She frowns, then reaches into Eddie's jacket pocket and draws out a phone.

"What?" I ask. Venus whimpers next to me. I place my hand on hers, and this time, she doesn't react.

Mercedes angles the screen to me. Caller ID: Luiz Suarez.

We need him down here. So let's get him.

Mercedes hands it over. I accept the call.

"*Davis, what's going on?* Get your—"

"You missed me."

There's silence across the line. Then, "Who is this?"

"You're smart enough to figure that out, Luiz."

Another long pause crackles over the speakers. I gesture at Mercedes to the janitor and the security guard. I mouth and mime, *Keys.*

She runs as Luiz's voice comes through the speaker again. "Where are you?"

"You walked right past me." Mercedes is madly searching belts and pockets. She seems to find something, but then quietly groans as if it wasn't what we need. "I'm in the main lobby with your friend." I hate the tone of my own voice, so flippant over a death, any death, but I need to get Luiz down here, and I need time to think.

"Stay there, or I will shoot through every floor of this building," he says.

Why does that sound like a bluff?

I chuckle into the microphone, a sound like a dark bell, frighteningly like his. He can't think he has me. He needs to think that I have him.

Somewhere near. Empty. Somewhere I can keep him busy until the police arrive, without putting anyone else in danger.

"Here's how this works." I work a smug smile into my voice. "You could shoot up the whole hospital, but you still won't have gotten me."

Luiz listens. I get an image of his finger curling around his trigger.

Mercedes nods, jaw set.

"I'm headed to outpatient across the way. If you can find me, you can have me. But it's a maze in there, so I'd get moving."

Let him wonder how I'm going to get in, how I plan on evading him, how Eddie's dead. Venus shudders. I touch my stomach; underneath the fabric of my shirt, the scar from the last time Luiz came after me bulges against my fingertips.

I raise my hand and grasp Elijah's necklace, the crucifix stuck to my skin with sweat. And I pray.

You said You'd never leave me. That needs to be now.

"You want me?" I tell Luiz. "Come get me."

49

I HANG UP AND TOSS the phone. A small sound—I can't tell if it's a laugh or a cough—bubbles from Venus' throat. I squeeze her hand. She feebly runs a thumb over the bump of a scar below my knuckles, the one that Luiz gave me.

Mercedes crosses the hall back to me and tosses a circle of black plastic onto the floor: a retractor for a large collection of keys, the wire torn off.

"Looks like we're breaking in," she says. The gray of her irises is like steel, unbreakable.

"*I'm* breaking in. He doesn't know you're here."

"I wasn't asking."

The mock confidence I had when I was on the phone slides away, but we don't have time for me to panic. *She* doesn't have time.

Steel and scar.

Venus nudges her hand to the side just enough to get my attention. A tiny sound pulls on her lips. "Go."

I bend forward and give her a light kiss on the head. And pray to God that Luiz doesn't finish her when he passes.

I stand and face the front doors, which are shattered open. A blizzard roars outside, spraying snow and glass. I step closer until

I'm inches from the border. The warm light of inpatient glows at my back. Black and harsh white swirl in front of me. Broken glass burrows into the bottoms of my shoes, the smallest shards glittering like snowflakes.

Mercedes steps out next to me. Strands of her turquoise hair whip free of her ponytail in the wind. She ties it all back into a snug knot.

And a few floors above me, Luiz is coming. With a gun. And I have nothing to protect either of us, except the outpatient building past the serenity garden.

"Let's go," I say.

Mercedes and I run.

My muscles are unused, stiff, weak. My joints are swollen. Wind bites my ears, but pain is a luxury I can't humor.

Thirty yards down. Sprint. Past the serenity garden, full of evergreen shrubs and trees, coated white, glimmering with crystals. I beat snow beneath my feet. Flakes like freezing rain cut at my face. Mercedes' ribs expand and contract steadily, arms pumping, stride fluid. That's probably the way she practiced with Elijah.

Twenty yards down.

How fast is Luiz moving? Will it be enough time for Mercedes and me to break into outpatient?

Ten yards. Will we be able to break in? What if the glass is stronger than we're expecting?

Time to find out.

We skid to a stop. My shirt absorbs wet flakes and sticks to my body with water and sweat. Outpatient looms over us, a skyscraper of frost-covered glass. The serenity garden is a few feet behind us. I keep the inpatient building in my peripheral vision, waiting for a shadow to dim the glow from the broken door.

"There has to be something to break it," Mercedes says, winded. Her head swivels.

I search the ground for a stone, but the sidewalk's clean, the snow flawlessly flat.

A shadowed form in inpatient's light.

I spin to face him. Luiz stands like death. His gun is trained on us.

I throw my shoulder into Mercedes' as the hum and hiss of space being split by lead rips past us. My elbow and hip crack against the ground. Cold and pain and gone. The bullet completely misses the building. Either Luiz is a poor shot, or the wind is blowing him off target. That won't last.

Mercedes is already on her feet, and she wrenches me up with her. Luiz strides down the storm. An aviator jacket whips loose over a zipped leather one. His finger is curled into the trigger guard.

There's only one thing between him and us: the serenity garden. "*Go.*"

We dart toward the shrubs, Mercedes and I at each other's hips, toward a wide, circular thicket of holly, large enough to give us cover, to buy time for us to think of something better.

Through the white curtain of snow, a fiery flash. Snow and waxy holly leaves are shredded off a bush, close enough that the shrapnel sprays us.

We dive into the thicket. Branches claw my face and hands. Mercedes leaves a clump of hair on a thorn. Her eyes are sparked with alertness and adrenaline, and flash to me, past me, around the garden. Mine follow. Circular thickets sprawl throughout, large enough for us to hide in or under. Walking paths weave through them. A pine and a dormant deciduous reach toward a window in outpatient. The clearing with the bench is dead center.

My muscles itch. We've been here too long. He saw us jump in, and our footprints in the snow lead right to it. They'll always lead to us.

Mercedes tucks her turquoise bun into her black hoodie. Her fingers are so pale they're almost gray, like frost. "Split up."

There's no time to argue—she's on her feet, and I'm on mine, ill body screaming. She tears across the clearing, past a large, gnarled tree trunk, and I'm bolting parallel with outpatient.

Another shot, and I dive under a low juniper bush. Grind my cheek to the dirt as the blizzard begins to fill my tracks.

Evergreen needles bow and tremble over me, striping my line of sight; dull blue berries bob on them.

I don't know where Mercedes is, but she must be hidden safely, because I would have heard if Luiz had injured her. I would have heard if he—

A crunch in the snow. Another. And then a young man to match them.

Easy, slow—arrogantly slow—Luiz saunters to the first thicket we dove into. He runs his fingers across the branches we snapped. Apparently comes upon something interesting and pinches it off. Turquoise strands.

He lets the wind sweep them away. Faces me.

Stay still. He can't see you yet. Stay still.

His hair is blown back, exposing his pearl-white scar. He scans the garden with small swings of his head.

The cold delves into my marrow and spreads outward. My body aches to shiver. Snow swirls across the clearing and smacks against the glass of outpatient.

Luiz's chin dips down to two trails of footprints, each in opposite directions. He stalks down their center.

A thicket rustles near the bench: Mercedes, her black hoodie under a prickly-leafed holly. Her pale, exposed fingers are hooked on a branch, visible only from my angle.

What is she doing?

Luiz gives no indication that he saw it. He traces the ground with his eyes.

Decides. To the right. To me.

My cheek stings on the ground. Crumbling earth enters the raw scrapes and dissolves into my arteries.

Do. Not. Move.

One step. Snow melts on his jacket and trickles onto the barrel of the gun, then off the tip.

Another step. The juniper branches over me block out his face. His ankle adjusts unsteadily on the snow. White cakes the cuffs of his jeans.

How long do I wait? How close do I let him get?

Snow creaks beneath his weight so near I could swear it vibrates in my teeth. His feet align. Too far for me to even attempt to get to him.

The wind has sapped my eyes of any moisture. Luiz's tennis shoes are beaded with water.

His stance shifts like he's ready to crouch.

Mercedes' holly bush near the bench rustles again, harsher, louder. There's a creak and the snap of a broken branch. Luiz spins around. Mercedes clutches the frayed-ended stick in her hand. I watched her break it on purpose.

My throat squeezes, but I don't move. I know her. If I move, she'll expose herself, and he'll kill her. Luiz is stock still for a moment. Then he pivots, and his gait is solid, purposeful, no longer searching but set. Toward Mercedes.

My teeth sink into my lip until warmth dribbles down them.

She'll jump out if you move, Paityn, you know it, and then she'll die.

She'll die anyway if he catches her. I have to take that chance. The muscles in my back coil. He's feet from Mercedes. The snow he kicks up sprays her face and the legs of the bench.

Mercedes lunges out of the holly bush, a hidden predator.

Reaches for the gun.

Gets ahold of the barrel.

There's a bang.

50

"LUIZ, STOP!"

I tear myself from the juniper bush and jostle onto one knee, my numb hands in the snow. Luiz whirls around, his index finger stiff over the trigger. Mercedes lies on the ground, her hood torn back, turquoise hair splayed and stained ruby on the snow.

I think she's breathing. I think her eyes, half open, are searching. It looked like she pushed the barrel out of the way. It looked like it only skimmed her. The arm of the bench next to where she was hiding is splattered with red where her head hit it as she fell.

Please.

"I'm the one you want." The tremor I've been hiding finally shakes my voice. I raise my hands. "Leave her alone."

Luiz's brown eyes flicker in the swirling snow. He wants her too. She was there the day his brother died. And I have no leverage. He could kill us both, and I'd have no way to stop him.

Luiz uses his foot to tip Mercedes from her side to her back. Her head lolls, but this time I'm sure I see it: her chest is rising and falling.

My heart hammers in my neck. Luiz considers her for a long moment.

He shifts his aim to me. "Fine."

And I wait. I wait as he approaches me, the barrel point blank. He stops when the front sights are inches from my mouth. Residual gun smoke curls up my nose; I can practically taste granules of it. "Back up," Luiz tells me.

I do. I back up until dirt becomes iced cement under my shoes and my back presses against the glass walls of outpatient. The bright windows of inpatient across the garden—where my mother is—glow, lit from the inside, unobstructed.

This won't be enough to protect her. This won't be enough to protect anyone.

Luiz's aviator jacket flows around his body, exposing the leather one underneath. And under that, I think there's a fleece collar. The front pocket of the leather one bulges.

He lowers the gun. Its smell fades and my face becomes colder without its aura of heat. He tucks it in the back of his pants' waistband. Slides two of his fingers into the bulging jacket pocket. Pulls out a folded knife.

He'll kill me. And there's nothing to stop him from coming back for them.

He unfolds the knife. It might be the same one that he used to kill Elijah.

I can't let him do that to anyone else. But I can't stop him from doing it to me.

Luiz braces both his hands on the hilt. I raise my eyes past his face, past his scar. The sky is black satin. Clouds like downy raven feathers are thinning. A couple of stars peer out. A snowflake lands on my cheek and melts. A second does the same just between my eyes.

Luiz prepares the point over my beating heart.

Elijah's necklace is warm on my neck.

Don't. God, don't let this happen. Don't let him hurt them. Don't leave us.

I bring my eyes back to Luiz's. They remind me of Elijah's. Not the shape—Luiz's are narrower, harder—but the rich, sweet brown color is the same.

Luiz clenches his jaw the way I do when I'm controlling emotion, when I'm refusing to shed any tears. The last time I saw that was when he stabbed Elijah.

The tip's already drawing blood like a thorn. It's shaking.

I slide my hands over his on the hilt. For a split second, his eyes soften. They clear up like they used to whenever he would see me.

Then that shadow's gone. His hands stop shaking under mine.

There's movement over Luiz's shoulder, at a higher floor of inpatient—a shadow in one of the lit windows.

Resolve solidifies in Luiz's eyes.

He thrusts his weight behind the knife.

51

GLASS SHATTERS.

Glass shatters under a gunshot from the second floor of inpatient. Luiz jumps at the noise and twists toward the shooter. But not before the blade drives in.

Metal through skin. Through muscle. To bone. Sinking deep. Cutting the air from my lungs, cutting the vision from my eyes, cold and straight and flawless.

All the way down. Into my shoulder.

He flinched.

My hands on his guided the knife the rest of the way.

My ribs drag air through my stunned throat. My shoulder slides on a layer of blood. Luiz's attention jerks to me. His eyes race up and down me, disbelieving as my chest heaves, very much alive, under his knife.

Another shot blasts through the night from inpatient's second floor, and this time, outpatient's glass wall behind me explodes. Luiz ducks and shields himself from the hail of shards, ripping the knife from my shoulder in the process. A groan snaps out of my body.

Luiz retrieves the gun from his waistband and returns fire.

I'm on my feet. Outpatient gapes before me.

Run.

Glass scatters under my shoes and gunshots hammer through outpatient's bottom floor—the entry hall, chairs, a large greeting desk. An abstract glass statue stands on the other end. This whole building is glass, waiting to be broken, to slash me and make me bleed.

Luiz lets out a yell and a groan. I don't know if that means he's wounded, but it doesn't matter. If he's shot, the person from the window still has a gun. And if he isn't, then both of them do.

I dart for the far side. Polished tile pounds under my shoes. My footfalls ricochet off the high ceilings. My shoulder's numb and limp. My lungs scream as they claw back the oxygen the stab took from me. I fly past chairs. The greeting desk is here and gone.

A different type of groan, frustrated and echoey, growls behind me. Glass clinks viciously under another pair of feet and rough breathing bounces off the walls.

I'm almost at the glass abstract—it rises and grows like a slick teal branch. Its wide base is black stone. I could swear I can feel the muzzle of Luiz's gun on my back, cold and unforgiving.

Behind me, he stops moving.

He's aiming.

I dive behind the statue's stone base. My elbow cracks onto the tile. The statue bursts into splinters and rains on me, and I shield my head with my screaming arms. A heavy piece of it skims my bad shoulder before smashing on the floor.

Get back up.

Glass slits my hands. The teal has become red.

The end of the building and a hall to the left are five yards away. I sprint into the open and cross it.

My good arm lashes out and grabs the corner so I can make

the sharp turn. The moment I touch it, a red smear and leftover specks of glass decorate the plaster.

A bullet zips a foot or less from my head. I throw myself forward, swing around the corner.

I make it.

The hall is wide and long. There are doors on either side. Footsteps hammer from the front entry. So many doors, so many locks, just *pick* one.

Signs and directions blemish the wall: cancer, mammography, biopsy lab, stairs, elevators, cafeteria—

Bathrooms. An alcove with the men's door facing me, women's on the opposite side. I coil my muscles and drive forward, into the alcove. A water fountain is dead center, women's on the right. I shove my good shoulder into the door. It swings on oiled hinges.

I ram the hydraulic hinge closed behind me and slide down to the floor. It's dark as death in here—no shapes, just black. I deaden my lungs. I have to breathe, but I can't, I can't, he'll hear me. My pulse pounds in my face, my throat, my shoulder. I can't contain a wince.

Tennis shoes squeal to a stop on polish outside.

I freeze. Glass is wedged in my hands. Blood weeps down my arm, slippery under my palm.

Tap. Another tap: rubber soles against tile, smooth and rocking. His breathing, heavy but methodical. Closer.

Wide mirrors and a bar of sinks are to my left. The walls are spread with mosaic tiles. A small space yawns between the door and the ground. And the tip of a shadow emerges. His shoe.

Don't move. Don't breathe. Don't move.

Hot fluid collects under my hand. I'm slipping. Slipping. My muscles rage to compensate.

Another shadow. Two legs. My fingernails bend backward against the floor. Blood has pooled under my hand and oozes toward the space under the door. Where he'll be able to see it.

One leg of his shadow moves. Raises, eases forward, lands. Stops. His breathing is quieter.

My hand is about to slip. If I change my position even a fraction, it'll go. Glass flecks grind in it.

The shadows adjust, but not like he's leaving. Like he's found something.

My lungs burn, convulse. My body wants to compensate with a scream.

Stay. Still.

The shadows are deadlocked. His breathing is inaudible.

He shifts so abruptly I almost cry out. One shadow of his leg leaves, the next following. The tapping recedes.

I let out an exhale, tiny enough that I'm sure he can't hear, then another, more complete. All out, full back in, the air smelling of disinfectant and hand soap.

I get my weight off my hand—the floor's a puddle—and droop against the door. How long ago did Mercedes set off the alarm? I replay everything in my mind. The phone, the garden, the knife, the shot, here.

I swallow dizziness and nausea from blood loss. Focus.

Three minutes. I'm going to guess it's been three minutes, which means there are another nine minutes to stall until the police get here.

How? If Luiz finds me, he'll kill me and run. If he doesn't find me, he'll give up and run. I have to keep him occupied.

What do I know? What can I use to my advantage?

I mentally run through everything I saw coming in: the wide-open waiting room, the deadbolted halls, the signs directing patients—

The stairs. A sign on the wall said there were stairs. But it's a miracle that this bathroom was unlocked, so what makes me think I'll get so lucky twice?

I have no other choice.

I push myself to my feet. I'm shaking, and my joints are rioting by now. As I rise, so does my reflection.

It's difficult without light, but I see enough. Rose-colored scratches stripe my face. My hands are tarred with blood. There's a tear in my shirt, too far left to be my heart.

Two eyes, bright, alive, blaze. No fear for him to see.

52

I PULL THE DOOR OPEN a sliver, then stop and wait.

The taps of shoes come back toward me.

Every cell inside me wants to close the door, but it's not far open enough for him to notice unless it moves. I make sure it's still, my palms stinging with flecks of glass, my muscles tingling with exertion and adrenaline.

There's an opening just wide enough for me to see. Not him yet, though; he's still too far away. I can only hear his steps. They're careful and waiting.

He'll see you if you move.

My arms shake. I wedge the toe of my tennis shoe against the side of the door to prop it there, to keep it secure where it is. And then he's in my line of sight, bundled in black. The tips glint on his lead-gray pistol. His back faces me.

He browses to his right, down the hall. To his left, back to the waiting room.

A swift stride, almost a lunge, and he yanks a doorhandle across from me. It doesn't budge. He spins around and crosses the hall, now out of my thin view, but from the sound of it, he tests a door feet from where I am.

The bathroom's next.

My throat almost closes. I have nothing to protect myself. Even if I did, it's point blank for him. I can't fight. Mercedes tried.

Luiz suddenly stops.

I catch the sound too: a second pair of hammering steps. Unrestrained panting sweeps through the hall and rubber soles shriek to a standstill on the tile.

Luiz gasps. A glare of light rages through the hall, and a boom pounds against my eardrums. Luiz curses and fires a return shot, and then his racing steps pound away from me.

The person with the second gun bolts past, gone too fast for me to recognize. Another screech of shoes tells me Luiz skidded around a corner.

Not yet.

I wait for a final screech—the second person pursuing—but it doesn't come. While Luiz's steps wane, the second set slows. Stops.

Come on, follow him.

Deep, cleansing breaths murmur from the direction they both went. I wait.

A few more steps, and they begin to sound blocked by a wall. Now.

I drag the door open until it accommodates my body and squeeze out.

Luiz's footprints of blood—my blood—race down the hall and around a corner at the end, followed by dropped pieces of glass that seem to flicker in the moonlight pouring through a window. I'm so exposed; I need to get out.

On the sign that will route me to the stairs, arrows point in two directions: one down the hall where Luiz and the other person disappeared, the other back toward the entry, where I came in.

Another isolated gunshot rings out. I run back toward the entrance and cross it, dodging broken shards so they don't clink under my feet, and make it to a hall I must have passed when I came in; it runs next to the serenity garden. I enter it, and five yards down, there's a recess in the wall. Next to it, another small sign tells me it's what I've been looking for.

A noise. I stop.

I'm not sure I really heard it, but if I did…someone's approaching.

I brace my knees and sneak into the recess, which is less than ten feet deep. A simple door is planted in the back, tan fake wood and an ugly chrome handle with a ragged keyhole.

Don't let it be locked, God.

I push down.

It doesn't budge.

My wrist quakes against the solid handle. I let go and lean against the wall, soundlessly stamping it with a red body print.

How long has it been? Another minute. If that. And I never took the storm into account. How much time will that add? Time I can't give them.

The walls of this building are made of glass. All Luiz has to do is shoot one and get away. I have to call him back, but if he kills me, there's no chance he'll stay. For now, he thinks he can find me. He'll keep searching.

I have to wait. Get his attention at the last minute or hide as long as I can until he tracks me down. And hope that's enough for the police to catch him.

I slide down—the swish of the cloth on my back slipping against the drywall is too loud—and tuck into a ball. A gag squeezes my stomach. How much blood have I lost?

It doesn't matter. It'll all be over in a few minutes. Because this time, the knife will sink true.

Breathe slowly. My pulse thuds in my ears.

Steps, uneven, almost limping, but intentional.

My head rips upright, and I drag myself up the wall. Not yet. Not yet. If he kills me, it's over.

His shadow creeps up on the recess. Stops and stands outside, where I can't see him. I crush myself against the wall, bite down on my lip.

A foot passes the edge.

He lunges.

53

HIS HAND CLAMPS OVER MY MOUTH and nose, killing a scream. The other braces the side of my face. His skin and his clothes are cedary. His eyes are green even in the dark.

A hot, wet path drains down my cheek onto his hand.

He came for me. After what I said to him, he came for me.

Tristan eases his hand from my mouth and puts a finger to his lips. Then he points at the tile floor. Scarlet prints in the shapes of my shoe, surrounded by small beads and splatters, lead into the hall. A perfect trail.

Tristan's eyes shift to the door that will let us into the stairs. His hand slips off my cheek; the other traces up the leg of his jeans to his pocket. He pulls out a keyring—the janitor's empty retractor.

Tristan steps to the door. The grip of a handgun—that must be Eddie's—juts out from the small of his back, secured in his belt. His arm shakes. My pulse slams in my wound as I stand with my back to the hall.

Where's Luiz? Is he close enough to hear this?

Tristan picks the first key of at least ten and slides it up the ring. He doesn't let the other nine jangle.

He pushes the tip to the jagged keyhole. It doesn't fit.

Second. Silver. He places the tip into the hole, and it slithers in.

Tristan's shoulders flex. He rotates his wrist to open the mechanism. And is stopped cold.

Tristan moistens his lips and extracts the key. It scrapes loudly as it comes, and he winces at the sound before moving on to the third key.

Approaching feet reverberate in the hall.

Every nerve in my body lights like tinder. Tristan wrenches his head over his shoulder. His free hand flinches toward the gun in his waistband. His gaze shoots past my frame, then settles on me.

I've never seen him so afraid.

He clamps the bulk of the keys in his hand to keep them from clinking, from betraying us, and tries the third key. This one fits too.

The footfalls come nearer.

Tristan turns the key with a click I can feel in my heart.

The chrome lever yields with the crunch and grind of springs. The hydraulic hinge hisses as Tristan drags the door open.

He jerks his head for me to get inside. I restrain my urge to sprint, and step without a noise, heel, toe, easy, legs screaming from bone to joint to muscle. Tristan pivots in behind me, keeping the knob twisted as he closes the door. Relocks.

No sound. No one approaching. No one retreating.

A wave of dizziness forces me to exhale.

Tristan looks at me, then drags the heel of his hand across his eyes to get rid of the water in them.

I grip the metal rail of the stairwell; the tiny slivers of glass in my palm are like teeth trying to bite past blood and into muscle. The steps, made of polished concrete, climb above us, switchbacking every half flight. The thin air smells of dust. This place is cold enough to be a tomb.

Tristan replaces the keys into his pocket. He's not wearing the sweatshirt that he had before—he's left in a long-sleeved maroon T-shirt. The bottom of it is rough like he tore off the hem. His gaze shifts from my hand on the rail to the other one limp at my side, to the gash in my shoulder. Then at the floor and the ever-present blood trail.

I grimace. I'll keep leading Luiz to us unless we can stanch it.

Tristan gestures at my shoulder and touches the ragged hem of his shirt. I nod.

He crosses the few steps between us. I was right when I heard him walking—he's limping a little bit. It doesn't look like he messed up a joint, but more like his shins hurt. He must have jumped from the second story he was on when he shot at Luiz.

He places his hand on my good arm and helps me lower myself to the stairs, my back supported by the wall. Out of the pocket that doesn't have the keys, Tristan pulls his father's knife. It's as black as the stairwell until he unfolds it. The blade shines silver, the same as...

Nausea sweeps over me, nausea and grief and dread, and I press the back of my hand against my mouth.

Tristan's shaking hand cups my jawline. When I meet his eyes, they're steady. Strong. And like they always have, they steel me.

I lower my hand from my mouth. It's a knife, but it can't kill me. And it can't kill anyone I love. Not while it's in his hands.

Tristan takes the blade to the bottom of his shirt and frees a large strip, which he bundles into a fistful. He closes the knife, dousing its deadly reflection, slides it back into his pocket, and raises the wad of cloth to my wound. It's not much pressure, but it lights up my synapses. I bite my lip and strangle a moan before it can escape.

Tristan waits patiently. He waits for me to gather myself, waits for my permission to save us both.

I look at the door. At the blood leading here. And I look at my brother.

Do it for him.

I take his free hand in mine and cover my mouth with it. He keeps it there after I release my own.

He mouths, *Ready?*

I nod.

One.

Breathe, Paityn.

Two.

Keep breathing.

Three.

His hand crushes over my mouth as he drives the wad into my wound. A groan claws at my chest, a groan or a scream, I'm not sure, but it must be a scream, it must be, because it burns like a scream as I drag it down.

Don't let it out, don't get us killed, don't get him killed.

He pushes it deeper and deeper into my vulnerable tissue, until I'd swear he's at the socket. Then the pressure releases. Not fully—the wad is packed in firmly—but his weight comes off it.

I exhale, my heart pounding. Tristan's eyes have that pinch, that ache at the corners, the one that shows up whenever he sees me in pain. His lips form the words, *It's over.*

That part is at least. Now where's Luiz?

Tristan's hand comes away from my mouth. He tips his head toward the polished cement stairs. I nod and clasp the hand he offers me. Now there's glass in both our palms, the flecks scraping against each other.

We take the stairs one at a time. I don't lean on him, but he supports me by my elbow anyway. We mount the first half-flight and follow the switchback so that the door we came in through is visible past the barred railing.

The doorknob jiggles.

Tristan's hand turns to iron on my arm. "*Run*."

54

TRISTAN GRIPS MY ELBOW AND THRUSTS me up the
next two stairs, but my toe catches the lip—my shoe sole skims
against the polished concrete with a screech. My heart clenches.

Orange fire lights up the stairwell, burns away my sight, hits my
ears like the blow of an ice ax. Lead bores through the lock. The
twang of a ricochet and the crack of splintered flooring.

"*Go!*" Tristan pushes me up another two stairs, but this time I
latch onto his arm and drag him with me, and then we're running,
tearing up the stairs, two, three at a time, Tristan hauling me forward
when I fall behind.

Second floor. Second gunshot. One more bullet, two at the
most, and the lock will have fallen apart. Tristan wrenches the gun
from his belt, strikes the clip with the heel of his palm to secure it.
He could be going faster, I know it, but I'm sick, and he's waiting.
He's hanging back for me.

Don't lose him. Keep running, harder, *go*.

We're halfway up the second floor and take another switchback.
A third gunshot. A clatter. A door crashing open.

Footsteps pound beneath us.

Third floor. Third floor and nowhere else to go.

Tristan rips the keys out of his pocket, jams the right one in. Luiz is half a flight down.

The door opens with a rush of fresh air and moonlight. Tristan shoves me through. A hall stretches away from us, and two stunted areas spread to our left and right. In the right branch, facing us, an alcove is carved into the wall.

There.

Tristan and I burst for it as the door slams open. I throw myself into the alcove, where the wall protects me. Tristan, behind me, pivots, raises the pistol.

Luiz's is already up. His eyes light up white in the explosion.

Tristan's back arches. My heart cuts off my throat.

A groan drives through Tristan's teeth. He hits his knees, then his stomach. There's a tear in the side of his shirt, and liquid trickles out. The gun clatters on the floor and slides toward me.

I dive for it, raise it, shoot. It's poor aim, but it does the trick: Luiz dodges away, and his next bullet buries itself into the hard carpet, not into Tristan. I sink into a low kneel and poise my one good hand, but Luiz throws himself down the other stunted hall into an identical alcove. My bullet, which would have split his spine, drills into the wall.

Tristan cranes his neck off the floor and claws himself toward me, toward protection. Luiz snaps a poor shot at us from his alcove. I shoot back. I'm not aiming at this point, only keeping Luiz busy, giving Tristan a few seconds. Tristan drags himself into the alcove. I retreat after him.

Now the only way for Luiz to get us would be if he came down this part of the hall, unprotected and point-blank. He's stuck as long as we can keep him there.

There's a ceiling-high window behind us and, outside it, the serenity garden. Tristan clutches his side; his hands glisten red. I help him sit against the wall. He gasps through gritted teeth.

A bang, and the window behind us spiderwebs.

Tristan flinches. I snatch our gun and fire, but it's no good. Luiz is as well protected as we are. How many more rounds do we have left? How many more can we waste keeping him over there?

Tristan struggles to control his breathing. I carefully strip his fingers from the wound and peer through the rip in his shirt. It's a puncture shot straight through. Gunpowder blackens the area. I pray the bullet didn't graze anything vital.

I fold his hand back over the wound and layer mine on top. Blood seeps through.

"Here it comes," I tell him. I add my weight to our hands.

A strangled inhale scrapes into him. Tendons turn to cords in his neck, but after a few moments, he relaxes, and it becomes quiet.

Too quiet. What is Luiz doing?

I lean out of the alcove to see past. Tristan twists to do the same. The hall is obscured farther down, but there's something at the end, something more than drywall. Hinges.

I listen. A click. Another. Testing a knob. A knob to a door. To a hall. To an exit.

"He's trying to run," I breathe.

The pain dissolves from Tristan's face. He braces his jaw, reaches for the gun, stances his fingers on it.

I stop him. Set my hand over his and bow my head.

Luiz can't get out before the police come. Which means we need to draw him from that corner.

One of us needs to let this gun be taken out of play. One of us has to walk out there with it. The other has to stay behind, weaponless, and somehow finish it.

I raise my eyes to Tristan's, and I know the same things have run through his mind.

"I'll do it," he whispers.

I shake my head; my eyes sting. I told him he should've died instead of Elijah, and I can't take that back, but I can show him I was wrong. Wrong to say it. Wrong to ever think that I meant it. "No. Tristan—"

Tristan removes his hand from his wound and places it over mine. "Please."

I look at him, tears burning down my face. I can't lose him. I can't. Not again.

I see the same thing in Tristan's gaze. And I see that even if I tried, he wouldn't let me take this.

Salt stings the raw scrapes on my cheeks. I squeeze his hand. Memorize the ridges of his knuckles. Imagine if this is how my foot felt under his hand each morning.

I release the gun. He exhales steadily.

Tell him. Tell him now, while you have the chance. "I—"

A gunshot splits my ears, and my hands fly up to them. Tristan clenches his teeth and reaches into his front pocket. He hands me the knife our father gave him.

Steady. You can take it. Use it. You have to.

I take it from him. A second gunshot blows at Luiz's door. It has to be now.

I point to the spiderwebbed window behind us. Tristan gets the message and fires. The window blasts open, and snowy air sweeps in. Luiz spins so that half of his body is exposed.

So fast you'd have no idea he's injured, Tristan shoves to his feet and braces his shoulder against the wall.

He locks gazes with me one last time.

And steps out. No fear in his eyes.

He fires. Deafening, over and over, he empties the magazine. The wall protects Luiz. And the return shots come, but no ricochets, no shattering glass or punctured plaster. Each bullet pierces my brother's torso.

A gasp. That same gasp.

Tristan collapses. The gun clatters away, far out of my reach.

Luiz emerges.

I press my hand over my mouth, barely able to swallow a sob, barely able to breathe.

He did this for you. Get up.

I fight to my feet and press myself into the corner where Luiz will have to turn to get to me.

I have one chance. Where am I going to make this count?

I unfold the knife. Glacial air curls in from the broken window. Luiz is wearing three jackets and who knows what underneath. There's too much of a chance I won't penetrate if I go for a lung shot. I have to go for something exposed.

Luiz is close enough that my neck prickles.

That's how to end this.

Shudders run down my body. There's a break in Luiz's pace, like he's stepping over something. Stepping over Tristan.

Sweat and blood slick my palm. I grip the hilt tighter. Grief threatens to choke me, but I swallow it.

Luiz's foot appears outside the alcove. His pistol raises. He turns the corner.

I plant my foot, throw every muscle I have. A scream of effort, pain, fear, resolve, tears from my body.

I sink all three inches of the blade. My fist, closed around the hilt, smacks against Luiz's collarbone. A flinch of a shot digs into the floor. Luiz's entire body stiffens to wire in a convulsion that spreads the wound in his neck.

He's gaping, staring at me. Not seeing me at all. Seeing me for the first time.

Finish this.

I shift, using the knife to give him no choice but to rotate with me. My foot rams into his solar plexus.

Icy wind whips through the window. He topples over the ledge.

My eyes are the last thing he sees.

55

LUIZ SCREAMS. It's a haunting sound cut short by breaking branches. By groans of pain. By the thud of a body on solid ground. Silence.

And in the silence, soft, labored breathing.

Tristan.

My breath leaves me in a broken exhale. I whirl around. Blood pools around his broken body. He's on his side.

I stagger forward and collapse to my knees next to him. His eyes are closed.

His lips move. It's so soft, so weak I almost can't make it out. But I hear him.

"Paityn," he whispers.

That's all he says. My name. And that numbness, that scar that has been keeping me safe is sliced open.

I lower my face until my forehead touches his cheekbone. Let my tears fall onto his skin and warm it. "I'm here."

His eyelashes brush mine. I ease my arms around his shoulders and slide him into the crook of my good arm. I cradle his cheek. Bloodstains have spread and mingled on his tattered shirt. His stomach. His chest. He's soaked.

"Breathe," I say. "Keep breathing."

His eyes make it open. Bright green. Fighting. Always fighting. "Paityn, please."

He tries to inhale and coughs, a weak contraction in my arms. Blood coats the side of his mouth and is painted into the seams between his teeth.

I draw him closer and wipe away the stains at his lips. Tilt his head toward me.

His gaze finds mine.

"I'm so sorry," he whispers.

I look into his eyes. The eyes I first saw when I was four years old. The eyes that have found me and wept for me and laughed with me at every moment of my life.

He grimaces, pressing a tear out.

"Hey. Look at me." I stroke the tear away with my thumb. "It's okay."

The pain melts from his face. His eyes well up, and he smiles like that was all he ever wanted to hear. "Thank you."

He reaches up with a shaking hand and brushes the side of my face. I hold it to my cheek.

I finally tell him.

"I love you, Tristan."

He smiles again. "I love you too."

And I smile back.

A few seconds. Seconds. Then his body starts to relax. His hand grows heavy in mine.

His eyes lose focus. He exhales. And he's gone.

I press him against my chest. Wrap my arms around him and bow my head to his. Shielding him, ready to take any blow for him even though it's too late.

And as I hold him, he's no longer a young man, dead, broken, shot. He's the little boy I found lying on the street twelve years ago. The one who murmured his name to me as I hugged him close. The one I promised I wouldn't leave until he was safe. The one I would've died for if he hadn't died for me first.

A voiceless sob crushes me from the inside out. I lower my lips to his face and press a kiss only a sister can give to his forehead.

56

I STROKE HIS HAIR. Innocent blond, once wind tousled and free, now blood caked and soaked with sweat. I comb through as if he can still feel it.

His eyes are open, their glow gone. My fingers, careful and light, close them forever.

There's glass beneath my knees. Blood soaks down my arm, where it mingles with his. I'd give it to him if it could bring him back. I'd give him everything. Take it. All of it.

The wind's gone. Only a few snowflakes drift outside the gaping window. The chill weeps over us. My body resists it; his absorbs it. He's cold, growing colder. I draw myself close to him, sharing my heat. It does nothing.

Sirens whine less than a few minutes away. They'll come. They'll take him from me.

They can't heal him. It's too late. They can't heal—

Mercedes. She's down there. In the storm, bleeding.

I nestle my face against Tristan's.

"I can't leave you," I whisper into his skin.

I can't leave Mercedes either. She's alone. And she might still be alive.

I fight myself. I fight the urge to cling to him as long as I can. I lay him down. Soothe back a lock of hair. Stand. Leave. Leave, even though it hurts more than anything I've ever done.

I go to my sister.

57

GLASS PIERCES THE SOLES OF MY SHOES. My hand is numb beneath my wound. I touch the jagged shards that are still connected to the pane as I step out of outpatient.

The garden lies before me, heavy with snow. To my right, glass decorates the branches of bushes. Larger shards are in the trees. An evergreen and a tree stripped of leaves stand together, their once touching branches shredded on the ground. There are red stains on the broken ends, bright as ink on the pale bark.

I push straight forward, toward Mercedes. The window on the second floor across the way is shattered. The one Tristan shot saving me. And in all the other windows, there are lights on. People alive. All thanks to him.

The cloth of his shirt overflows with my blood, and droplets seep down my arm and follow me in the whiteness. Broken branches and a lifeless mass stay in my peripheral vision.

Mercedes is where I left her, but not the way I left her. She's propped up against the bench, her head supported by the armrest. She's not awake judging by the angle of her head, so she must have been moved. She's wrapped up in a sweatshirt with the hood up.

I kneel next to her. The sweatshirt is Tristan's. He was wearing it when he came to see me. Her arms aren't through the sleeves, but it's secured over her torso. The hood protects her face from the storm. When I brush it back, a different piece of fabric peeps out: torn rayon, a strap bandaging her bloodied head—the same material that's in my shoulder.

I place two of my cold fingers on her neck. A healthy pulse beats beneath them.

I cup her face in both of my hands, grinding through my injured arm to do it, and inhale. I get a waft of his cedar and her cinnamon, sweet and clean and familiar.

Her eyelids flutter.

I touch my forehead to hers. "Thank you."

The sirens are closer now. Two minutes or less. I wish I could get her somewhere warm, wake her up, but there's nothing I can do.

I pull back and let my hands drop. I've left a burgundy handprint on her cheek. In my peripheral vision, a small cascade of snow falls—bloodstained snow from bloodstained branches.

Mercedes is as warm as I can make her. I gaze at the mass inside the ice-covered branches.

I stand and walk.

I don't know what I think I'm doing. I stabbed him in the neck; I pushed him out of a window.

He's on his side. The knife's gone, nowhere near him—it must have come out in the fall—and his blood has melted the snow around his neck and face. A branch slants across his jaw. His right arm is partially beneath him, his wrist contorted in a strange direction. His knee is forty-five degrees sideways.

I kneel next to him and clear away the branch from his face. His nose is shattered. His lip is split.

I roll him onto his back without any resistance. His aviator jacket is splayed open. His leather jacket is freckled with snowflakes and soil. I unzip it and the second one beneath it. Now there's only a thin shirt between me and his chest. The stab is livid, flush with his collarbone. Not his neck. A flesh wound.

I lay my ear over his heart. He's warm beneath me. More than warm—he's burning up. I would guess he had a fever if I didn't know better.

And spearmint. Always spearmint.

I listen. I feel.

A low, quick pump like a frightened child's. A firm pulse pushing against my skin.

I sit back on my heels, blank.

He survived. Tristan died, and he survived.

In the little light there is, everything around me sparkles: snow, glass—and a lead glint only a few feet away. His gun.

I stand. Pick it up. My hand fits perfectly into the frame. It's flawlessly balanced. My finger parallels the barrel, and a shudder runs through me.

Luiz stirs. My thumb curls back and cocks the hammer.

His eyes wrestle open. He grimaces and makes a move to push himself onto his hand until he realizes his wrist is destroyed, and slumps to his elbow with a shocked wince. He blinks for a few seconds before his good hand gropes toward his collarbone. Glistening crimson flows across his fingers. When he pulls his hand back, he stares at the blood, at the strange angles of his opposite wrist and his knee.

Then he sees me.

He recoils at the expense of his bad wrist, and with a groan harsh enough that I can feel it in the pit of my stomach, he crumples to his shoulder.

My left arm hangs helpless at my side. I come closer.

Luiz raises his gaze. Shifts it to the gun. Back to me.

"Finish it," he says.

The muzzle's trained on the ground. I stroke the trigger.

Is this what he wants? Is this what he's wanted all along?

His scar is reopened. Blood trickles down his hairline. He's waiting for this barrel to rise and for the bullet to blaze. Waiting for me to end it for him. End his pain.

He does—he looks like he's in pain. And he looks tired. The same young man who once knew he could come to me bleeding. The same young man who knew I was the one who would let him cry on my shoulder.

My index finger straightens off the trigger. I release the gun's magazine, aim behind me into a cluster of evergreen bushes, and fire to clear the last round in the chamber. And when the recoil's over, the bullet gone, the light and the smoke cleared, I drop the gun on the ground.

I turn back to Luiz. His breathing is torn.

My head's light. The police are down the way, less than half a mile from the sound of it.

I kneel next to Luiz. Fumble for the crucifix on my necklace. And break the chain.

I raise my left hand and guide his uninjured wrist toward me, palm up. The muscles in his forearm constrict under my touch.

I press the necklace into his palm and close his fingers around it. They're cold and stiff and smooth. My blood coats his knuckles and is already starting to freeze on them.

His eyes have been fixed on our hands. Now they come to my face. "Paityn…" My name comes out of his mouth like he hasn't said it in a while, like he hardly remembers how.

"Tell them where Tristan is." The words are hoarse, less than a whisper.

Luiz is silent for a moment, staring at me like I'm something beautiful and fearsome and painful all at once. Snow melts off of his hair, gathers in a bead near the corner of his eye, and flows down his bruised cheek. It runs through his blood, which dyes it scarlet before it falls somewhere in the broken branches beneath us.

He tries again. "Paityn—"

I'm already gone. I stand and stumble back toward Mercedes. She stirs, takes a deeper inhale, shifts her shoulders. Sirens wail behind me. Her face and the snow are tinted with alternating flashes of red and blue.

I lower myself to the ground. The snow is a cushion beneath my bleeding body.

I let unconsciousness overtake me.

It's done.

58

"PAITYN, WAKE UP."

That voice—I know that voice.

Air rushes into my lungs. Hard, slicing pain spears through my left shoulder. I blink away fluorescent light and search for whomever spoke. I'm in a hospital room. It's empty.

I heard someone. I know I did; I know that voice.

I try to raise my head. It hits the pillow as soon as the shredded muscles in my shoulder contract, a phantom knife carving in.

My sister bleeding from her temple, her blond lashes just barely fluttering. My brother, broken, shattered in my arms.

A hot pearl of moisture rolls down my temple, catches on my ear, and flows into it. What did they do with his body? And where's Mercedes now? How long have I been here?

Blue and red lights dye the night outside the window on my left. On my right, a door opens. I jolt, yanking at my shoulder wound.

Nurses mill in the hall behind him. One stares right at him, considers, then carries on, as if he's supposed to be there.

The one from all my dreams. From the cemetery. From the garden. His striking eyes are fixed on me.

He approaches my bed until he's close enough to rest his hand on the guardrail. I let him. I should be uneasy, but I'm not.

"Who are you?" I say. "What are you doing here?"

His eyelashes are wet. "I think you know who I am."

"I have no idea—"

"Paityn." He touches the side of my face with the length of his hand, tilting my head to guide my gaze.

Straight to His.

My air, my straight thoughts—they cut off.

I know Him.

He sets His hand on my forehead. Gentle. His touch, His eyes, His voice. "I think you have someone you want to talk to."

I try to ask one of a storm of questions.

I'm out and dreaming before my eyes close.

59

MY ROOM AT HOME IS UNLIT. My feet are bare against the laminate flooring, except it doesn't feel like laminate—it's not smooth enough. It's prickly and almost crystalline under my soles.

My heart pounds. I grope for my nightstand to see if my phone is where it should be. Everything I touch—my down blanket, my pillow, the nightstand's flat top—all has that rough, uneven surface. I rub some of it off, and it melts against my fingertips. Frost.

I find my phone lying on its face and turn the screen toward me. With my thumb, I wipe off the layer of frost. The time blinks up at me.

3:59 a.m.

What...

Something tickles the back of my neck. I reach behind me and touch it. Hair. I have my hair back.

Dull pain burns the front of my shoulder and spreads in fibers across the rest of me. My breath pops delicately as the hot vapor in it freezes.

My phone buzzes with a text message.

My hand shakes. The shaking rides up my arm, my spine. It takes over my whole body.

It can't be. He died. I saw him. I held him. I closed his eyes.

I close my own—they sting behind my lids. I must be dreaming. Nothing more.

It doesn't feel the same, though. I know when I'm dreaming. This is different.

My thumbs hover over the phone screen. His name and his message twinkle back at me.

And if it is a dream? I have nothing to lose.

I' m here.

My stomach squeezes when I send it.

Hesitant steps. The knob turns. The door eases open.

"Paityn?"

I back up until my legs bump the bed.

It's him. Thick hair trimmed and sideswept. Green eyes that light up the dark. Tall shoulders that always stood between me and the world. "Paityn, it's me."

This is more than a dream. It's too real.

I think you have someone you want to talk to.

"It's you." A crack splits my words down the middle.

Tristan casts his eyes down with so much pain my heart twists inside me. "I know you probably don't even want to look at me—"

I cross the distance between us in two strides and throw my arms around him.

He's completely still for a moment. Then his chest shrinks under me, an exhale riddled with tears. His arms ease up and around me, protecting me. He holds my head in his long fingers. I hold his in mine.

I press my temple into his neck, crush his body closer to me. I remember this. I remember his jawline against mine. I remember the strength of his body as he breathes tears.

I weep, inhaling his scent of body wash and laughter, and exhaling the pain, my chest rising and falling with his. I don't know how long it is. Forever and not long enough, but eventually, I let him go. And I get to see his smile for the first time in far too long.

"It's so good to see you again." Tears sparkle in Tristan's eyes.

Mine spill unchecked. I take his hand. "Just...tell me what happened."

His eyes well up again, the way they did when I held him dying. "After Dad—" His voice snags. "Tony blamed us for his father getting arrested, so he found me and told me I needed to pay protection. I'd do everything he said. Keep quiet, keep my head down, or he'd make sure all of you were dead before I had a chance to do anything."

My hand in Tristan's begins to shake. He tenderly squeezes until it's steady again.

"I wanted to tell you," he continues, "but I knew you'd want to help me. And even if we got Tony arrested, he said he'd make sure someone else finished it. I wasn't willing to test if he was bluffing. I couldn't lose—" A tear slips down his cheek, then another right behind it. "I had no idea. About any of the attacks."

I wipe his tears away. He smiles, and two more fill their place, one on each cheek. I let go of his hand so that I can hold his face. When I do, the warm water, shining like mother of pearl over his skin, drains onto my wrists. The salt paths they leave look like scars of their own. Scars we share.

"How...how were you there?" I ask. "At outpatient."

He guides my hands back into his own. "Venus and I were in the parking lot when Luiz and Eddie came. Luiz was already gone by the time we got in, but Eddie was his lookout. Venus—" He clenches his jaw before the next words can get out.

"She was alive," I tell him. "When Mercedes and I ran out, she was awake." A faint, beautiful light rises in his face. A light I would have loved to watch grow. "But why were you and Venus at the hospital at all?"

He squeezes my hand again, his thumb brushing over the knife scar on the back. "I never left."

He didn't leave after I...

Regret spills down my cheeks.

"I'm sorry." I am, with every part of my being. With every part that broke but turned away when I saw the pain that I had put him in. "For what I said. I—"

"Hey." He reaches up and tilts my head toward his, and we meet halfway, our foreheads touching. I close my eyes. His voice whispers in the air we breathe. "It's okay."

Tears stream down my face. I tuck myself into his arms again.

"Thank you," I whisper into his neck.

He broke his life to save ours. He gave us up, let me think he was less than he was, to protect us.

He holds me as tightly as if I were the only thing keeping him alive. "Are they okay? Mercedes and Mom and the baby?"

I don't know. Are they even—

A pang rips through my body, and my knees buckle. Tristan's arms stiffen around me, and he catches me before I hit the ground. His ribs constrict as he lowers both of us, barbed frost flattening beneath our weight. Tristan's hand is under my head; his arms support me.

I pry open my throat. "What's happening?"

"I don't know." His eyes are wide.

The pain spreads, following my blood vessels like a disease. I grip Tristan's arm. I won't let him go. Never again.

He draws me to him and presses me close, his jaw next to mine. His heart beats on my chest. His heart, then my heart, one right after the other, as if his is what is allowing mine to beat after it, as if he's pouring his own life into me.

He begins to rock me.

"God, please," he whispers.

I'm still clinging to him when my vision fades.

60

I CAN'T MOVE. When I try, nothing happens, like someone slit my spinal cord and left me to bleed. I'm walled in by my closed eyelids.

I can hear, though. A familiar voice. Dr. Tahan.

"The storm's over. The snow is beautiful."

Why would she say that? Who is she talking to?

"You never cease to surprise me, Paityn."

What?

Why is she talking to me? And why does the way she's talking make it sound like she thinks...

Like she thinks I'm dying.

"Sweetheart." Dr. Tahan's never called me that before. It's tender. "Your injury got infected. It went septic."

Sepsis. I have no immune system.

She does think I'm dying. That's why she's talking to me. She thinks she may be the last voice I hear.

No. No, I can't. Where's my mom? I have to know that she and the baby are all right.

"Mercedes is fine."

I can't leave Mercedes; I can't leave any of them.

"They're keeping her for a while. She's fighting to get out and be with you." Dr. Tahan's voice tremors, and that's when I know.

She doesn't think I'll last that long.

"Sweetheart, I don't know if you can hear me."

I can. I can, and it doesn't matter what you have to say. Just keep talking to me.

"I think you might have a few hours left. But..."

I strain so I don't miss a word.

"You're a rare case." A warm hand—she's not wearing any medical gloves—clothes the curve of my head. "Surprise me, Paityn."

I will.

Everything fades. Her voice, my consciousness. The pain.

I'm asleep.

61

THIS ISN'T MY HOSPITAL. Not any real hospital. An IV is slid in my arm, and there's a bright strip of lighting overhead, but the walls are hand-brushed black, decorated with crimson and gold swirls. My hair is braided beneath me. An elegant chair of ebony and wine-colored leather stands guard next to my bed.

The bottom of my vision is lined with red. My throat is flooded with hot, iron-tasting fluid. My heart pulses with strain as I draw my fingers to the raw, burning section of my chest. Warm moisture spreads across them.

I startle when, to my right, the wall splits open in a perfect line—a camouflaged door. My vision blurs scarlet; I blink two thick tears.

"Elijah," I whisper.

He's the same as when he died. The black jeans, the torn cobalt shirt—the stain in the center is wet, as if he's still bleeding. The only thing that's different is his hair. It sparkles with a thin layer of frost.

I recognize his lithe strides, the ones that mean he's coming, that he's safe and so am I.

He shifts the ebony chair so that it's facing me and sets himself onto the edge. He takes my hand in his.

"I'm here," he says. I thought I'd lost his voice forever. His voice that protected me and went silent for me. A tress of curls rests on my forehead. He carefully tucks it behind my ear.

My shirt is soaked, my hand slick. My heart beats under a spearhead.

A groan gurgles up from the pit of my stomach. Blood tickles in my throat, but I can't cough, so it flows back down.

Elijah wipes my cheeks and the corner of my mouth. His hand comes away smeared with red. "I know."

Am I bleeding out of my eyes or am I crying blood? Or is that his own blood, from his shirt, from where he took the knife for me?

"I'm sorry," I whisper. In a spasm, a convulsion, I cough. My chest erupts. Blood drips over my lip.

His hand cradles my face, cool and strong.

Underneath, I can feel my own fading pulse. It feels exactly how his pulse did right before he died.

"This was my choice," he says. "And I'd do it again."

I know he would—and I'd do the same for him if I could.

Blood collects in my eyes. More blood is in my lungs. I don't know how I know; I just do.

"What about my mom?" I say. "And the baby?"

Elijah smiles. "Her name's Kestrel."

Kestrel.

She's alive. They're *alive*.

For a moment, I think I can see her. My baby sister. Feel her weight in my arms, her head cupped in my hand, her cheek against my collar. Watch her as she learns to raise her head, turn over on her own, and wrap her tiny fingers around mine.

And my mom—our mom—will be there to see it. To nurture her and protect her.

To teach her. Teach her what it means to live. To love. And teach her to remember me.

Black creeps into my vision. I claw through it to Elijah. Because I know this will be the last time I'll see him. The last time while I'm alive.

My pulse against his hand slows.

62

AND SHE'S ALREADY HERE. Her hand strokes me the way I never thought I'd feel again.

Mom.

I wish I could cry. I wish I could ask about the baby, about Kestrel—it's bursting inside me.

Thank you. Thank you, thank you, thank you.

It's the best I can give Him.

My mother's skin is on mine, and there's a whiff of wood and roses from her clothes. She's weeping, tattered inhales and exhales that crack in the middle every so often—followed by the familiar click of a door.

Immediately, there's the scrape of a chair's feet on the floor and eager footsteps from both my bedside and the door's direction. Cloth snaps in the way that only means two people embracing each other.

"Oh, honey," my mom says. Mercedes. "You made it."

She's okay. She's okay.

Mercedes is crying. "Is she still—"

"Yes."

And skin is back in contact with my own. Hands surround

mine, never letting me go, one on each side. My left hand begins to shake in my mother's grasp. Harder and harder, and my mom—my strong, brave mom—is breaking.

They're both here. Mercedes' tears skim my face, warm and gently acidic. They're with me, and my baby sister—Kestrel—is all right.

My terms are fulfilled.

63

UNTOUCHED SNOW SPANS FOR MILES, shin deep. Ice, snow, and evergreens, needles blotted white and branches bending low under a thick layer of frost. Dew has frozen on the tree branches and forms perfect beads that reflect the light. The sky is also white, but not blinding. Cloud cover donates its smell to everything beneath it.

I turn a slow circle. At a distance is a lone building. It's identical to outpatient, down to the shattered windows at the base.

Cold air slips out of my lungs warm. I stand in the clothes I wore for the fight: wrap top, khakis snug around my ankles, except I have no shoes. Snow melts and smooths until it's spongy beneath my soles, but it isn't biting, just cool, almost a tickle.

A placid crunch and swish of snow beneath feet. And there He is, the One from the cemetery, my dreams, the hospital. He wears a black shirt rolled up to the elbows. His shins leave trenches in the snow; He stops a few feet in front of me, head and shoulders taller.

"You're…"

He nods. "I am."

The frozen beads of dew on the branches clink as a breeze I can't feel knocks them together.

And I laugh. It's feeble, but a laugh all the same.

I can't say I'm not surprised, but I think I've known. I don't know since when. Certainly after I saw Tristan one last time, but maybe before then. Maybe it was at the cemetery two months ago, when He first told me He knew me.

In this light, the hazel of His irises is almost iridescent.

He gestures with His head. "Walk with me."

I follow Him. His strong legs displace snow powder, but the way He walks is delicate—it's the way I walk when I have a fever, when every motion is pain.

I weave in the trail He leaves; red droplets stain the snow in His wake.

He leads me to outpatient. Glass shards stick out of the flawless white blanket, but none of them touch me. More make the perimeter of the broken pane ragged. The pane, if this is the same building, that Tristan shot.

The snow is shallower inside. The main entry is so much larger, so much more welcoming in the light. The glass abstract is broken on the other side, but He leads me down the nearest hall. The door to the stairs is blasted open. When we get to the top, the window is also shot through. My feet are wet and clean.

He leads me past it all, down the straight hall, and into a room that doesn't belong in outpatient. It shouldn't, anyway. Outpatient wouldn't have a bed and an IV rack.

He sits on the edge of the bed. Hooked onto a lower bar of the rack is a needle already attached to an infusion tube; He reaches for it.

"Go ahead," He says as He unhooks it.

I don't take my eyes off His hands as He eases the silver point into a vein between His knuckles and His wrist. "What?"

He adjusts the needle and winces. He nods to me. "Ask."

I brush my fingertips against the wall, collecting frozen dew. "Where were You?" When I got sick. When Luiz came to me bleeding. When Tony threatened Tristan. When they attacked Mercedes and my mom. When I killed Tony. When Luiz came for me at the hospital.

When Tristan died. Elijah. Damien.

"Paityn, look at me."

He extends His right hand. Underneath the needle, a straight, pale line cuts across it.

Luiz's knife from the day Elijah died.

Suddenly, they all seem to show themselves. Two carved marks tracing half of His neck. A slit down His left forearm. A scrape scar on the side of His face. White slices on the sides of His feet. A pale skim shot at His temple.

And the trail of burgundy in the snow has been coming from a spot that the black of His shirt hid—over His left shoulder.

"I've been there the whole time," He says quietly.

I slip my hand into His. Trace the thin raised scar and let its shape chisel into my memory, careful not to shift the needle He pierced His own body with.

The pain wells up—the grief, the anger. It aches. A lone, hot tear splits the cold on my cheek. His hand brushes the tear away and tips my chin up. There's an identical wet path down His face.

Then I'm tucked in His chest. His arms are strong around me. And His heartbeat—it's like fire and oceans and wind…but also just a heartbeat. It matches my mom's. Mercedes'. Elijah's. Tristan's. Mine.

The loose curls, the scars, the salt stain down His cheek. So human.

A breeze flicks our hair. The snow sparkles. And lights up another scar: a silver line from the center of His forehead all the way across to His temple.

He raises His eyebrow, daring me to guess and telling me I'm right.

A shiver runs down my spine, and goosebumps rise on my arms. My left shoulder begins to throb. This is ending. It's all ending.

He extends His marked hand to me. I take it, needle and all. It matches mine. Our bones jut out from a thin wrap of skin. Our knuckles are swollen. We both flinch at the pressure of each other's grasp but refuse to let go. My raised scars press into His hand. His scars press into mine.

He exhales unsteadily. The sound sparks a memory of a high fever and a cool cloth and a heartbeat against my ear.

"Don't leave me," I say. "Stay with me. Please."

Through the needle, He grips my hand like He'll never let anything take me away. "I promise."

64

CINNAMON ON MY RIGHT. Rose on my left. Ebbing, but there if I concentrate. I wish I could inhale deeply.

Their hands are on mine, my mom's callused and strong, Mercedes' soft but scraped, the raw patches smooth on my nerves. Even that's getting harder to feel.

My body is slack. Numb. An EKG chimes slower and slower.

I don't want to die. My mom, Mercedes, my baby sister Kestrel—I have more than enough reasons to live.

He won't leave them.

The cinnamon, rose, calluses, scrapes—they fade to nothing.

I don't want to die.

He doesn't want me to die, either. But for a reason that I don't know, that I can't understand, He lets it happen.

A scar on His hand. His temple. His neck. And so many more that I've never seen: He pays the price.

I'm dizzy. I don't know what's coming next.

Damien's voice in my mind. *Your unafraid eyes.*

My mom's. *No shame. Your terms.*

Unafraid. On my terms. With Him.

65

MY LUNGS COLLAPSE.

It's coming.

They won't expand again.

I'm coming.

And it hurts.

He's coming.

I'm not afraid.

I slip under. And everything starts to go.

One at a time.

Every organ,

Every cell,

Releasing.

66

AND FIRE. WIND. OCEAN.

Soft, warm, passionate. Free, beautiful, adventurous. Deep, powerful, inviting.

A heartbeat.

Human. Bleeding.

"I'm here, Paityn."

His chest, His touch, feels so much like my mom's. Tristan's. Elijah's. Damien's.

Or maybe, this whole time, their touch felt like His.

There's no more pain. They're waiting for me.

And I'm finally at peace.

EPILOGUE

LUIZ

MY GOOD WRIST IS CUFFED to the rail of the hospital bed. Like I'm going anywhere.

My throat aches, referred pain from where she stabbed me. My stitches are sharp and snug. I can still feel the metal piercing my skin, sliding deep inside me, scraping against my collarbone. I can still feel the blood gushing up and hiding how cold her hand was against me. I can still see her eyes, unafraid, like wildfire.

I swallow, beating back the pain, refusing to acknowledge it. Tony wouldn't have.

I turn my head to stretch the gash in my neck. There's no window in this room, just four walls, the vitals monitor, and the IV drip. The plain wallpaper is a blanched stone blue, and fluorescent lights hang in bars. My snapped wrist and knee are both shelled in casts. And tucked in my cuffed hand, so securely and discretely that no one has found it three days later, is her necklace.

Her dried blood flakes off inside my hand from when she pressed it into my palm. From when she dropped the gun.

The muscles in my forearm coil. Everything inside me wants to let it fall, throw it, let them find it and take it, get rid of it somehow. I can't bring myself to do it.

I grit my teeth until they grind. She's gone. To me, at least.

I crush my skull into the flat pillow. My hair and skin are oily from being strapped here for so long. Sleep tugs at my eyes, but I fight to keep them open. In my nightmares, someone always dies. Is killed. She kills Tony. I kill her friend. She kills me. I kill her.

My body doesn't give me the choice. Within a few minutes, I'm asleep and dreaming.

My hands and knees submerge in chilled crystal water. Everything around me is covered in it. The sky is like white gold.

I'm at Paityn's house, on the sidewalk out front. Her lawn stretches beneath the water, the grass lush and green and reaching for the surface. The hydrangeas in her small garden pierce through, their small flowers beaded with dew. Through the glass storm door, I have a view of her entry hall, framed pictures hanging on the wall, and her living room. It's clean, like it always was. Safe.

Four points jab inside my palm. Heat swells on my forehead, and warm fluid silks down the side of my face. It drips off and stains the diamond water ruby, then dissipates until the water's flawless again.

I draw out my hand and trace the smooth stream up my face.

There's no pain—just split skin where there should be a scar.

My hand aches as badly as my throat, the pain threading up my wrist and forearm. I ease back onto my knees, water trickling around me, and unfold it. Pierced wounds are torn open: one for each point of the crucifix.

It's the first time I've looked at her necklace since that night. The whole thing, medal and broken chain, is covered in blood, except at the tips, where the silver spears through. My blood. And her blood.

Tears flash up, and I barely stop them. I drive my teeth into each other so hard my jaw pops.

Her door opens.

She stands halfway out, one thin hand poised on the handle. Her hair has grown back, full and curly and rich brown, bundled into a thick ponytail. Her jeans and jacket are white.

She smiles at me, gentle, quiet, closed-lipped.

I stagger to my feet. The water around me is knifed with ripples as the splash echoes down the street.

She steps out and lets the door swing shut behind her. Her hands slide into her pockets, and she wades toward me, the water around her shins burbling.

My heart thuds. A sick heat grows in my stomach as she approaches me. There's no fear on her face, no anger.

I search around my ankles for a gun, a knife. Because that's what always happens, and I want it over with.

There's nothing. Just the necklace in my hand. I step back. "What do you want?"

She shrugs the way she always did when she wanted to put me at ease. Her face is serene. Contented, even. "I already died, Luiz."

A void inside me clenches.

She's not dead. She was bleeding and exhausted, but she spoke to me. She walked away and laid herself down, and when they found her, they said she was breathing. She's alive. She has to be.

This is my dream. So why would she say that?

She nods, a wild curl falling over her shoulder. "Sepsis."

No one told me that. I didn't hear anything about her after they took her away.

Her quiet smile grows, just barely. "Do you want proof?"

"You can't prove it," I say, my voice rising. "You're gone."

She looks at me with an intensity that makes my heart slow. The rest of the world around me falls away until she and I are all that's left.

"Tony's going to be fine," she says.

Everything goes still. My heartbeat. My breathing. My blood. It all stops.

My voice shakes. "What did you say?"

Her eyes well up to match her smile. "You heard me."

An exhale torn to shreds escapes my mouth. I stare at her, my body stone. Nothing that originated from my mind would have said that to me.

She steps toward me, and this time, I don't maintain the distance. The gentleness in her eyes digs into my chest.

"Why didn't you kill me?" she asks.

I stiffen, my fist clenching around her necklace. I know the reason. I've always known, and that's why I came for her the second time—because I couldn't live with myself until I had finished it.

Blood drips between my fingers from her pendant. "I couldn't look you in the eyes."

Not after her friend. Not after he looked at me, then down at the knife, my hand on the hilt.

She takes another step. This is how close we were when I held the same knife to her chest.

The ache weaving up my forearm sharpens. I raise my hand and pry it open. The crucifix sits inside.

Her warm, smooth fingers brush mine. I tense at her touch—I never thought I'd feel it again.

She lightly folds the necklace back into my grasp, careful of the puncture marks. Same as last time. The pale line from my knife lights up the skin below her knuckles.

I back up, taking the necklace with me, disturbing the tranquil water. "It's too late."

"No, it's not."

"*Yes, it is.*" My body is convulsing with tremors, but my voice is as cutting as the blade I stuck into her friend. Into her. "You know what I've done. You know who I am."

For a minute, she stays where she is, the compassion on her face never wavering. Then she closes the small distance again. Water laps at my shins. The sheen hasn't left her eyes—a thin pearl of it sparkles on her cheekbone.

I turn my head away and tighten my jaw. She used to do the same thing. I can picture the muscles bulging under her ear.

A soft touch on my face. I flinch.

She brushes the backs of her fingers against my temple, against the bleeding tip of my wound.

"I know who you are," she whispers.

Her eyes hold mine.

Years. For years, I have drowned and beaten and numbed the pain. Now it wells up fresh and raw, and I break open the way I only ever have with her.

I tilt my head into her hand. She smells like lemon and lavender. She always has.

I remember this. The gauze and the hydrogen peroxide. Her cheek against mine, absorbing the tears that I was too ashamed, too afraid to shed anywhere else. *I got you.*

The scars on her face from when I pinned her to the ground are pale like ivory, like starlight. They're beautiful. She's beautiful.

"I'm going to wake up, and this is all going to be gone," I say. She's going to be gone.

With her thumb, she spreads a wet band across my face. "Is it?"

I savor her touch until she lets it slip away. She turns and begins to wade away from me.

"Wait," I call. She stops and faces me. My blood slicks her hand. It slicks mine as well and flows over the crucifix. "Why didn't you kill me?"

She gives me that same smile from when we were kids.

"I saw you, Luiz," she says.

I gasp.

Every muscle in my body cinches and tears at my wrist, my leg, the stitches in my neck. The fluorescent lamps glare, and I blink away the harsh light. Sweat soaks my back and hair. Leftover blood is caked on the side of my face and on my collarbone. The points of her necklace, of that crucifix, pierce my skin.

And there's the ghost of her hand on my face. A memory of lemon and lavender.

My heart rate scribbles unevenly on the vitals monitor hanging over me. I raise my head off the pillow and withdraw my cuffed hand from the bedrail as far as it will go, with a clunk of metal on plastic. My palm's crimson. My sweat has changed the dried blood to liquid again. Her blood.

I ease my broken hand to the cuffed one and loop the silver chain around it. The links are warm, the same as when she pressed the necklace into my hand. Closed my fingers around it and wrapped hers around mine. And that wasn't a dream.

For the first time since she held me that night at her house, I let the tears fall.

"Thank you," I whisper.

I press the crucifix to my chest.

Acknowledgements

There are so many people I have to thank for helping me get here—I'd better get started!

First things first: to God the Father, Daddy; Jesus, Big Brother; and Holy Spirit, Best Friend. Thank you for so much love and mercy and grace—not to mention the complete blast I had writing this book. You are amazing, and I love You.

Thank you to Our Blessed Mother, my guardian angel, St. Theresa of Avila (I got Paityn's prayers from you), and all the saints and angels for your prayers.

Next, thank you to Mamma: you inspired this novel way back in middle school, and you've had my back as I've worked on it ever since.

Thank you also to Sissy, the world's most incredible cheerleader, who has known (and loved!) Elijah as long as I have, and to Babbo, who has been excited since the moment I told him about my book.

Thank you to Corinne O'Flynn, my mentor, who first introduced me to indie publishing and guided me every step along the way. Every time I had a question, you were there with me for hours on Zoom or for a late-night email. I am so grateful to have you as my teacher.

Thank you to Corinna Turner, for being so generous in your support of me, my story, and the process of getting it into the world. Your critiques were indispensable, and I cannot tell you how grateful I am that you imparted your knowledge and advice to me.

Thank you to Dani Edwards, my editor, for making my writing shine and for bringing a perfect sense of humor and fun to every edit and email. Also, thank you Amy Scott for connecting me with Dani and guiding me through my very first editing process. You both lit up my experience with your kindness.

Thank you to Stefanie Saw for your phenomenal work on my cover. When I first saw it, it took my breath away. I couldn't ask for a more talented—an unbelievably friendly—cover artist.

Thank you to my absolutely incredible band of beta readers and critique partners: Liane Miller, Isa Miller, Diane Donovan, Lauren Hoppestad, Maria Ferraro, Bekah Wright, and Lily Jacinowski. Without you guys, the story wouldn't have gotten to where it is today. I am deeply grateful to you for letting me share my story with you first.

Thank you to Mattie Gonzales for voicing Tristan in my book trailer and to Mike Haberkamp for jumping in to voice Tony. It was beyond fun and a blessing to make this with you. I'm so thankful for your generosity with your time and talent.

And, of course, thank you to all the people who offered to take a look at my book; I truly, truly appreciate you!

Finally, thank you to all the friends and family who have supported me in this project. I can't find the words to thank you for every moment of encouragement. Please know that I notice every time and I am beyond grateful that God has placed you in my life.

Until the next story!

PLAYLIST

"Hero" by Faouzia

"Arcade" by Duncan Laurence ft. Fletcher

"Déjà Vu" by Dionne Warwick

"Speechless" by Naomi Scott

"This Mountain" by Faouzia

"Strange Sight" by KT Tunstall

"Speechless" Epic Version by Frostudio Chambersonic

"Enemy" by Tommee Profitt, Sam Tinnesz, Beacon Light

"Gangsta's Paradise" Epic Version by 2WEI

"I Have Nothing" by Whitney Houston

"Gone" by Ionna Gika

"Sacrifice" by Alan Lennon

"Hero" by Elizaveta

"Survivor" by 2WEI ft. Edda Hayes

"Strange Sight Reprise" by KT Tunstall

"Dos Oruguitas" by Sebastián Yatra

"Thick and Thin" by Faouzia

GABRIELLA BATEL is a young and vibrant Catholic woman with an adrenaline craving and a passion for God, her family, movies, and all things YA fiction. *Don't* is her debut novel, and she's already working on the next thrill ride.

Manufactured by Amazon.ca
Acheson, AB

15752265R00189